FIRST
BLOOD

D0835189

BOOKS BY ANGELA MARSONS

DETECTIVE KIM STONE SERIES
Silent Scream
Evil Games
Lost Girls
Play Dead
Blood Lines
Dead Souls
Broken Bones
Dying Truth
Fatal Promise
Child's Play

OTHER BOOKS
Dear Mother (previously published as *The Middle Child*)
The Forgotten Woman (previously published as *My Name Is*)

Angela MARSONS

A D.I. Kim Stone NOVEL

FIRST BLOOD

GRAND CENTRAL
PUBLISHING

New York Boston

Copyright © 2019 by Angela Marsons
Cover design by Mimi Bark. Cover photo from Shutterstock.
Cover copyright © 2022 by Hachette Book Group, Inc.

Grand Central Publishing
Hachette Book Group
1290 Avenue of the Americas, New York, NY 10104
grandcentralpublishing.com
twitter.com/grandcentralpub

First published in 2019 by Bookouture, an imprint of StoryFire Ltd.
First Grand Central Publishing edition: August 2022

Grand Central Publishing is a division of Hachette Book Group, Inc. The Grand Central Publishing name and logo is a trademark of Hachette Book Group, Inc.

The publisher is not responsible for websites (or their content) that are not owned by the publisher.

The Hachette Speakers Bureau provides a wide range of authors for speaking events. To find out more, go to www.hachettespeakersbureau.com or call (866) 376-6591.

ISBN 9781538701942 (mass market)

Printed in the United States of America

OPM

10 9 8 7 6 5 4 3 2 1

This book is dedicated to Amanda Nicol.
For all that you do.

PROLOGUE

"Are you scared yet?" I ask, peering down into your soulless eyes.

You are prostrate and trapped. This time it's you that is helpless.

If not for the gag in your mouth what would your last words be? I wonder. Would you beg for forgiveness? Would you plead for your life? Would you make promises? Would you apologize?

I bend down and remove the gag to satisfy my curiosity.

"Let me go, you fucking..."

I shove the gag back in. You are not in charge. You have absolutely nothing of interest to say to me. Of course there's no remorse. That's okay. It doesn't change a thing if you're sorry or not. Your fate remains the same. Your failure to feel anything other than for yourself makes my task so much sweeter.

Your expression mixes anger with fear.

"Not so much fun on the other end, is it?" I ask, enjoying myself. But I want to be sure I'm clear; that you understand.

"Make no mistake, you are going to die," I say, waving the knife in front of your face to make my point. "And I'm going to make it hurt."

I read your expression again and now there is only fear. Finally you believe me. Your eyes shift from side to side as your brain turns toward desperate self-preservation.

"There's nothing you can do. It's too late," I say to put you out of this misery. I want your eyes full of fear. I don't want you to have any hope for your own life. There is none.

"It's all about you, isn't it? You care for no one but yourself and your own sick perversions. Well, now's the time to pay for everything

you've done and I know it all, my King. I know every bad thing you've ever done."

The urine stain that appears at your crotch gives me pleasure.

"You've pissed yourself," I laugh, waving the knife around your cock. Your weakness gives me strength. I am now satisfied that you have suffered. You've tasted the fear you've inflicted on others.

For me, that will have to do. It is time to end this.

I stand above you. I have taken all your power. Now I am bigger, stronger and in control.

"Do you feel my power now?" I ask.

You nod vigorously as though that will make a difference. You think you can appease me, identify with me, befriend me to save your own life.

"Now you're going to die."

My fist tightens around the handle of the blade I've been holding. It is itching, almost to the point of a spasm, to carry out the wishes of my brain.

I bend down. My hate-filled face will be the last thing you ever see before you leave this earth for your final judgment.

I savor this triumph for just a second before I slice the knife across your throat.

There is horror. There is fear as the blood spurts from your body taking with it the light from your eyes.

I watch as the last signs of life depart. I feel peace as you gurgle your last breath. I feel cleansed.

You are dead. And that should be enough, but it isn't.

What I've done already is for others, to save them pain and suffering, but the rest is just for me.

I grip the bloody knife with all my strength.

It's time to get to work.

CHAPTER 1

December 15, 2014

The 7 a.m. winter darkness felt like the middle of the night as Detective Inspector Kim Stone dismounted the Kawasaki Ninja, removed her helmet and surveyed the concrete and brick building.

West Midlands Police, as the second largest force in England and Wales, was responsible for policing an area with almost two million, nine hundred thousand inhabitants and covered the cities of Birmingham, Coventry, Wolverhampton and her own patch in the Black Country. The area was divided into ten Local Policing Units. Dudley was the LPU under which Halesowen Police Station sat.

The three-story structure offered a mixture of darkened windows and bright shining lights. The top floor remained the darkest. Just like every other station the brass resided at the top and most likely were not yet out of bed. It was similar throughout the borough. And she should know—she'd worked at most of them. A case here, a case there, sometimes longer, sometimes shorter. Her most recent placement at West Bromwich had been shorter than most. She'd been seconded to work an armed robbery of a small greengrocer two streets away from The Hawthorns, the home of West Bromwich Albion Football Club, when the DI in charge had been struck down with a sudden case of peritonitis.

The case had been two days old and witness statements had been confusing and lacking in detail.

With a team of one sergeant and three constables she had worked through the statements one by one and eventually established that not one witness had actually seen the perpetrator flee the scene, except for the son of the owner, who had been on his way in to assist his father, and had offered them the only description they had. Male, approximately six feet tall, faded jeans, blue jacket and black balaclava.

In the absence of CCTV Kim had attended the scene and inspected the premises. The shop was on the end of a row of five shops with a narrow one-way street leading to a car park at the rear. A gate led from the car park back into the store. The owner's son, Ricky, had accompanied her as she'd toured the premises and unlocked a small, damp, decommissioned outside toilet at the rear of the shop.

The toilet had been removed and the space filled with old racking, paint tins and a couple of chairs. She had taken a quick look around and turned to Ricky.

"So, you saw the man and he was…"

"About six feet tall, jeans, blue jacket and black balaclava."

Kim rubbed her chin and nodded. "Anything like that black balaclava there?" she asked, pointing to the corner of the space where the woolen item had been thrown, and forgotten.

His face had immediately contorted with guilt and the case had been solved. Opportunistic criminals had not honed their methods, learned their craft over time. They made mistakes, they forgot things. They were clumsy and nervous. And this nineteen-year-old had been refused the eight hundred quid to go partying in Ibiza with his mates, he'd admitted back at the station.

That evening DCI Worthington had insisted the whole team meet him at The Dog for a celebratory drink. She had attended but had not taken a drink. She never touched alcohol. Two hours later she'd been told she was off the team and to await her next placement.

The rest of the team had been surprised.

She had not.

And now she was about to meet her second DCI in as many weeks.

She used her fingers to ruffle her short black hair, flattened by the helmet. A quick look in the bike mirror confirmed that the fringe was resting untidily on her eyebrows without obscuring her dark brown eyes.

Let's see how long this one lasts, she thought, stepping through the automatic doors of her newest work placement.

The first thing she noticed was the Christmas tree: a battered artificial affair with limbs missing and the remaining ones arranged haphazardly as though someone had become bored by the task. A few mismatched baubles and a one-line zigzag of tinsel arranged to cover the maximum area did not a festive vision make.

Not that she had any interest. Her own home had not turned up for school on the day they were giving out Christmas and that was just how she liked it. The season of goodwill and present giving did not appeal to her natural disposition.

"DI Stone," she said, showing her ID to the desk sergeant.

"Jack Whittle, Custody Sergeant," he said, offering his hand across the desk.

She ignored it.

And so, it began. New station, new people, new ground rules.

And unnecessary touching of other people was one of them.

"DCI Woodward is expecting me," she said as the custody sergeant's arm retracted to his side of the desk.

"I'll buzz you through," he said, nodding toward the key-coded automatic doors.

Kim remained where she was and said nothing. It was a three-story building that she'd never been in before.

"Top floor east corner," he offered, coolly, catching on quick.

Maybe Jack was going to be all right after all, tolerable for the duration of her stay. However short that was going to be.

She made her way along corridors and up staircases that were pretty much generic in all of the OCUs she'd worked, and one office of beaten-up mismatched furniture was no different from the next.

Except of course for Head Office at Lloyd House, in Birmingham. From what she'd seen it was furnished very nicely and was the benefactor of the hand-me-downs to the smaller stations.

She knocked on the door with the brass nameplate and forced herself to wait for instruction. Hating time-wasting, she was always tempted to announce her arrival with a single knock and enter immediately. After all, he was expecting her and how many other meetings did he have planned for 7 a.m.?

She heard the instruction to enter and did so. It was her first day after all.

DCI Woodward stood and offered his hand.

She approached and shook it. His grip was dry and firm.

"Welcome to Halesowen," he said, taking a seat and indicating she do the same.

"Thank you, sir," she said, taking a moment to appreciate the brilliant whiteness of his shirt against the smooth, dark brown skin. Rimless reading glasses were perched on his nose.

A memorial photograph of a young man closely resembling the man behind the desk graced the wall.

She hadn't heard a great deal about DCI Woodward before she'd been seconded and she hadn't known if that was a good or bad thing. Was he lazy, unremarkable, perhaps treading water until retirement? She'd met all of the above. A bit of digging into his performance as a DCI had told her that his team satisfaction percentage rate was in the high seventies and his successful prosecution rate was in the mid-nineties. There were more statistics available but it was these two that interested her the most. He ran a decent team and put bad people behind bars. And yet she'd never seen this man on press conferences hogging the spotlight.

"I thought it prudent to have a brief chat before putting you to work," he said, lacing his fingers together and resting them on the desk.

Here it comes, she thought, preparing to adopt the correct expression. It was time for the chat. If true to form of every other DCI there was very little chatting involved. It was a one-sided conversation where he laid down the law, told her how it was going to be and what he expected, a bit like how she remembered her first day at school. There would be no questions and no response required from her until the end when she would be expected to offer total acquiescence. There you go. Job done. She could get up and leave right now. She knew the drill. She'd listen, nod in the right places and then follow the rules she agreed with.

"So, Stone, why is it that practically no one wants to work with you?" he asked, surprising her from the off.

Firstly, because it was a question that required an answer. Secondly because it was direct and thirdly because he hadn't launched into an immediate lecture.

"Sir, in all honesty, I'm probably not all that easy to get along with," she answered and saw the hint of a smile tug at his lips.

"And why is that?" he asked.

"I'm not good with people. I don't like them very much."

"All people?"

"Most, so it's safer to assume all and generalize."

"I see, so you take full responsibility for the fact that this is pretty much the last station that will take you?"

She thought for a moment and then recalled his own directness.

"No, sir. I work hard and like to do a good job. I am direct and not everyone likes that, but I will not stop until I've exhausted every opportunity open to me. Not everyone likes my style, and

I just didn't feel it prudent to detail some of the knobs that I've worked for who also happen to be your contemporaries. Not on our first meeting anyway."

He surprised her by throwing back his head and roaring with laughter.

"There may be some I actually agree about but clearly that stays in this room."

And she hadn't expected that.

"Talking of which, what exactly happened with you and DCI Worthington?"

She said nothing.

"Some kind of communication issue, he cited as your reason for transfer?" he pushed.

Kim thought back to the night of the celebration in The Dog. Her sudden movement of standing up at the table had sent a pint of bitter and half a bag of pork scratchings hurtling into his lap. He'd caught her outside and asked what the hell that had been about. She had told him that if she saw him patting one more female officer on the behind she'd put in a formal complaint against him herself. He had claimed it was just "banter." Tipsy or not it wasn't acceptable and the detective constable being pawed hadn't looked like she was enjoying the "banter" all that much.

"Yes, sir. A communication issue is exactly what it was."

"So," he said, removing his glasses. "No big speeches but just to say I don't judge you and you don't judge me. And we'll take it from there."

"Fair enough," Kim said, unsure if he was playing with her. It was the shortest, most direct welcome speech she'd had yet.

"It'll be a small team to start but you'll have two DSs and a DC. Needless to say there'll be other resources available but today I'd like you to focus on getting to know your colleagues, their strengths and weaknesses and then I'll move some cases around to give you something to get your teeth into."

A whole day getting to know folks she wouldn't work with for very long? She'd worked in her last team for four months and still didn't know everyone's name.

Seemed like a waste of a day to her.

"Sir, to be honest, I'd rather just get stuck into..."

"I'm sure you would, Stone, and I'd rather we just did it my way."

She nodded her agreement while thinking that once she and the team had introduced themselves she'd put the feelers out with Dispatch for any active cases.

"Any clues on who or what I'm getting?" she asked, standing.

He shook his head. "I'll leave you to sort that out yourself. The CID office is on the second floor next to the general admin office. I suggest you head there and await the arrival of your team."

CHAPTER 2

DCI Woodward let out a breath as the door closed behind her.

She hadn't recognized him and he hadn't realistically expected her to. It had been a long time since their last meeting. But he'd remembered every second of it.

He'd heard much about the detective inspector from all of his fellow DCIs. He hadn't bothered to mention to her the two condolence cards he'd received that were in his drawer.

He'd been fully briefed about her bloody-mindedness, her lack of social skills, her inability to work well with others. He'd heard about the complaints that had been received about her manner. He knew there were times when she broke the rules without breaking the law but sailing close to the line.

He had read her personnel file cover to cover. Followed her journey since their meeting all those years ago. He'd read about every slap on the wrist, just as he'd read about every case she'd worked and her impeccable success rate.

He also had a rough idea about what had happened between her and Samuel Worthington. He knew the man. He'd trained with him years ago and had felt back then that he was a sexist, chauvinistic oaf with little room for improvement. How he'd survived in the changing diverse landscape of the police, he was unsure although even he knew that the political correctness training and directives were white noise to some officers. Something had occurred between them and yet she'd chosen to keep it to herself. He felt the seed of respect being sown somewhere in his mind.

He thought again about the sympathy cards in his drawer from her former bosses who felt he'd been lumbered with the force's problem child, when that hadn't been the case at all. He had actually requested that the unmanageable, rule-bending, taciturn officer be allowed to join his team.

And for better or for worse that's what he'd got.

CHAPTER 3

DS Bryant checked his reflection in the mirror. His customary dark suit and light blue tie with white shirt looked back at him.

Only yesterday his wife, Jenny, had said that he was starting to remind her of Bradley Walsh, the guy who presented that Chaser program or something.

He'd started to argue with her until she'd told him with a wink that she quite fancied Bradley Walsh. He hadn't been sure how to take that until she'd convinced him that she only had eyes for him. And after almost a quarter century together, he'd take that.

He removed the tie. The damn thing was refusing to knot properly.

"It was fine," Jenny said, startling him. He hadn't realized she was awake but she was sitting up in bed, her knees bent, watching him.

"And it was also fine the three times before. What's wrong?"

"Ah, just new boss, that's all," he said, snaking the tie beneath his collar again.

"You met her before?" Jenny asked.

He shook his head.

"It's not because she's a . . ."

He turned away from the mirror before she'd even finished the sentence and offered her a look. "You really have to ask that?"

She bobbed out her tongue to show she was joking, and he turned back to the mirror.

"I've worked for women and I've worked for people younger than me before. She just happens to be both. That doesn't bother me."

As both a police officer and as a detective he'd witnessed the horrors that people could inflict upon each other. He understood the coping mechanisms employed by some of his colleagues: drink, drugs, adultery; all of the above. In fact, anything to distract the brain from the images it held onto. He understood that the need for a crutch came from the absence of balance. Every crime scene was horrific, every crime he dealt with had a victim: loved ones, grief, despair, anger, hatred, death. Every case was a negative. Few police officers were called to investigate a cake bake. It reminded him of the Samaritans' helpline. You were never gonna get a call from someone telling you how great their day had been.

His own crutch had been thirty cigarettes a day. Stressful situations had been followed by a few hits of nicotine which had helped relax him and bring him back to normal. He had known the cigarettes weren't really relaxing him, just deadening his muscles in response to the poisons he was ingesting but it had felt good while he'd been doing it. Until after one chest infection too many, when the doctor had told him he was in danger of shortening his life by ten to fifteen years if he didn't stop.

The thought of missing those years from the life of his nineteen-year-old daughter had prompted him to buy every patch and gum pack available. The sudden chest infection that had knocked him off his feet for three weeks had shown him just how poor his lungs were. He had eventually returned to work with the help of Menthol Lyptus extra-strong sweets and had been trying to kick them ever since. But he was almost two years smoke free so the addiction to sweets he could live with.

Only thing was, since quitting he'd worked hard not to voluntarily place himself in stressful situations that might have him reaching once again for the smokes.

Attending crime scenes and interviewing witnesses were unavoidable but he tried to keep his working relationships easy-going, pleasant and without conflict.

And from what he'd heard about his new boss, that was likely to be nigh on impossible.

"So, what have you heard?" Jenny asked, as though she'd traveled along his entire thought process with him.

Always knowing his thoughts was one of the many things he loved about her. As was her insistence on forcing him to speak those thoughts so he could hear the words outside of his head.

"That she's difficult, arrogant, rude, hates working with anyone for too long."

"Well, *if* she is all those things it may be good that she'll want to move on quickly."

"If?" he asked.

"Absolutely. If you've never worked with her, you can't possibly know if these rumors are true. Remember when we went…"

"To Marbella," he finished for her. "Yes, I remember. Bill and Helen told us it was bloody awful and reeled off everything they'd hated, making us wish we'd never booked the damn holiday until we got there and loved it."

"Am I that predictable?" she asked, rubbing sleep from her eyes.

"No, it's the thing you always quote when you're trying to tell me not to take other people's opinions as my own."

"Then my work here is done," she said, dusting off her hands and getting out of bed.

She stood in front of him and straightened his tie. He didn't bother to resist the urge to lean down and kiss the top of her head.

"And beautiful," he said. "She's apparently very good-looking."

Jenny shrugged and tapped the knot of his tie. "There you go. Perfect."

"You're not even a bit threatened, are you?" he asked.

She shook her head and smiled up at him.

"I love you," he said and meant it.

"And, that's why I'm not threatened," she said, moving away but tapping his behind. She paused at the bathroom doorway. "So, you okay about this then? There's nothing else bothering you? It's got nothing to do with the other thing?" she asked.

He shook his head and felt the tension seep into his jaw.

Right now he didn't even want to think about the other thing.

CHAPTER 4

It is time to take out the book.

The book.

I both love and hate this fucking book. I hated it as a child. I feared it as a child. But now it guides me and tells me what must be done.

The first three pages bear straight black lines, shooting diagonally from corner to corner. They are done.

I turn to page 4 with the pen in my hand and realize I can't mark it complete quite yet. Should I do a part line, halfway across the page until I complete this task?

I sit back, pondering, giving myself a minute to relive the memory of your death. I smile. I enjoyed every second of your demise.

Each one soothes another layer of my pain.

You got into my car so easily, you stupid bastard, because you thought I was just like you. You were tempted by my promises of the freedom to satisfy your disgusting pleasures. You didn't know me but I knew you. You see, I've listened. I always listen, it's what I do and I know everything you ever did.

I made you piss yourself, King Louis. A bonus, an added pleasure and a true exhibition of terror. You could not have gratified me more; the stench of the urine as it seeped through your clothes was like the aroma of a sweet summer flower to me. Because it stank of your fear.

You see, that's exactly what I was after, you bastard. It's your fear I wanted. It feeds my soul. It satisfies me. It's what I crave and so far you're the only one to exceed my expectations.

How did it feel, King Louis, given your own reign of terror?

I wish I could have felt your distress but I have felt plenty enough of my own. And now no one will fear you ever again.

My thoughts are now tired of you and return to the page. I hate that I cannot put a line through and mark it complete. The King is dead but the Queen still lives.

My gaze catches a few words from the page and I cannot help the tears that spring to my eyes.

I brush them away. Those emotions are no good to me. They didn't help me then and they don't help me now.

Rage is better. Blind fury gets the job done and there is still so much to do.

But it's too late to stop that damn memory seeping into my brain.

A soft, cajoling voice that says,

"Go on, it's time to fetch the book."

CHAPTER 5

Detective Sergeant Kevin Dawson opened one eye and employed every sense he could locate before fully emerging from the cocoon of sleep.

Where the hell was he this morning?

Okay, there was no sheet beneath him, his legs were bent and the fabric of the sofa was velour, green velour.

The single pillow beneath his head had a faint smell of Chinese takeaway.

Terry's flat, he realized, as the man himself came through the door from the kitchen with a mug of something.

He smiled gratefully, not even sure what the liquid was.

"Cheers, mate," he said, inhaling the aroma of strong black coffee. He took a sip. Too bloody strong. "Where'd we end up last night?" he asked, looking around for his stuff.

"Where didn't we?" Terry asked. "After your fourth pint, I couldn't get you to listen to a word I was saying. You had a skinful."

Dawson remembered telling his friend that he only wanted to go for a couple, just to take the edge off his misery, and to calm down his anger.

At many things.

Not least that he'd been pulled from a big team in Brierley Hill to work in a smaller team, in a smaller station with the biggest bitch in the force. He had the unnerving feeling of sitting facing forward but moving backward, like being on a train. And forward movement was the only thing he was interested in.

Not that he'd ever met her but he'd heard the stories, knew she couldn't work with anyone for longer than a case or two. She'd been moved around the borough more often than the five-a-side football trophy. As far as he was concerned, there was no smoke without fire.

And besides, he'd been happy in his old team. Yeah, fair enough they weren't what you'd call over friendly and he hadn't made any lifelong friends, but sometimes being in a bigger team worked for him. Never too much attention on one person. Some days, like today, when you were a bit hungover you could let the others pick up your slack a bit and the boss was none the wiser. And DCI Church had been an okay guy to work for. Dawson felt the guy would have been a decent bet for putting him in for the DI exam if he'd had the chance to work on him a bit longer. He'd already started laying the groundwork to shine in the boss's eyes, much to the irritation of his colleagues, but he'd had no problem taking credit for others' work now and again or throwing his hand up enthusiastically for a task, to get noticed for his keenness before quietly delegating the job to a meek and unsuspecting detective constable. It was survival of the fittest and he fully intended to survive.

He'd worked out how to play every single one of his bosses so far and he didn't intend to stop now, he decided, trying to cheer himself up. All he had to do was watch her, analyze her weaknesses and play up to them.

"What you smiling about?" Terry asked, removing the pillow from behind him. "You were a right grumpy bastard last night."

"Ah nothing, I'm just forming a plan."

"Well, mate, I hope that plan includes finding somewhere to stay tonight cos Louise is off nights and she ain't gonna be chuffed with finding you on the sofa when she comes down for her cornflakes."

"Ah, shit, Terry, I've got nowhere to..."

"Sorry, mate, but unlike you she pays half the rent and like err…lives here."

Dawson ran his hand through his hair wondering which mate he could tap up for a bed tonight.

Terry sat in the single chair and shook his head.

"Beats me why you can't go home, mate. I've seen your missus and she is one tasty…"

"Hey," Dawson warned.

"You know what I mean. Whatever has gone on between you two can be worked out, surely. She's bloody worth it."

Dawson said nothing as he pulled on his socks and his shoes.

He couldn't think about that situation right now.

It was time to get to work and meet his new boss.

And he couldn't fucking wait.

CHAPTER 6

Detective Constable Stacey Wood smoothed her hand over the tight black curls lying close to her head, enjoying the feel of her own hair against the palm of her hand.

Her last weave had recently been taken out and she was glad to see the back of it. Only two weeks in it had been clear that the hair had been sewn in too tightly, causing pain and discomfort to her scalp. She'd stick with her own hair and wear it proudly for now.

She viewed herself in the full-length mirror, a donation from Uncle Cedric. Like most things in her new flat, it had come from either members of the family or the wider Nigerian community in and around Dudley. That was how smaller communities worked, like one big family. She remembered when her father had been made redundant from his printing press job. The news had been whispered around the streets of Dudley and each night a bag or box of groceries and essentials had been left at the front door until he had found work again. No names, no need for thanks or repayment. Stacey was proud of her Nigerian heritage even though she had never stepped foot outside England and was equally proud to be British.

She took a deep breath to expel the anxiety caused by all the change in her life that seemed to have come at once.

Just one week after receiving the keys to her new flat she'd passed the detective constable exam and right now it felt as though she was living someone else's life. Just one month ago she was working eight-hour shifts in uniform and then going home to a freshly cooked meal from her mum.

Yes, she had wanted that independence. As a woman just starting out in her career she'd realized that she needed to rely on the protective support of her parents a little bit less.

She had envisioned independence as euphoric freedom. Evenings of wine and experimental cooking with friends.

It wasn't until she'd moved out that she'd realized that she actually didn't have that many friends. She had police colleagues with whom she'd worked for the last few years who had become surprisingly distant since she'd passed the detective exam.

In the stillness of her own home she realized just how many hours she spent online in the fantasy land of *World of Warcraft*.

At home, with her parents fussing around she had felt it was an escape, a diversion from the job. Sitting alone in her flat with nothing else around her, she realized it had become her entire social life.

She pushed the thought away. That was for another day.

Today, her immediate problem centered on whether she was dressed appropriately for her first day. New detective, new team, new boss. And the new just kept on coming.

Eventually she had settled for cream slacks, one-inch-high court shoes and a plain white long-sleeved shirt. She had seen members of CID in all kinds of attire: power suits, mismatched suits, jeans, chinos. She'd never worn a power suit in her life and didn't intend to start now, although her father's words burned in her brain.

"I know, Dad," she whispered to her own reflection. "You never get a second chance to make a first impression."

And she so desperately wanted to make a good first impression, she admitted to herself.

Despite trying to shake it off over the years she knew she was a people pleaser. She knew she wanted people to like her as well as respect her capabilities, and that trait had accompanied her since little Courtney Jackson had refused to sit beside her on her first day at school.

She had wondered what she could do to make the little girl more comfortable. She had smiled as widely as she could manage. She had pulled her chair further to the left to give Courtney more room. She had offered the girl the first toy from the toy box and in some way or another she'd been doing the same ever since.

She surveyed her appearance once more before reaching for her satchel, and resisted the urge to send a picture of herself to the new phone she'd bought her mum, to check she'd got her appearance just right.

Twenty-two-year-old detective constables didn't do that.

She expelled another deep sigh as she locked the door to the flat that did not yet feel like home.

She stretched the tension from her jaw by smiling widely.

Folks warmed quickly to people who smiled.

CHAPTER 7

Kim appraised the set-up of the squad room from the glass partitioned bowl at the far right corner of the room. Her office; clearly erected for someone who liked to observe their team from behind some kind of barrier.

On the other side of the glass were four desks, two sets of two, facing each other with a walkway through the middle of the office that led from the door to a row of cupboards supporting a printer and a filthy-looking kettle. She'd rather drink from the slushy puddle outside than from that. Due to her need for coffee to get through the day that was a situation that would be remedied at the earliest opportunity.

Her thoughts turned to the imminent arrival of her team. She wondered who they were and where they had come from. Were any of them difficult to work with? Had they all been the broken cog in otherwise well-oiled teams? Was DCI Woodward throwing a bunch of bad eggs into one basket?

She was saved any further ruminations as a figure appeared in the doorway.

The man rose up to around six feet high wearing a dark suit, blue tie and beige overcoat.

She left the bowl to greet him and realized that he reminded her of someone but she couldn't think who.

"DS Bryant," he said, offering his hand.

She shook it briefly. "And I bought coffee, Marm," he said pleasantly while stating the obvious.

"Good call on the coffee but points lost on the Marm," she said, lifting the lid on one of the drinks.

"Duly noted and they're all flat whites," he said, looking around. "Wasn't sure how many of us there were…"

"Another two I'm told," Kim answered, taking one of the four cardboard cups. Another good call on the number. "And guv or boss will be fine," she clarified.

An uneasy silence dropped between them and Kim remembered what DCI Woodward had said about getting to know her team. Trouble was there was nothing she cared to know. How he could do his job would become evident.

It was going to be a long bloody day.

She was saved from trying to think of an appropriate question to ask by a second new face at the door.

"Hi, is this CID?" asked the black woman with a satchel crossed over her frontage.

Kim nodded, as the woman stepped in with a wide smile and an outstretched hand.

"I'm Stacey Wood, police const … I mean detective constable, and I've been assigned to this team."

Kim introduced herself, and Bryant rushed forward to take her hand and give his own name.

She appeared reassured by his presence and welcoming demeanor. Kim could tell she hadn't been a detective long as she'd almost introduced herself under her old rank.

"Well, pick your desks, folks," Kim said, taking a sip of her drink.

Bryant placed his overcoat on the back of the door and then took the desk closest to the bowl, with his back to it.

Stacey removed her satchel and took the one across the aisle from him and so they were both facing the door.

Kim idly wondered at DCI Woodward's logic at giving her two detectives at opposing ends of the career ladder. It would be just her luck that she had one who knew nothing and another who didn't want to do anything except twiddle his thumbs right up to retirement.

She found herself praying for something in her last team member. Just as another face appeared at the door.

Her heart sank. Never touching the stuff, she could smell the alcohol on him and it wasn't from his aftershave.

Before speaking, his eyes swept the room dismissively and rested on her. She caught the quick up and down and she did the same thing.

What she noted immediately was the navy trousers crumpled at the knees and the crotch. The light blue shirt had a mark to the right of his bright pink spotted tie, the knot of which appeared to be keeping a respectful distance from his open shirt collar.

And if he'd shaved he'd done it in the dark. Only his dark brown hair appeared to have turned up ready for work.

Kim knew she was seeing the Sunday night version of the man and not the Monday morning model.

He slapped his right hand against his temple in a mock salute and smiled.

"Detective Sergeant Dawson reporting for duty, Marm."

She saw Bryant's cringe and shake of the head from the corner of her eye, and the detective constable didn't seem to know where to look.

Aah, confidence. She liked that in a person, provided it was substantiated by ability and results and that it didn't cross the line into arrogance.

"Not Marm, thank you," she said, calmly. "And pick a desk."

Unsurprisingly he chose the one that he was closest to, which was nearest to the door and faced Stacey.

She took another sip of coffee as the other two introduced themselves across the room.

She noted that the young detective sergeant took a drink from the cardboard tray without either a request or an acknowledgment. And the detective constable had taken nothing.

"Okay," she said, perching on the edge of the spare desk, "right now, we appear to have no active…"

Her words trailed away as a phone rang. They all looked around.

"It's me," said Bryant, reaching for the handset.

He listened, eyebrows raised, and thanked the caller before replacing the receiver.

"Looks like we have got a case after all. Body found on the west side of the Clent Hills."

She gauged their facial reactions as she stood. Bryant—expectant and alert. Stacey—fearful. Dawson—excited and almost salivating.

"Who's going, guv?" Bryant asked.

"Well, seeing as I barely know your names yet, never mind any of your strengths and weaknesses, I guess we'll all go."

Bryant reached for the receiver.

"Shall I call for a squad car to take…?"

"No one here drives a car?" she asked, looking around. Squad cars had better things to do than ferry detectives around.

Stacey shook her head.

Dawson looked horrified.

"Astra Estate if that's any good?" Bryant offered.

Hardly a muscle car that was going to get them there in record time, but it had four wheels and a roof unlike her mode of transport.

"Go fire it up then," she said.

Bryant headed for his jacket, and Stacey followed closely behind.

Her own placement in the doorway blocked DS Dawson's exit.

"Not you," she said, watching the anticipation fade from his eyes.

"Go home, get ready for work properly and meet us up there."

As she headed out of the office she couldn't help wondering if she'd just made enemy number one. And if so, that was a record.

Even for her.

CHAPTER 8

Kim found her right foot pressing down on an imaginary accelerator in the passenger foot well of the Astra Estate. Oh, how she wished he had dual controls, but he'd made sure to observe every speed limit, red light and zebra crossing en route. It wasn't as if they had a crime scene to get to.

Neither he nor Stacey had asked as to the whereabouts of the younger DS when she'd reached the car and told Bryant to drive.

The four-mile journey to Clent was made in silence, and given the speed her colleague had driven she was surprised when they reached the site before sunset, which in the short days of mid-December never seemed that far away.

The Clent Hills range consisted of Wychbury Hill, Clent Hill and Walton Hill continuing toward Romsley, attracting approximately a million visitors per year.

They had arrived at Clent Hill, the most popular hillwalking summit in the range, and had been told to access the climb from Nimmings car park off Hagley Wood Lane.

She got out of the car, glad to be away from the magnetic light-up Rudolph the Reindeer on DS Bryant's dashboard before the damn thing gave her some kind of seizure.

She made her way through three squad cars, an ambulance and the pathologist van all parked close to the visitor center and café not yet open. Two police officers were guiding dog walkers back toward their cars.

She followed the trail of yellow jackets as though they were bread crumbs dropped around the visitor center and across an open field with picnic benches. Beyond which an officer stood at the end of the path that led into a wooded area.

Inside, the path was more rustic and trodden than originally planned. It wound around fallen trees that had developed into an unofficial playground. Right at the center was more high-visibility tape than a builder's construction site.

A diminutive man stepped away from the crowd and approached her. She guessed him to be mid-fifties behind his pointy brown beard.

"Who are you?" he asked, peering over the top of his glasses.

She held up her warrant card. "Same question."

"Joseph Keats, Pathologist."

"ID?" she asked.

"Really, Inspector?" he replied, meeting her gaze. She didn't blink or look away. He opened his jacket to reveal the lanyard around his neck.

"Where's Tony?" she asked of the easy-going, friendly white-bearded man she'd dealt with in the past.

"Retired," he answered, buttoning up his jacket.

Oh, she hadn't even known he'd been close.

"And in case you're interested I've transferred from South Staffs, but I'm sure I'm not the person you've rushed here to see."

Rushed, not so much, she thought, glancing back at her new colleague.

She made to step forward when the man blocked her path.

"Not without these you don't," he said, holding out shoe coverings. He looked behind her and reached for more.

All three of them donned the footwear to avoid contamination.

"Happy now?" she asked, offering the pathologist a stern look.

"Satisfied would be more appropriate," he said, leading the way.

The sea of white tech suits parted.

"Bloody hell," she said.

"Oh my God," Bryant offered.

And Stacey Wood simply gasped out loud.

"Yes, quite," Keats added. "Although not the worst attempt I've seen in recent years."

Kim looked down at the naked body of a man in his late-twenties. His skinny frame was milky white from head to toe. His legs were open wide and staked to the ground at the ankles by oversize nails. His arms were stretched wide from his hairless chest and staked into the ground at the wrists.

She counted fifteen stab wounds around the body, not deep enough to cause severe blood loss but enough to inflict pain.

She suspected those wounds had been a warm-up for the main event; a bloody mess of flesh and skin at his center where his genitals had once been.

She stared at the wound for just a minute, feeling the rage that must have been present to inflict such a vicious attack not only on the genitals but all over the body.

What did you do to deserve this, matey? she thought to herself.

"Mugging gone wrong?" Bryant asked, drily.

"Well, there's no wallet," Keats retorted, with a half-smile.

She hadn't received a half-smile. What did Bryant have that she did not? The question didn't stay in her mind for long because she didn't much care.

"In fact, there's nothing left except the body," Keats continued. "No phone, no money, no clothes. Nothing."

Kim paused for a moment, working through the possibilities of the pathologist's words.

She knew that some killers would take an item from a crime scene as a keepsake. Something onto which they imprinted the memory of the event to relive it over and over. That was more common with sexually motivated killings and the killer normally took one item, not the whole lot.

The killer might also have been concerned that they'd left DNA or trace evidence on the clothing or items, but she'd never seen a victim stripped of every single item.

The word *stripped* stayed in her mind. Stripped of everything: clothing, belongings, possessions, pride, life.

She continued her walk around the body, taking in every limb position, every detail to keep the scene fresh in her mind until the photographs came through.

She noted the swallow tattoo on his left arm. She noted the dirt caking his fingernails telling her that death had not come quickly, despite the fact his throat had been cut.

And not very tidily either. She frowned at the marks on the flesh from the tip of the blade. And then peered down at the wound more closely.

Keats was watching her intently: Bryant was following her around the body and Stacey still had one hand covering her mouth. She was learning more about her new team with every passing minute.

"Stacey, go back to the car and point Dawson in the right direction when he finally gets here."

The detective constable nodded gratefully and left the area.

Even Kim had to admit that this was one hell of a gruesome scene to view on your first day in the job.

"You see that there?" she said to her left-hand side.

Bryant looked to where she was pointing. To what she had thought was simply the dark stain of blood beneath his neck. But it wasn't red. It was black, like soil.

As though she could see through his throat to the ground.

She looked toward the pathologist. "Has this man's head been removed?"

Keats nodded slowly.

"Yes, I'm afraid to say that this poor fellow was beheaded."

CHAPTER 9

Kim just wanted an approximate time of death and another look at the tattoo before heading away from the crime scene when DS Dawson put in an appearance, looking more like she would have expected.

The suit was fresh, the shirt was clean, the tie was more subdued and the face was shaven.

He looked at her expectantly. She said and offered nothing. She was not into congratulating someone for turning up to work appropriately attired.

She was more impressed that his younger colleague had chosen to walk back with him and take another look at the scene.

"You got a close-up of that tattoo?" Kim asked the photographer.

He nodded but she took one with her mobile phone anyway. There was something familiar about it.

"Well, he got his dick handed to him on a—"

"Time of death, Keats?" Kim asked, cutting off Dawson's smart-arse comment. She was all for gallows humor. It often kept people in their profession sane, but there was a golden rule: it had to be funny and not just inane.

"Liver probe tells me it was 11:45 and twenty seconds," he answered, with the hint of a smile.

She didn't smile back. She simply waited.

Dawson continued to walk around the body with his hands in his pockets. Tracing the exact route she had.

When he reached the area of the dismemberment he crouched down and took a closer look.

"I'd place his death between 11 p.m. last night and 1 a.m. this morning, and if you want any closer than that I suggest you ask the murderer when you catch him."

"Oh, I will," Kim said, as Bryant returned from speaking to the person who had found the body.

"Jerry Walker, guv," he said. "Twenty-nine years old. Runs this way every morning come rain or shine. Still in shock but got his details for follow-up."

"Anything off?" she asked.

Bryant shook his head. "Don't think so. Seemed legit to me. His address and the route make sense but..."

Yeah, they'd check him out anyway.

Dawson's circuit had ended and he had come to rest behind them.

Keats looked up at the four of them standing together.

"I say, how many detectives does it take to screw in a lightbulb?"

As already noted in her own mind, gallows humor was supposed to be funny.

"Postmortem time?" Kim asked.

"Tell me something, Inspector," he said, fixing her with a stare. "Are you a prime example of what I've got to look forward to working with here at West Midlands Police?"

"Not at all. You'll find some of them are dead miserable so enjoy me while..."

To her surprise he threw back his head and laughed out loud.

She hadn't even been joking.

He checked his watch. "I have something to finish up so make it 2 p.m. on the dot."

She nodded her thanks as she headed back to the car. Once there she stopped and turned to her team.

"Okay, we have a male victim, nailed to the ground, naked and no possessions. What's the very first thing we need to do?"

No one spoke.

"Jeez, guys, there's no penalties or punishments for wrong answers."

Again, she asked the question and Dawson was the first to speak.

"We need to give our guy a name."

"And that's the answer I wanted."

CHAPTER 10

"Okay," Kim said, heading back into the squad room. "DCI Woodward has been briefed so let's get cracking on trying to identify our guy."

In every case it was her top priority. As a product of the care system she had been called "child" or "hey" or "girl" or something that took no effort from her carers to know her name and it had always stayed with her. Being nameless made you irrelevant and their victim was certainly not that.

The trip out to the crime scene had eaten away at a chunk of the morning but she'd learned a great deal about the small team she was managing.

"And thank you to whoever got the coffee," she said, seeing the collection of canteen disposable cups.

Bryant raised his hand in acknowledgment.

"Right, Stacey, it's a long shot but I want you to start looking at any potential CCTV leads in the area. We have a rough time of death so work your way back from that. And don't forget that there are a couple of different routes to that location, so we want to cover private residences, petrol stations, industrial buildings."

Stacey nodded and turned toward her screen.

"Dawson, I want you to get onto missing persons and see if anyone matching his description has been..."

"Bit early for that, isn't it, boss?" he questioned.

She had thought the same thing herself. He was an adult male who had been killed less than twelve hours ago but you never knew what might come up.

"Yeah, but do it anyway."

He hesitated then nodded.

"Bryant, start checking into our witness and see if there are any nasty skeletons in his closet."

"On it, guv," he said.

She took her coffee into the bowl and fired up her own computer but she had the feeling that wasn't where the information she sought was stored. She'd seen that tattoo before; it may be a coincidence, or it may have a connection to the crime. Some tattoos were more common than others.

She'd seen plenty on folks she'd put away time and time again. The numbers 1488 were common on white supremacist prisoners, representing fourteen words of a quote by Nazi leader David Lane and the "88" standing for the eighth letter of the alphabet repeated: HH for Heil Hitler.

The cobweb she knew typically represented a lengthy term in prison and the teardrop often signified that the wearer had committed murder, or attempted murder if it was simply an outline.

She understood that rappers and other celebrities had recently popularized the teardrop and hoped none of them ended up in prison, because newbies with teardrops made a lot of enemies.

Although she'd never been tempted to get one herself she understood that for some they were a personal expression; some were sentimental, some were statements but many were about a sense of belonging to some kind of group or gang both in and out of prison.

Every gang she'd heard of had some kind of mark. The Crips had many; some linked to disrespecting rival gang The Bloods.

Even Hells Angels had a marker—AFFA, standing for Angel Forever, Forever Angel.

Gangs, the swallow.

"Aha, got it," she said, tapping her nails on the desk.

She grabbed the jacket that had been off her back for less than fifteen minutes and headed back into the general office.

"Forget Jerry Walker for now, Bryant. I need you to come with me."

She knew where she'd seen this particular tattoo before.

CHAPTER 11

It was a thin line that separated the D for Dudley postcode from the B postcode for Sandwell and mattered very little for most people but a hell of a lot for two groups of people.

The Deltas was a gang that had grown out of the Hollytree estate back in the Eighties when the place had turned into the council's dumping ground for evictees from other estates.

Over the years the gang had spread out from the estate, and despite the occasional turf war with the B Boys, both gangs had maintained an uneasy peace since a revenge war between two particular families on different sides of the dividing line had ended in a nine-year-old boy being stabbed to death during a fight. The whole of the force knew it was a tentative cease-fire and could be sparked back into all-out bloody war at any time.

Kim dragged her thoughts back into the car and tried not to show her frustration at the leisurely pace at which her new colleague drove the Astra Estate. After her Kawasaki Ninja it felt like a whole lot of metal.

"You wanna check the cost of putting me on your insurance, Bryant. I'll pay."

He laughed politely.

"Yeah, I'm not kidding," she said, as he neared the location to which she'd directed him.

Twice already she'd felt like a speeding car in her mind with the brakes suddenly slammed on. She expected her mode of transport to keep pace with the thoughts and developments in her head.

"Okay, stop here," she said, as they reached the Holy Trinity Church in Old Hill.

"Don't they congregate down by what used to be the Blue Oyster chippy?" Bryant asked, of the local faction of the B Boys.

"I don't want all of them," she answered. "Just one of them."

And she knew exactly where he'd be.

"Wait here," she said, as Bryant unclicked his seat belt.

She got out of the car and headed to a small underpass that led onto the Riddins Mound estate.

Built near the Halesowen Road overbridge in the 1960s, Riddins Mound consisted of 547 homes across three tower blocks, seven three-story blocks of flats, nine maisonette blocks and four bungalows. Due to the estate falling into decline by the early 1990s one of the tower blocks was demolished while the rest of the estate was refurbished and community facilities improved.

As she'd suspected she saw a man sitting huddled on the ground. His jacket, although dirty, was of good quality and his shoes had better soles than hers. His hair was as long and straggly as she remembered it.

He held out a metal can, shook it and a couple of coins rattled.

"Cut it out, Dundee," she said, coming to stand before him.

"Aw, shit, what you want?"

This was a man she knew well and who also knew her. She'd arrested him for low-level drug pushing more times than she'd had hot dinners. If he emptied his pockets she'd be able to stay high for a month.

When Dundee's shop was open he tied a bandanna to the balustrade at the top of the underpass, and right about now folks would be looking out of their windows to see if Dundee's weed store was open.

He'd been inside countless times and every time he was released he just came right back to this very spot and carried on as though nothing had happened. But as far as she knew the man didn't sell to kids.

And he was also a member of the B Boys gang.

He turned his face fully upward, toward her, his skin bathed in a jaundiced glow from the yellow light above.

She looked around at the dark, gloomy, depressing area.

"You really choose this as your office?"

He shrugged. "It's warm."

"I need something, Dundee. Information."

He shook his head, looking to both ends of the underpass. His customers would start to arrive soon and it wouldn't look good if he was talking to a known police officer.

"You got the wrong guy. I ain't no snitch."

"I don't want that kind of information. I want an identity," she said, taking her phone from her pocket.

She scrolled down to the photo of the tattoo. "One of yours?"

Traditionally a swallow was linked to sailors: they would get a set of the birds inked on their chest. The story went that if he or she drowns the swallows will come down and lift the soul to the heavens.

In England, the swallow tattoo was often the symbol of working-class pride, fast fist, meaning these fists fly. The swallow tattoo used by the B Boys had a feather missing from its right wing.

Dundee shrugged.

"Look closer," she said, thrusting the phone into his face.

"Could be."

She waited.

"Yeah," he said. "But do you know how many of these have been inked over the years?" He took another look. "But he's a fucking pansy whoever he is."

"Why so?" she asked.

He rolled his eyes. "Cos the more prominent place you get inked denotes your gang loyalty," he said, pointing to his own, smack bang in the middle of his forehead. "Shows you're never gonna try and leave."

"Any names?"

"Nah, way too many..."

"How about now?" she asked, showing him a photo of the dead man's face. She'd hoped to avoid it, but she wasn't going to get his identity any quicker and their victim needed a name.

"He dead?" Dundee asked, looking closer, but a hint of recognition passed over his features.

"You know him, don't you?"

He shook his head.

"Dundee, you're lying. Give me a name or I'll have the squad car that brought me parked up for the next hour for your peak trading time."

His eyes challenged her but she'd arrested him enough times for him to know she was good for it.

"Luke Fenton and that's all you're getting; but I can tell you that swallow has got no place on that fucker's neck. Shoulda been burned off with a red-hot poker."

"You mean he should have been thrown out of the gang?" she asked, surprised. The B Boys weren't normally so choosy. A soldier was a soldier.

"He was thrown out of the gang," he said, spitting to his left.

"For what?" she asked, moving closer. She'd never heard of any other gang member being thrown out of the B Boys.

He shook his head resolutely. "Never gonna happen."

Damn that sense of gang loyalty that prevailed over all else. Regardless of what he'd done to get himself excommunicated from a criminal gang, and to earn the disgust of a low-level drug dealer, Dundee still wouldn't tell her the whole story.

"Dundee, I can have that squad car here in seconds..."

"You can bring the whole bloody fleet for all I care but I'm not telling you one more thing."

CHAPTER 12

"I've gor a name," Stacey said, putting down the phone to the boss.

"Good for you. Mine's Kev," her colleague offered, glancing again at his phone.

"For our victim," she clarified.

"No shit," he said, dismissively, without looking at her. "But it kinda gets me off the hook with trawling through mispers," he said.

"You wanna start looking...?"

"Nah, you're okay. I need to pop out. Be back in a bit," he said, grabbing his overcoat.

Stacey watched him go and tried not to let her mouth fall open. He was senior in rank to her so she couldn't really question him about anything, but she was unsure just how much trawling, as he put it, of missing persons he'd actually done. Unless there was some kind of app on his phone for it, she didn't think he'd done a lot.

And what should she tell the boss if she asked? Was she supposed to be honest or cover his arse? She didn't yet understand the politics of CID after half a day, but he was still pissing her off, causing her to wonder if she had the word "mug" tattooed on her forehead.

A tiny voice whispered that he might have some kind of personal problem and needed support. A bit of leeway. Everyone needed that sometimes, didn't they? she asked herself, aware that she was trying to excuse both his behavior and his attitude.

People pleaser and now people excuser.

More importantly, would she land herself in trouble for not saying anything to the boss?

From what she'd seen of the boss so far, she was direct and forthright. There was nothing warm and fluffy there. *Nurturing* was not a word that sprang to mind but Stacey found herself not minding that. One of the worst things for a people pleaser was not knowing where you stood, wondering if you were doing okay or totally messing things up. She had the feeling that with DI Stone she wouldn't have to wonder for long, and Stacey was grateful that the boss had given her a reason to step away from the crime scene. But that had just made her want to return with Dawson. Just to show that she could.

So, on her first morning as a detective constable she had met a new team, visited a crime scene, watched a pathologist at work, got CCTV to check and a name to research.

And that was before she tried to analyze the seed of discomfort that had settled in her stomach when she'd looked down at the body.

There was something in the back of her mind but for the life of her she couldn't tempt it to the front.

CHAPTER 13

"Fuck," Dawson said to himself as he walked out into the freezing cold. He took a few steps away from the entrance to avoid nosey parkers.

He was pissed off on so many levels.

He didn't appreciate being humiliated by his boss in being sent home to change. Although she'd done it privately, the others knew exactly what had happened and now he'd lost face with a trudging DS of equal rank to himself who, despite being in his late forties, hadn't made it past sergeant. Not to mention being humiliated in front of a detective constable on her first day, for God's sake.

Thank God Ally had been at work and he'd been able to sneak into the house, shower, change and grab a few items of clothing to keep him going.

He'd felt a bit of a pang as he'd entered the home they'd started renting seven months earlier. They'd had some great times in the house already and in some ways, he missed her. He was pretty sure he loved her even though he said it rarely. He'd never felt this way about a woman before and eventually she had managed to turn him monogamous, for a while. But then he'd remembered the last time they'd been together and the angry, bitter words they'd exchanged. His blood had run cold and he'd hot-footed it out of the house as though the devil was nipping at his ass.

And as if that wasn't bad enough he'd returned to work, and not only had the boss not even acknowledged his efforts, she had proceeded to give him the grunt work of trawling through missing persons. He sneered to himself, glad he hadn't even bothered with that fool's errand.

But right now, he had a more pressing problem like where the hell was he going to spend the night.

He'd sent text messages to all of his friends. Some hadn't even bothered to reply and the ones that had replied hadn't bothered to cushion their refusals with excuses. Just two-letter responses, but Jesus, he couldn't turn up for work again tomorrow looking like shit and his overdraft was at its limit.

He scrolled back through the list of contacts on his phone, half wishing he'd been nicer to his new colleague. Maybe she had a spare room going.

A smile began to tug at his lips as he had an idea.

His relationship with Ally had turned him *almost* monogamous. But not quite.

He scrolled down to a certain number and pressed.

The call was answered on the second ring, which offered him a ray of hope. A part of him expected her not to answer his call at all.

"Hey Lou, how are you doing?"

"What do you want?" she asked, coldly, but the emotion in her voice gave her away.

He silently fist pumped the air. He knew just how to play this one.

He hesitated for just a few seconds before lowering his voice.

"I've been thinking about you a lot. There's something...I dunno what it is but there's unfinished business. I don't know if I made a mistake when I broke it off with—"

"But didn't you ditch me for the love of your life?" she spat angrily, giving him even more hope. She still had a lot of emotion coursing through her at losing him. Perfect.

"It's not how I thought it would be, Lou." He paused again for dramatic effect. "It's not how it was with us. None of it," he said, meaningfully.

He knew she'd get it.

The sex had been explosive.

He heard an intake of breath and knew she was recalling exactly what he'd intended.

"I mean...I dunno...maybe we should meet up. Just chat about stuff?"

She hesitated. "Okay, maybe we..."

"Seven at our usual place?" he asked, tremulously, humbly, hopefully.

More hesitation.

"Okay, I'll see you there."

He ended the call and smiled widely.

Now he could concentrate.

Because now he knew he had a bed for the night.

CHAPTER 14

Kim was surprised at how much bigger the morgue seemed under Keats's supervision. The three metal dishes were lined up as they had always been.

The fixed shiny metallic work surfaces hadn't been moved or rearranged since her last visit, but there was something different.

Keats's predecessor had filled the space with his height and girth, and although the area had not been what she would call messy it was now positively sterile. Folders and books and measuring guides had been moved to the small desk in the far corner and all tools had been arranged onto a movable trolley that sat between the first and second dish.

She remembered the first time she'd attended a postmortem. For a full two minutes she'd been unable to rip her gaze away from the tools. The pathologist had talked her through the different types of forceps; some for bone cutting and some for bone holding and others used just for arteries. Amongst the knives, scissors, retractors, clamps and chisels the most unnerving tools had been the selection of saws. She had expected the tools to look drastically different from the ones in the hardware shop. She had expected something that looked more gentle, less intrusive, more respectful, somehow.

She was disappointed to see all the dishes empty. The workspace had been arranged to reflect the man's tidy, efficient mind, but maybe it would have been time best spent arranging the body for postmortem at the agreed hour.

Because she was right on time.

She put her hands on her hips. "I mean, anytime you'd like to start on the reason we're here so..."

"The postmortem on Luke Fenton has been completed."

"Excuse me," Kim said, as the pathologist reached for a clipboard.

"My lunch was a cold sausage sandwich and surprisingly I wasn't all that keen, so I decided to crack on."

A low chuckle sounded from her colleague.

"And my motivation for speed has absolutely nothing to do with getting you in and out of my workspace as quickly as possible."

"Your very tidy workspace," she noted, ignoring the jibe.

"A tidy mind and all that, Inspector," he said, placing his clipboard behind him.

"Vital statistics all recorded and will be sent in the formal report but in short our man was five foot ten and weighed around one hundred and fifty pounds. All major organs are of normal weight and size and exhibit no particular lifestyle vices. His last meal was some kind of Chinese dish with beef and noodles, and a full toxicology report will be with you once I have it back."

"Is that it?" she asked.

"Give a man time to pause for breath, Inspector, for goodness' sake."

"Sorry to rush you but anything useful would be great," she said, offering what she thought was an accompanying smile.

"Please don't do that again," he said, frowning. "It's not an expression that sits naturally on your face."

Yeah, he was right. It did feel kind of strange.

He reached for a stack of printed photographs and laid three down.

The snaps showed the victim's hair parted to reveal a sizable lump on the back of the head.

"Wow," Bryant said.

"Yes, our man was hit with great force with an object that was almost sure to have rendered him unconscious."

"Giving our killer time to get him into position," Kim observed, remembering the scene that had met her.

"And strip him," Bryant added.

"Okay, that's mildly helpful," she said, nodding toward the three photographs.

"Well, as it's my only priority to try and impress you, I shall continue."

He laid out another three photographs and these needed no explanation.

"The genital area," he said, which had been photographed from all angles. "The mutilation took place after death and although looks haphazard and frenzied was not. The cuts to the penis are amateurish but assured. There are few start and stop wounds so I'm guessing your killer knew exactly what they wanted to do."

"But it wasn't the main event," Bryant offered quietly.

Kim looked his way.

He continued. "The nails were probably hammered in while the victim was unconscious. The genital mutilation was performed after death which pretty much leaves the neck work as the main course."

Kim agreed.

"Keats, do you have the close-ups of the neck?"

He took more photos and laid them out while gathering the others. "There are three modes of dismemberment, which are: disarticulation around the joints, which is basically the separation of two bones at their joint either by injury or surgery; transection of bone via chopping; and transection of bone via sawing."

"And we have?" Kim asked.

"The head was cut off with a saw," he said, pointing to a close-up of the jagged edge of the flesh where it had been chewed up by a heavily serrated saw.

Even on the photo Kim could see that the wound that had been inflicted to kill him was an inch higher than the saw marks, and it was that first cut she wanted to understand. The psyche of someone who could get on their hands and knees and saw someone's head off she would consider later. But as Bryant had noted, the victim had been beheaded after death so the kill wound was the priority and told them more about both the crime and the criminal.

"Bryant, would you mind lying on the floor?" she asked.

The two men looked at each other and then back at her.

He didn't move.

"Guv, are you...?"

"Look, I'll lie on the floor if you want. I just need to..."

"Okey dokey, I'll do it," he said, removing his jacket and lowering himself to the ground.

"Adopt the position of the victim," she instructed.

He put his arms out to the side and opened his legs wide.

"Jeez, I can't even think what's been on this floor," he said, turning his head to the side. "Hey, Keats, there's a pound coin under your fridge."

"Noted," Keats said, keeping his eyes on her.

She walked in between Bryant's legs. His eyes were watching her closely.

"If you couldn't move, how would you be feeling right now?"

"Well, my hands are itching to cover my knackers quick smart."

"Give me an emotion, not an action," she said, peering down at him.

"Vulnerable," he admitted. "And please don't let this leave the room."

Kim continued to stare down at him.

She changed her position and stood with her feet either side of his waist.

"How about now?"

"Not so much but I can see your expression better. I feel like I can read your eyes now."

Kim held her hand out. "Keats, you got something...?"

A ruler was thrust into her hands.

Watching her, following her thought process and anticipating her next move, definitely earned him a couple of Brownie points.

Kim continued to move up her colleague's body. The tips of her boots were almost touching his armpits.

"How do you feel now?" she asked, staring down into his eyes.

"Intimidated, powerless, maybe just a little freaked out seeing as we only met a few hours ago."

Kim lowered herself and placed the ruler half an inch below Bryant's ear. He swallowed deeply but her eyes never left his as she slowly pulled the ruler across his throat.

"Okay, you can get up now," she said, stepping aside and handing the ruler back to the pathologist.

"Strangely compelling," he said, placing it on the work surface.

"Hmm...so what are the rest of the photos in your hand?" she asked, as Bryant jumped to his feet with more agility than she would have expected.

"Observant, Inspector," he said, laying out the last three prints.

She looked closer. "What's that?"

"Brown paper," he said. "Placed just inside the mouth. Nothing written on it. Just a perfect square about an inch wide of brown paper. I suspect it's the kind used for parcels and packaging, but it's gone off to the lab for analysis so there may be something more to come from that."

"Accidental or intentional?" Bryant asked.

Kim shook her head. She really had no idea.

"Anything else, Keats?" she asked, edging toward the door. He shook his head.

*

Bryant waited until they were in the corridor before speaking.

"Guv, that wasn't some kind of first-day initiation prank, was it?"

"No, Bryant, it was a whole lot more than that."

"Such as?"

"It told me what this murder was all about."

"Go on."

"Intimacy, Bryant. Intimacy and power."

CHAPTER 15

Stacey considered holding out her hands to see which ball in the air would fall down first.

She was trying to research the life of their victim and pin down his last known address. Once she'd got that she could approach the phone companies to see if they could offer any details on his phone. She was still trying to check the CCTV of the areas around the crime scene and the feeling of not putting something together in her stomach was not going away.

And DS Dawson was staring out the window.

Admittedly he'd returned to the office after lunch with a smile and a whistle and had then proceeded to do bugger all.

"Hey, do yer fancy giving me a hand with...?"

"I'm thinking," he said, looking past her and out of the window. "There has to be an easier way." He looked pointedly toward the papers strewn across her desk. "And it ain't the method you're using."

"You mean good old-fashioned police—"

"You got a washing machine?" he asked, cutting her off.

She frowned. "Of course."

"Did you know they used to hand-wash every garment at one time. Hot soapy water, squeeze, rinse and mangle?"

Of course, she knew. Many years ago she'd watched an elderly aunt do it.

"Well, folks don't wash that way anymore, you know. There are easier, quicker, less labor-intensive ways of doing things," he said, as his face broke into a smile.

He pushed back his chair. "You just sit there and keep hand-washing, Stacey, but I think I've got a better idea. See you later."

Stacey opened her mouth to say something and then changed her mind. She knew it would make no difference to her colleague at all. He wanted a quick, easy fix to finding their killer.

He wanted a fast food solution. He wanted to drive through Maccie's and come out the other side with a Happy Meal, a McFlurry, the killer's name and address and current location.

She idly wondered how often that actually happened in CID. In uniform the whole process of policing had been divided into sections with neighborhood teams, traffic teams, firearm teams. She had attended jobs and then never known the outcome. Jobs were passed on and dealt with by close-knit teams who…

Her thoughts trailed away as the reason for the knot in her stomach made itself known to her. She'd overheard something on her last day at her old station. Only three days earlier. She'd been in the locker room at Wolverhampton station, clearing out her stuff. Two of her colleagues came in to clock off. They hadn't spoken to her and she hadn't taken too much notice of them, but she knew they'd attended the discovery of the body of a homeless man in the city center, and although they'd been whispering she'd heard the words "genitals" mentioned before they'd lowered their voices even more.

She turned to her computer and searched for the news article. She skim read it and then pored over it in detail. The news report offered no identity and had quickly been buried under the news that a foreign diplomat's daughter had been abducted. The report was brief and mentioned nothing of genital mutilation, but perhaps that was one of the details being withheld by the team running the case. It would explain why her colleagues had been whispering as they would have been briefed at the scene.

She tapped her fingers on the desk. What if this had happened before? What if this wasn't the killer's first victim?

She took a deep breath as her email dinged and one of her balls in the air fell into her hand.

She had found Luke Fenton's last known address, and it was time to call the boss.

CHAPTER 16

"Please tell me you have the address, Stacey?" Kim said, answering the call. She was eager to learn more about their victim. This murder was one of the most personally intense crime scenes she'd ever witnessed and she already felt sure that knowing more about Luke Fenton would lead them to his killer.

"Gor it, guv," Stacey said. "And texting it to Bryant right now."

"Okay," Kim said, hearing a note of trepidation in the young detective's voice.

If she was texting the address why the need for the phone call? "And?"

"Err...boss...it might be nothing but...err..."

"Out with it, Stacey," she said.

"Well, the other day, as I was finishing up at Wolverhampton I overheard..."

Kim was about to chivvy her up as Bryant took out his phone to read the text message, but realized that what she was hearing was nervousness. She closed her mouth and let the girl finish.

"...two officers talking about a crime scene they'd attended in the city center and..."

"The homeless guy?" Kim asked. She'd heard the news report. From the sparseness of the details she'd assumed that the death was a result of a fight over a bottle of beer or some other item. She was sure she'd heard the man had been stabbed.

"Yeah, but they were talking about genitals and I just wondered if there was anything there we should..."

"You heard them say the word *genitals*?" Kim asked, raising an eyebrow in Bryant's direction.

"Yeah, I mean, I know it ay..."

"See what you can find out," Kim said, noting that Stacey's Black Country accent became stronger the faster she spoke. "But don't spend too much time on it," she advised. Luke Fenton was their priority, although Stacey's call had dusted off the memory of something she'd heard and forgotten.

She ended the call and scrolled down her call register.

"Hey, Keats, got a minute?" she asked, not really caring if he was free or not.

"Just about to perform a—"

"Great," she said. Just about to do something was not yet doing it, which in her language meant he had a minute. "You said something earlier about our victim's mutilation not being the worst you'd ever seen. What were you talking about?"

"A case a few years ago in Stoke. Single stab wound to the heart but a right mess of the testicles."

"Any other similarities to our guy this morning?" she asked.

"Well, the man still had his head but I can't remember every detail." He paused and let out a breath. "But I will take a look at my report later and see if there's anything that jumps out."

"Thanks, Keats," she said, ending the call.

Just like Stacey's lead it was probably going nowhere but it didn't hurt to check.

CHAPTER 17

Darkness was already dropping by the time they were a mile away from the property in Amblecote that Stacey had called through to them.

"So, you work with DS Dawson before?" she asked idly.

"No, thank God," he said and then turned her way. "Sorry, I shouldn't…"

"It's fine. Just wondered what you thought," Kim said. She'd form her own opinion on the detective based solely on his performance under her remit, but she was curious as to whether their paths had crossed. As Stacey was a new detective, she knew he wouldn't have worked with her, and Kim's opinion was already forming on that score.

"Sorry, guv, but don't like to speak ill of the brain dead."

She hid her smile at his humor. "I'm gonna take that as a no."

"Didn't realize quite how lucky I'd been," he said, pulling off the main road, leaving her in no doubt about his opinion.

"Just up here," Bryant said, checking the satnav.

The house itself was one of four narrow properties that had been built on a plot previously occupied by a decent-sized bungalow, judging by the other properties along the road.

The empty frontage was a sliver of tarmac wide enough only for a medium-sized car, and Kim would not even have called it a driveway.

Bryant negotiated the waiting squad car and pulled in. There was no way of avoiding stepping onto the neighboring property as they got out of the car.

"You tried the door?" Kim asked of the constables ready and waiting.

"Locked, Marm," the guy on the left answered.

Kim glanced around at the prying eyes looking out of brightly lit windows, aglow with flashing fairy lights.

"Okay, let's do it," she said.

The officer nodded and headed for the squad car.

Anyone not yet looking probably would be shortly, she thought, as the PC returned with the big red key. Forensics had not informed them of any possessions found at the scene leaving them little choice but to force entry. His house keys had gone along with the rest of his stuff.

The PC offered her one final glance before getting the tool into position.

She nodded her instruction to proceed.

"No car, guv?" Bryant asked.

Strange, she agreed. No vehicles had been found at the scene either.

The door gave way on the first hit and bounced back off the internal wall with the force of the blow from The Enforcer, which applied more than three tons of impact in its 16kg weight.

Kim pushed the door open and stepped into the narrowest of hallways, made more hazardous by a bicycle leaning up against a small radiator.

Kim carried on through past the stairs on her left. She'd entered many properties that were deceptively spacious on the inside despite the external appearance, but she quickly realized this one really was a poky little house just as it said on the tin.

The downstairs area consisted of two rooms. A kitchen that looked out to the front and a lounge that looked out onto a fenced area approximately twenty-five feet long.

She headed into the kitchen first. Three basic wooden chairs and a round table sat immediately to her left. A car magazine with the pages open caught her attention. Two of the cars listed were circled.

"Must be getting a bit chilly on that bike," Bryant said, also glancing at the magazine and seeing the markings.

She took photos of the contact details of both cars to see if their victim had ever made a call.

She stood in the middle of the room and looked around. The units and appliances were cheap and functional. A few tea stains marked the work surface on their journey from cup to the spoon rest, which was half full of used tea bags.

Immediately she suspected that no woman lived here. But it didn't hurt to check.

"Bryant, ring Stacey and see if anyone else is listed on the electoral roll."

He nodded and stepped back into the hallway.

She wasn't exactly house-proud herself but those tea stains would have driven her mad.

Also, she detected a thin film of dust on pretty much everything other than the kettle and the percolator.

Dried spill marks littered the floor and followed a trail from the work surface to the nearest chair.

"No, guv," Bryant said, putting away his phone. "Stacey says he's the only one listed on the electoral roll for the last three years. The whole time he's lived here."

She nodded her acknowledgment and moved into the lounge. Another small space darkened further by an oversized three-piece suite and heavy velour curtains that dropped and then spread out on the floor. A small television and a games system occupied the far corner. A football mug and snack plate had been left on a small glass coffee table to the right of the single chair.

Lying on the far cushion of the three-seater sofa was a closed laptop.

Kim wondered if they'd find out more about the man from that than they would from his home.

Footsteps sounded behind her.

"Hey, Roy," she said to the heavily bearded man.

"Got a call from your constable to meet you here." He took a look around the empty room. "Left the crime scene at Clent for this?"

Kim had worked with Roy a few times before. His analytical and enquiring mind made him the perfect forensic technician, and she had learned to ignore his moans. She'd swear that a Euro millions lottery win wouldn't put a smile on that face.

"Can we get that bagged?" she asked, pointing at the computer.

"Is that it?" he asked, clearly miffed that he'd been called away.

"Who knows? We haven't checked upstairs yet," she said, hoping that there wasn't actually another body.

He took a suit from his bag and started to climb into it.

"No forced entry," she elaborated. "Well, until we got here so I'm not thinking anything took place here, but we are looking for clues."

He offered a grunt of acknowledgment, and she headed upstairs.

Bryant followed. "Happy chappie."

"He's okay. Just likes to be where the action is. I'll take him over the pathologist any day."

"Hmm...not so much," he replied.

The hallway was small with three closed doors.

The first she opened led into a bathroom with a shower above the tub. A quick look around confirmed he didn't bother to clean the area often. Toothpaste specks mottled the glass of the bathroom cabinet. Black tidemarks circled the bath like the age rings in a tree trunk.

"My missus would throw a hissy fit," Bryant remarked from the doorway.

Kim stepped out of the room and back onto the landing as she heard Roy below ending a call.

"Hey, Inspector," he called up. "You give your boy the instruction to be a pain up our arse?"

Kim looked at Bryant, who shrugged.

"Didn't hear you, Roy," she said, playing for time.

"Your sergeant, Dawson. You tell him to turn up at the lab hassling for the chemical compound of those nails?"

Kim didn't hesitate. "Yeah, I know he's keen but we need the info. He ain't leaving until he's got it."

"Yep, that's what he said too."

Kim turned away, hiding her brief smile.

The fact that she hadn't instructed him to do so would be dealt with at another time, but if his presence at the lab got the results any quicker she was happy to leave him to it.

She opened the second door and almost walked into the end of a king-size bed that was too big for the modest bedroom space, leaving room for only one bedside table and lamp.

"I'll check the other room," Bryant offered.

Kim suspected he would find it empty.

She inched crab-like past a heavy oak wardrobe, her leg tripping on the overhanging quilt cover from the unmade bed.

She opened the drawer of the bedside cabinet to find underwear, some stray screws and a pair of glasses. The second drawer of the unit was empty.

"Bloody hell," she said, wondering if anyone had known this man.

She was about to turn away when something caught her eye from beneath the stack of pillows.

She pinched her nails together and tugged at it gently. It was the ribbing of a sleeve cuff, pink. She frowned and continued to pull. An arm, a front, back and hood. She slowly and deliberately exposed the whole garment.

A small pink hoodie with the word "Princess" sequined on the back.

"Hey, guv," Bryant called from across the hall.

She lifted her head and could see straight into the smaller bedroom and to what Bryant was pointing at.

It was unmistakably a child's bed.

She looked again at the small pink hoodie that their victim had kept close to him at night.

Now she had even more questions about Luke Fenton, but the one that was flashing brightest in her mind was where the hell was the kid?

CHAPTER 18

Stacey replaced the receiver after her call from the boss. She'd been nervous that the boss would ask after her colleague and she would be placed in a difficult position.

Her relief turned to puzzlement. Why hadn't she asked? Did the boss know something she didn't or had she given up on him already?

Maybe he'd been transferred off the team and they were to get a replacement tomorrow.

She could hope.

But in the meantime, the boss had found an old telephone bill and she now had a direct route back to the service provider. She fired off an email.

The boss had told her to leave the CCTV for now and concentrate on the background of their victim.

She'd heard the pause at the end of their conversation. A pause that should have been filled with Stacey's update on the murder of the homeless man in Wolverhampton, except that she had nothing to offer. She'd left a message for Robyn, the one female police officer who had still been semi-friendly toward her after she'd passed the National Investigators Exam and Advanced Detective Training course.

Gradually, during her two years as a trainee detective constable, people she'd classed as friends had spoken to her less and less, but Robyn had still occasionally struck up a conversation in the canteen. Now and again their eyes had met and Stacey had fleetingly wondered if there was an attraction between them. The very thought had frightened her to death. She'd never once acted on her attractions to other women.

She took out her phone and dialed the woman's number again. She was mildly surprised when the call was answered on the second ring.

"Hey Robyn, I left yer a…"

"Yeah, I know. I just got it."

Stacey raised an eyebrow, trying to analyze the tone in so few words. Forced politeness. She couldn't help the emotion that gathered in her throat. At the very least she'd hoped they were still friends, but it appeared that Robyn now also viewed her promotion as some kind of betrayal against all female uniformed officers.

Stacey swallowed before speaking and put effort into keeping her voice light.

"I wondered if you'd heard anything about the murder of that homeless guy in the—"

"Tommy Deeley?"

"Yeah, that's the one," Stacey said, although she hadn't previously had a name. "Anything weird with his injuries?"

"Single stab wound to the chest is what killed him," she said quickly, and Stacey knew there was something else.

"Any genital mutilation?"

Stacey heard the sharp intake of breath and knew she had it right.

She pushed forward, knowing the two of them were not going to speak again. In for a penny in for a pound.

"Anything else withheld?" Stacey asked.

Silence.

"Look, we're still on the same side, finding the bad guys, and I promise not to bother yer again if you just tell me, okay?"

"A small bell, like from a bird's toy, was found in his pocket. No idea what that's all about but…"

Her words trailed away and Stacey could tell she was eager to be off the phone. There was nothing more for either of them to say.

Maybe there had been something there once but it was now gone.

"Thanks, Robyn. Tek care," Stacey said, putting the woman out of her misery.

She made a few notes from the brief conversation. At least now she had something to tell the boss later.

She returned to the job she'd been tasked earlier. Finding out more about Luke Fenton.

She'd already found that he had no prior convictions and was not known to the police. Any Google searches of his name brought up nothing but a couple of social media accounts.

She logged into Facebook and found his profile.

The man had a total of twenty-three friends and had last posted three days earlier. His information told her that he worked as a storeman at a furniture warehouse on Brindley trading estate.

She scrolled down his timeline looking for anything of interest but his posts were mainly shares of other people's posts or Unilad videos. Each post had one or two likes but no interaction. His friends appeared to be a mixture of other workers from the warehouse and a few people of similar age that she guessed to be old school friends. She continued scrolling through his timeline, thinking how strange the profile was. He'd liked no pages, had no games, had joined no groups and so far, had posted nothing to give her any indication of the man he was.

Finally, a month earlier, she found a post from the man himself.

Stacey frowned at the one-word post, placed on the Facebook wall of a woman by the name of Lisa Baywater.

The post simply said "Gotcha" followed by a big yellow smiley face.

CHAPTER 19

Kim's brain was working overtime as they pulled away from Luke Fenton's address. There was something about the man that was not sitting comfortably in her stomach. They had found no further evidence of a child in the property: not a toy, no clothing, no bedding. Just the bed and the hoodie. All they had gathered from the home was that he rode a push bike and was looking for a car. She hoped Stacey was having better luck back at the station.

"Stop the car," she called out, suddenly.

Bryant halted the car in the middle of the road, much to the annoyance of the driver behind.

"What, where . . . ?"

"Jeez, I meant pull over, man," she said.

"Bloody hell, guv, I thought I was about to hit a small child. What got your attention?" he said, pulling in.

"That place there," she said, pointing to a brightly lit window.

He followed the direction of her finger. "You want Chinese food?"

"Not right now," she said, as he turned off the engine. "And you'd best stay in the car cos you just pulled onto double yellows."

She got out of the car and headed into the restaurant-cum-takeaway that occupied two shop frontages.

The combined smell of ginger and garlic hit her as she opened the door, reminding her that she'd barely eaten a thing all day.

She accepted that her relationship with food was estranged. It wasn't that she didn't want to eat or that she didn't enjoy certain foods, it was just that she tended to forget that it was a necessary part of her day.

She approached the counter of the empty takeaway and glanced into the restaurant. One couple sat in the furthest corner but she was guessing that fiveish wasn't their busiest time. Probably around seven for teatime meals and then half ten after the pubs shut.

A slim Chinese woman appeared from the space next door.

She smiled. "Eat in or...?"

"Neither, thank you. I need to ask if you know a man called Luke Fenton."

She shrugged, looking puzzled. But the common sense in her said that Luke would favor a Chinese restaurant close to home, being without a car, and this was the first one they'd passed. His last known meal had been Chinese food.

"About my height, slim, blonde hair, late twenties, here last night?"

She shrugged, "Sunday, busy night."

Kim took out her phone. She scrolled through the pictures searching for one where the man looked less dead.

She turned the phone. "This man."

The woman appeared to recognize him immediately, so Kim turned the phone away to prevent her from looking too hard.

"Oh, him, he not nice man. He stiffened us once and now we make him pay before he eat here."

"And did he eat here last night?" Kim asked.

She nodded.

"Was he alone?"

"Yes, always alone. Unless he order for takeaway and then he order more."

Kim filed that away for later.

"Any idea when he left?"

"Nine thirty," she said, definitely.

"You're sure?"

"He not nice man. Glad to see him go."

"Okay, anything strange about his behavior, different in any way?"

"Yes, he rush out and he only eat half his meal."

CHAPTER 20

"Really gonna need that phone stuff, Stacey," Kim said, as they entered the squad room. "Pretty sure our victim got disturbed from his supper by some text or call or message from someone, cos he left in quite a rush. Also need to check for CCTV in the area. I'm guessing he was picked up. He had to get from the takeaway to Clent somehow, and if he'd booked a taxi he wouldn't have needed to leave half his meal."

"Sent a follow-up email ten minutes ago, boss, but I'm not hopeful for a response before…"

"Damn," Kim said, cursing much of the working world for finishing around 5 p.m. Her gaze swept across the wipe boards on the wall, noting information that hadn't been there earlier.

"What's that?"

"All I could get about the homeless man. His name, the fact he'd been genitally mutilated and that there was something about a bell found on his person."

"Bloody good work, Stacey," Kim said, surprised. "I'll speak to Woody tomorrow and get the case from Wolverhampton. Given the similarities there's no way it won't get handed over to us."

The first thing she'd do is get Keats to go over the postmortem report to confirm they were the same killer, and then she'd start looking into Tommy Deeley's background, searching for links to Luke Fenton. Her mind was whirring with ideas but she could do nothing about it tonight.

"Okay, in the meantime we've brought a present back from the victim's home," she said, placing the computer on the spare desk. "Time to try and break the password and see what he's all about."

"May I?" Stacey asked, almost salivating at the laptop.

"Be my guest," Kim said, stepping aside. She only knew a few password cracking basics that she'd been told about dates and names.

Stacey sat down and started typing.

Kim had collected laptops and phones that had taken hours if not days to crack. Such was the information guarded within. She was hoping this one was going to be like a window to the man himself.

"I'm in," Stacey said, dejectedly. The laptop had presented no challenge at all.

"Already?" Kim asked.

"More him than me," she said honestly. "His password is his first name and his date of birth."

"Oh," Kim said, feeling the constable's disappointment. Something so easy to access was unlikely to hold anything valuable.

"Can I just have a nosey around for a few minutes, boss?"

"Of course, fill your boots," Kim said, grabbing the marker pen and updating the wipe boards with everything they'd learned that day.

"Guv, shall I go get...?"

"That would be great, Bryant, but from tomorrow we share."

Much as she appreciated the stream of caffeine, he was not going to become tea boy.

Kim watched out the corner of her eye as the constable's fingers flew over the keyboard. Her eyes were focused and her body hunched forward. Clearly the officer had the start of a fire in the pit of her belly, but the intensity of her stare, her concentration told Kim where both the skills and passion of this detective lay.

"Permission to speak freely, boss," Stacey said, as Bryant entered the room with two coffees and a bottle of diet cola.

"How did you know that's all I drink?" Stacey asked, wide-eyed.

Bryant smiled at her. "Well, it could be that my super power is that I'm psychic or it could be the empty can in the bin that wasn't there this morning."

Stacey smiled her thanks.

"Speak, Stacey," Kim instructed. "And this isn't the army. You don't have to ask."

"Okay, I'm feeling there's something not quite right here."

"Go on," Kim said, wondering if the constable could put into words the feeling that had been dogging her since they'd learned his identity.

"For a single man in his twenties it's like we're only getting part of the story, half the man. I can only find him with a half-hearted account with just one weird post. This computer ay even got Facebook on it."

"Could do it from his phone," Bryant observed.

Stacey nodded her understanding. "I get that but if this is his only computer he literally has no life at all. We all like easy access to everything: on our phones, computers, tablets. I have everything loaded on 'em all. He doesn't even have his emails hooked up to this computer and there's no search history at all."

"Deleted?" Kim asked.

Stacey shook her head. "Still leaves a trace."

"Is the computer new?" Bryant asked. "Perhaps he's in the process of switching stuff over."

"He's had this laptop for eighteen months."

Kim sighed heavily. The constable had, in fact, located the unease in her stomach.

"Ten hours on and we know very little about our victim, except that apparently he was not a very nice man," she said, quoting the lady at Wing Sun.

"All I've found is this," Stacey said, returning to her own computer and turning the screen.

Kim frowned at the one-word post on Facebook.

"What the hell does that mean?"

Stacey shrugged.

"Okay," she said, checking her watch. "Get into that tomorrow and the phone company but we'll call it a night. It's been one hell of a first day," she said, fully aware that she was addressing only two thirds of her entire team.

His absence had better be worth it.

CHAPTER 21

Kim turned the Ninja left as she headed out of the station car park.

She knew full well that she was on borrowed time in the mid-December weather and that she would have to bench it and use the ten-year-old Golf that sat on her drive. But every day was like a gift of the freedom to be herself.

She tried to put her thoughts of the day behind her and just enjoy the feel of the bike obeying her commands.

That thought led her straight to DS Dawson, appreciating the irony that the officer she'd seen the least had occupied her thoughts the most. A part of her was impressed he'd had the gumption to do what he had. But that wasn't the biggest part of her. That larger portion was pissed off that he'd been unable to follow her instructions or assist his colleague once the workload had increased.

You couldn't always force someone to be a team player and she sensed he was an ambitious young man, but his career aspirations were in serious jeopardy if he thought he was going to treat her like a mug.

She hadn't voiced any of her aggravation, because he would be dealt with and she would do it in her own way, in her own time.

Her thoughts inevitably turned to their victim, Luke Fenton, who had been killed and tortured in the most horrific manner, and all they knew was that he wasn't a very nice man because he'd stiffed the local Chinese. Somehow she knew that was not going to help them find his killer.

How was there so little of his life imprinted on the computer?

Suddenly she thought about her Golf, sitting on the driveway, used for nothing more than the odd few bad weather days.

Horses for courses.

She approached the next traffic island and rode all around it.

Home could wait. There was somewhere else she needed to go.

CHAPTER 22

Dawson checked his watch for the third time in as many minutes. He knew he was cutting it fine to make his date with Lou. He had to get back from the West Mids Police Forensic Department at Ridgepoint House in Birmingham, and after all the effort he'd put in to secure a bed for the night he didn't want to have to text and say he was going to be late. Something told him that would lead to another night spent in the car.

He took out his phone and checked it. He'd been expecting a call from the boss for hours, had almost been hoping for it. He had his answers all ready. His explanation of the sudden idea he'd had about trying to trace the origin of the nails used to pin their victim down. Hell, he'd even had an insincere apology waiting in the wings in response to the lecture he'd been expecting. He'd wanted to bait her into a reaction, had wanted to show her that he wasn't to be controlled, that he was an independent thinker. He had wanted to give her something to think about, but now all he could do was wonder about her silence.

As the tech he'd been waiting on finally gave him the thumbs-up, he couldn't help wondering who was playing who.

CHAPTER 23

Kim arrived back at Luke Fenton's property just before 7 p.m.

Roy greeted her in the hallway.

"Quite the exciting search we've got going on here, Inspector," he said, telling her they'd found nothing of interest. "So, what brings you back?"

"Just a hunch," she said, walking into the kitchen.

Horses for courses.

"You do know we're not done yet and you could have just called and…"

"Ssshh…give me a minute," she said, standing in the middle of the kitchen.

This was the room in which they'd seen the most signs of life.

"What exactly are you looking…?"

"That wasn't a minute," she said, glancing at the tea-stained counter and the film of dust that covered most surfaces.

She walked over to the chair that their victim had used to flick through the car magazine. She sat down, noting the burn rings all in the same area of the table.

She looked around the room from this angle, noting the dust on the shelves, on top of the cooker hob, on the oven door handle.

Her eyes fell to the utility drawer beneath the oven, used for storing pots and pans.

No dust.

Roy continued to watch her from the doorway, glancing at his watch.

She pushed back the chair and took the three steps to the cooker.

She opened the bottom drawer and found the missing part of the puzzle.

A second laptop computer.

CHAPTER 24

It was almost eight when Kim pulled the Ninja into the garage and closed the shutter.

The thirteen-hour day had stretched into the middle of next week, or so it felt.

She struggled to believe it had been only that morning that she'd left the house with no team and no case. And now she had both.

She switched on the percolator before removing her jacket. It was a job she did every morning, prepare the coffee machine for her return. She knew she'd down the pot, whatever the time.

She didn't bother to switch on the TV or the radio. She'd never needed additional sounds to fill the house. And she didn't plan on spending too long in the living room anyway.

A coffee at the breakfast bar followed by a shower and change and then she'd be headed into the garage to work on the explosion of bike parts that would eventually turn into a fully restored 1951 Triumph Thunderbird.

It was a passion she had adopted from foster family four. A middle-aged couple called Keith and Erica who had no children of their own.

From the age of ten to thirteen she had known how it had felt to be part of a family. To be surrounded by love. They had not tried to fix her after the trauma of her first six years. They had not tried to repair the break in her heart from the loss of her twin brother. They had not tried to get her to relive the pain of living with a paranoid schizophrenic intent on killing one of her own children. And succeeding when he was six years old.

They had not tried to wipe away the children's home she'd been sent to, or erase the three foster homes that had come before them. They had simply loved her like their own, before being killed in a motorway pile-up just after her thirteenth birthday.

They had given her love, affection, a sense of worth, security and a love of bikes both old and new.

Working on the Triumph held the power to erase the stresses of the day. If her hand was holding a screwdriver, ratchet or spanner she was focused on putting together the jigsaw of parts. Except she wasn't sure that tonight it was going to unwind her.

Her brain wanted to chew over the events of the day. It wanted to work through all the data.

From the second she'd arrived at the horrific crime scene she had been intrigued as to what this man had done to deserve such hatred and they had found out nothing. Sure, the lady at the Chinese takeaway wasn't over keen, but stiffing them on a bill and being rude wasn't usually motivation for beheading and genital mutilation.

Only at the last second had they found the second computer, and whatever was on there was going to tell them something on the man himself.

Roy had arranged to have it sent straight into the lab but she was guessing no work would begin on it until tomorrow. Once she had the second case from Wolverhampton they could start looking for links between the two of them. If she had her way, she'd be heading toward Wolverhampton right now to demand the case files, but she did understand that processes had to be followed. And she wasn't all that popular at the Wolves station anyway.

Her thoughts turned to her team.

There was something instantly likable about DS Bryant. His height and demeanor screamed solid and dependable. There was a calm friendliness about him that put people at ease. An asset she would probably use exhaustively for the duration of this case, to compensate for her own shortcomings in the personable department.

Stacey Wood was keen and constantly smiling. Kim wondered how long it would be until that stopped. Soon, she hoped, because the woman was trying to please too much, even in the face of a corker of a first case. The crime scene had winded her but she'd chosen to come back. Kim liked that she had spent most of the day working alone without complaining while her colleague was shirking, and Kim respected that, but she had no intention of allowing it to continue. But the real passion, the moments when the false, appeasing smile had dropped from her face, had been when she'd been busy at the computer.

And DS Dawson. Where did she even start? She'd met many Dawsons during her career. He was ambitious and not necessarily for the right reasons. Dawson wanted attention; he wanted reactions. He wanted to rebel against his new boss. She got it but she wasn't going to take it.

All she had right now were opinions, observations of her team based on one day of work.

It wasn't enough.

She switched on her laptop to find out more.

For tonight the Triumph would have to wait.

CHAPTER 25

Kim was ready and waiting as the team filed into the squad room.

She was unsurprised to see Dawson trail in last. A quick appraisal told her he was wearing the same clothes as yesterday, but he at least appeared clean and had shaved. The stench of a brewery hadn't followed him in today, which was surely an improvement from the day before.

To her eye he appeared more subdued. His eyes met hers expectantly.

Oh, it appeared he was still awaiting her reaction from yesterday.

She pointed to the brand-new coffee pot she'd picked up from the 24-hour superstore on her way in.

"The pot is full. If you want to drink anything else, bring it yourself and if you pour the last cup, make a fresh pot."

They all nodded.

"Okay, to recap, our victim is twenty-nine years old, worked as a storeman at Wainwrights, enjoyed Chinese takeaway, had a child's bed and hoodie in his home and hides his computer away. So, where do we go now?"

"Neighbors, workmates?" Dawson offered.

"Yep, well volunteered, Dawson," Kim replied.

"Still need to know about phone records first and the CCTV second," she instructed. "I want to know more about this woman that Luke Fenton contacted on Facebook. What is she to him—is this the mother of the child who was in his home?"

Stacey nodded her understanding.

"And Bryant, find out who is running the murder investigation in Wolverhampton."

She had a meeting with Woody in ten minutes and she just wanted the heads-up on who was going to be doing the handover.

She reached for the phone as she stepped into the bowl. They really needed to find out what was on that second computer belonging to Luke Fenton.

Roy answered on the second ring.

"Good morning to you, Inspector."

"Anything?" she asked.

He paused.

"Yeah, good morning," she offered as an afterthought.

"Jerry's working on the computer right now but it's locked up tighter than a duck's..."

"Don't you have software that can break in?"

"You know, for a police officer you watch way too many cheesy cop shows. Yes, we have software and no sooner it's been tested and implemented some spotty teenager comes up with a workaround. We have to make sure there's no destruction software that will annihilate the data if we get too close to it."

"Annihilate?" she questioned.

"Using terms you can understand," he said, with a smile in his voice.

"Yeah, thanks but if you've got nothing in the next few hours, I'm finding the nearest spotty teenager and sending him over to assist," she said, ending the call.

Her fingers began drumming on the desk in frustration. Whatever the hell was on that computer was important. Her mind pictured a hammer crashing down on it to open the whole thing up. But until they could access the info it looked as though they were all going door to door to find out more about the man.

She reached for her coat as her ears tuned into the conversation beyond her door.

"So, what age did you make DS?" Dawson asked Bryant.

"Thirty-two," he answered, without looking up from his two-finger typing practice.

"Jesus, that old. I got there at twenty-five," he crowed.

"Good for you," Bryant mumbled.

"You take the exam?" Dawson pushed.

"Yeah, I took it."

"More than once?" Dawson asked, keenly, as though he was scoring points with every answer.

Bryant ignored him.

"Cos if you fail it twice, statistically that means you're never gonna…"

"You wanna talk statistics, Dawson?" Kim asked, standing in the doorway. "How about the fact that in the last five years Bryant has achieved a total of one hundred and forty-two arrests as opposed to your record of ninety-six. Or shall we talk about conviction records based on those arrests? Bryant's arrests have accumulated a conviction rate running at ninety-three percent against yours which is in the low eighties. So, which one of those statistics would you like to?—"

"Guv," Bryant interrupted.

She ignored him. "This is not a competition, Dawson."

The jumping muscle in his cheek told her she'd made her point.

"So, let's get back…"

"I've got something, boss," Stacey said. "Umm…sorry, I day mean to…"

"It's fine, Stacey. What have you got?"

"An address for Lisa Bywater, the woman Luke contacted on Facebook."

"Good work. Text it to Bryant," she said, heading out the door. "And once I've got this second case transferred to us we'll find out what this woman has to say and who exactly she is to Luke Fenton."

CHAPTER 26

Kim knocked on the door of DCI Woodward for what she felt was a foregone conclusion. If he was worth his position he would already have been making calls to Wolverhampton.

"Enter," he called back.

She stood just inside the door, as far away from the seat as she could be. This shouldn't take more than a minute and she could be on her way to speak to this woman, Lisa Bywater.

"Take a seat, Stone," he instructed, looking over his glasses.

"Sir, I'm fine stand—"

"Take a seat, Stone," he repeated, but in a deeper voice as though she was a child refusing to put her toys away and the request process had increased a defcon level.

She moved forward and sat. She had learned with her superiors to choose her battles wisely.

"How was your first day with the new team?"

She narrowed her gaze. "Sir, if there'd been any problems I'd have let you know."

This wasn't why she'd requested the meeting. Any issues with her team she would deal with one way or another. She'd never yet sought her superior officer's help with people management and she wasn't about to start now.

"I understand that Sergeant Dawson can be a bit…"

"Sir, can we talk about…?"

"And I understand that having an officer so fresh to the job might be difficult."

"Honestly, I have no complaints at the moment about—"

"But Bryant appears to be a steadying influence, which can only—"

"Sir, they're all good, now when can I collect the case file for Tommy Deeley?"

"We won't be taking the case from Wolverhampton."

"Wh-what?" she spluttered. Nowhere in her proposed chain of events was that even an option. Now this was a battle worth fighting.

"May I ask if you've requested it?"

No matter how she phrased the question in her head it sounded rude on her lips.

"I spoke to DCI Redford late last night."

So, he had read her briefing document, seen the similarities and made the call last night. So, why were the case files not already on her desk?

"And?"

"It's got nothing to do with our case."

"Sir, how can you even think that given the similarities to—"

"Because they already have their killer. A man confessed to the murder last night."

CHAPTER 27

Bryant remained silent as they headed down the stairs, which was good because after the ridiculous conversation with Woody, she was in no mood for idle chatter. She stepped out into the freezing cold morning and right into a woman with long blonde hair wearing a trouser suit and impossibly high heels.

The notebook told her everything she needed to know.

"Are you the detective working on the naked man case?" she asked, blocking Kim's path.

Not a move that impressed her. Her personal space was guarded with alarms, barbed wire and motion sensors.

"Get out of my—"

"Is it true that the body had been mutilated?"

Kim ignored her and attempted to walk around her.

"Is it true that?—"

"Contact press liaison," she said, attempting to dodge the woman again.

"You wanna give me a name?"

"Rumpelstiltskin and this here is…"

"Of the victim," the woman clarified.

"No shit," Kim said, shaking her head and weaving around her once more. "Because my refusal to answer your first two questions would lead you to believe I'd give you that."

"Ah, I'm guessing you're DI Stone," the woman said, offering her hand. "Tracy Frost from the *Dudley Star*."

Kim glanced at the outstretched hand. "The pleasure is all yours."

"Look, Detective, we..."

"Inspector," she corrected.

"Okay, Inspector. You should know I can be a great help to you. Write your side of the story."

"Oh, get out my way," she said, aiming for Bryant's Astra Estate. There was no side of any story. There was just the truth.

The woman continued to walk by her side.

A snippet of a memory came back to her.

She slowed. "Hang on. I remember you. Didn't you report on the suicide of that fourteen-year-old girl from Tipton?"

The reporter's face appeared to lose color.

Kim continued. "The girl who was being bullied online about her weight. You attended the inquest and then wrote an in-depth piece about her including all the gory details about how she did it, totally disregarding the Samaritan guidelines."

Kim knew research had shown links between media coverage of suicides and an increase in suicidal behavior. This had prompted a whole set of what to do and what not to do for reporters. These included: avoiding detail, steering away from melodramatic depictions of suicide or its aftermath and to aim for sensitive, non-sensationalizing coverage. None of which had been adhered to by this woman.

"And what happened?" Kim continued. "If I remember, the day your piece came out a fifteen-year-old tried to copy and do the exact same thing. Lucky for everyone she didn't succeed."

"That piece was about bullying and the effect—"

"It was written to sell newspapers, Frost, and don't pretend otherwise. But what I can tell you, even though you've not yet posed it as a question to me, is that no one in the West Mids Police force likes you very much."

Tracy Frost's face hardened and Kim knew the battle lines between them had been drawn.

"Well, from what I can gather the same goes for your popularity too."

Kim offered her first genuine smile as her palm rested on the door handle. "Thing is, I couldn't give a shit."

She opened the door and got in as the woman hobbled away in shoes that were clearly too high for her.

"Well, that exchange woke me up," Kim said, waiting for Bryant to start the car.

He stared forward.

"What are we waiting for?" she asked, watching the reporter get into a white Audi; a car she would now remember.

"You know, guv, I don't need you to fight my battles for me."

Ah, he was pissed off about what she'd quoted at Dawson.

"I wasn't fighting anyone's battle. It was information that I didn't think you had right at your fingertips."

"And you did?"

"Strangely, yes," she said, buckling up even though the man's driving didn't require it.

She had taken the time to research them all the night before. She'd also found out that Bryant had been put forward for the promotion by two separate inspectors who thought he was good for it. And he had failed the exam both times.

Dawson had been right, statistically speaking. Bryant was unlikely to make it but she hadn't appreciated the younger officer trying to rub the man's face in it.

"Well, whatever it was, please don't do it again. I can handle Dawson."

"Noted," she said. "Now will you please start the bloody car?"

Kim glanced out of the window as the Audi pulled off the car park.

Well, so far today she'd pissed off two thirds of her team and the local journalist, and it wasn't even nine o'clock.

That might be some kind of record.

Even for her.

CHAPTER 28

"What the fuck are you looking at?" Dawson snapped at her as she glanced at him over the top of her screen.

"An arsehole," she said, before she could stop herself.

She instantly looked down, regretting what she'd said, but the words had popped out as though firing directly from her brain.

"I wasn't lying," he said, defensively. "The old man has tried for promotion twice and failed twice. Loser."

Stacey noted how he had conveniently forgotten the figures quoted to him by the boss. And DS Bryant didn't seem like a loser to her. From what she'd seen he was steady, attentive and friendly.

But calling her colleagues names like that was not going to help her to fit in.

"Look, I didn't mean…"

"Forget it. Your opinion doesn't matter to me anyway," he said, grabbing his jacket and leaving without another word.

Stacey shook her head. That guy had some serious issues.

She turned her attention back to work. The boss had told her to get cracking on phone records and CCTV.

A terse return email from the mobile phone provider had confirmed they were working on her requests, and she guessed that hassling them every few minutes was not going to get the results any quicker.

She pulled up the crime scene photos and grabbed a notepad.

As a constable, she'd always been encouraged to see the bigger picture, explore all the information available, dig as deep as you could. It was that need to go further that had driven her to want to be a detective, to find clues, to look at things from every angle, hold things up to the light and think outside the box.

The photos no longer filled her with the horror they had the previous day. This morning she wasn't looking at a man, a human who had been brutally murdered. She wasn't feeling the pain or fear of the victim as the knife had sliced across the flesh.

She was looking at the artistry of the kill. The skill, the cunning, the planning.

The killer had taken their victim to a secluded area in the Clent Hills, late at night, a spot where he'd known he wouldn't be disturbed.

He'd taken something heavy to render the victim unconscious. He'd taken nails to secure the victim to the ground. He had cut the man's throat and then taken the time to mutilate the genitals and totally sever the head.

Stacey remembered a time when she was thirteen and a group of girls had dared her to pinch some pick "n" mix from WHSmith in Dudley town. They'd said she could go to the cinema with them if she did it and so she had.

But she remembered the feeling of fear. She'd walked in, her heart thumping, the blood pounding in her ears. She had grabbed a handful and walked quickly back out of the shop.

She hadn't hung around after the deed was done.

She looked again at both the killer's planning and execution. He'd been in no rush to leave the scene once Luke Fenton was dead.

She prepared to start looking at the CCTV in the area of Clent, but she really hoped they were going to get the details from Wolverhampton soon, because everything she'd ever learned about the anatomy of a murder told her that this wasn't their murderer's first kill.

CHAPTER 29

Dawson sat in his car for just a moment before starting the engine.

Despite the cold sunshine there was a fucking rain cloud that had been following him from the moment he'd woken up.

His plan had gone swimmingly. He'd made it to the restaurant with just minutes to spare.

Filled with the triumph of having got one over on the boss he'd eaten a good meal, had a few drinks and enjoyed himself in the company of a gorgeous woman.

Two hours later he'd been in Lou's flat and in her bed. And all it had taken was a few false promises.

He'd fallen asleep content.

And yet when he'd woken up, turned and seen Lou sleeping peacefully beside him, that contentment had gone and left behind nothing more than a sour taste in his mouth. He had showered quickly and left before she'd even woken up.

He couldn't put a name to this shadow that was following him, but he did know that he was now thinking of Ally more than ever.

He had tried to cheer himself up by having a little fun at Bryant's expense. Just banter. But the boss had stopped him dead. Banter was not allowed. Noted.

And then his other colleague had called him an arsehole. Timid, smiley little Stacey had called him an arsehole.

Fuck 'em, he thought, starting the engine. He didn't give a shit what any of them thought of him.

He could out-police them all without even breaking a sweat and that's what he fully intended to do.

CHAPTER 30

By the time Bryant pulled up in front of a high-rise tower in Bilston the air appeared to have cleared between them.

Thankfully the man was not a sulker.

"Eleventh floor," he said, looking up as they got out of the car.

The area of Bilston was first referred to as Bilsatena in AD 985 and in the Domesday Book as a village called Billestune. Two miles southeast of Wolverhampton the area was extensively developed for coal mining and terraced houses built in the nineteenth century to accommodate the labor force. These dwellings had since been replaced with modern houses and flats on developments like Stowlawn, the Lunt and the estate they were at now called Bunker's Hill.

This was one of the nicer tower blocks she'd visited in her time. And although there was an intercom system someone had wedged open the outer door for the benefit of a furniture delivery team.

"Ooh, lift works," Bryant said, as a young couple with a pushchair got out.

They hopped in and Bryant pressed the button to take them up to the eleventh floor.

He sniffed the air. "Ah, I know what's missing. It's the smell of piss."

Kim smiled her agreement. Yes, she'd been preparing herself but the only smell was the lingering perfume of the woman who had just got out.

The lift landed and they followed the signage to apartment 11c, where a second intercom greeted them.

Bryant pressed and a crackly voice answered. Kim detected wariness in that one single word.

Bryant introduced them and asked if they could have a quick word.

"How did you get into the building?" she asked, still not opening the door.

Kim spoke into the intercom, explaining the delivery van, to signal to the occupant that there was a female presence.

Eventually the door was opened by a woman Kim guessed to be in her early to mid-twenties. Her brown hair was pulled back into a sleek ponytail and she wore little makeup.

She pointed to her clothing, which was the green uniform of the local superstore.

"What's this about? I have to get to work."

"May we come in?"

The woman looked behind her as though checking for something. She stepped back and pointed to a door on the left.

Kim stepped into a light and spacious lounge with three-quarter-length windows that had dark, heavy curtains tied back. The room was sparsely furnished with mismatched items that all seemed to bear battle scars. A stain here, a small rip there.

"I'm sorry to rush you but..." she said, pointedly tapping her watch.

Kim took a seat on the single chair that had no relationship with the three-seater sofa.

"Miss Bywater, do...?"

"Mrs.," she corrected.

Kim acknowledged the incorrect assumption with a nod and continued.

"Mrs. Bywater, do you know someone by the name of Luke Fenton?"

The color dropped from her face as she took a seat.

"How did?...Where?...I mean..."

Kim remained silent, not wishing to divulge that the only contact they could find for their victim was on Facebook.

"Are you related?" Kim asked.

The woman's hands had found each other in her lap. They were flexing and releasing as some kind of tension entered her body. "Please tell me what this is about."

"I have to know if you're related," Kim said, not unkindly. This could be the mother of his child. Whoever she was she was about to get one hell of a shock. Damn it, she hated this part of the job.

Lisa Bywater nodded. "Luke is my brother."

Oh shit, now she really hated this part of the job. And this sibling knowledge would have been useful to them ahead of time.

"Parents?" Kim asked.

"Dead," she answered, shaking her head.

Liking the job less and less.

"Mrs. Bywater, I'm sorry to inform you that we believe your brother is dead."

Not one solitary muscle moved on her face as the words appeared to bypass her ears completely. Her expression said she was still waiting for the actual reason for their visit.

"Mrs. Bywater, your brother has been killed, I'm sad to say, murdered."

The woman began to shake her head. "No...no...you're wrong...he can't be..."

"I'm afraid he is," Bryant said, firmly. "We're in no doubt."

She blinked a few times in quick succession as though the action was helping to get the information into her brain.

Her head dropped into her hands. Her elbows resting on her knees. Her body began to shake with emotion.

Bryant reached across and laid a gentle hand on her shoulder.

"Is there someone we can call?"

She shook her head.

Bryant removed his hand but continued speaking. "We're so sorry for your loss, Mrs. Bywater, but—"

"Are you kidding?" she said, raising a dry-eyed, color-infused face. Her eyes were alight and animated. "It's the best bloody news I've had in months."

CHAPTER 31

"What the hell was all that about?" Bryant asked as they watched Lisa Bywater drive away.

There was no grieving time for this lady, no call to the workplace to explain her loss and forthcoming absence. Brother or not, his death was not going to make her any later for her shift than she already was.

"And her refusal to answer any further questions about . . . well anything," she noted.

The woman had pretty much ordered them out of the flat and would speak no further.

"Shocked you got her to agree to the body identification, guv, to be honest."

Yes, Kim was surprised at that herself. She had asked as the young woman was pushing them out of the door. At first she had started to shake her head and then changed her mind and said she'd love to.

"On a scale of one to ten of weirdest notifications of a death, I'd rank that an eleven," Bryant offered.

Kim could feel her own frown. "Yeah, I get that they might not have been close but to get actual joy from his . . ." She stopped speaking as she had a sudden thought. "Bryant, how far away are we from Wolverhampton?"

"Just a couple of . . ."

"It was rhetorical and not even a question, more like an instruction for you to start heading toward."

"But you said they had their man."

"Well, let's just swing by and see if he's our man too."

CHAPTER 32

It had been two years since Kim had set foot in Wolverhampton Police Station and she hadn't missed it one little bit.

Most CID teams were territorial over their cases, and she'd been called in to assist in a double murder that was two weeks old and growing colder by the hour. Her presence had been met with suspicion, hostility and downright bad manners. In fact, the man she was hoping to see had asked her to fetch him coffee in front of eleven members of staff at the first briefing she'd attended. She had simply smiled and folded her arms in response and remained standing exactly where she was. The three female officers in the room had all lowered their heads but not before she'd seen the smiles they were trying to hide.

"Inspector Lennox, please," she said to the desk sergeant, showing her identification. He took a good look at her name and reached for the phone.

She moved away from the desk and Bryant followed.

"Never met him before. You?"

"Yeah," she said, and left it at that. If she updated Bryant on every inspector she'd clashed with they'd never get anything else done.

"Is he the type of guy who might respond to a polite request to view the footage of the interview?"

"Looks like we're about to find out," she said as the doors opened.

The man had changed little since she'd last seen him. He'd probably gone to the next notch on his trouser belt and there was a touch more gray in his full head of hair, but his open-necked shirt with the hint of tidemark around the collar was still evident.

Neither she nor Lennox offered their hand as they appraised each other.

"What do you want, Stone?"

She wanted to view the taped confession that DCI Woodward assured her they had, and she tried to remember a time when Lennox had ever been pleasant or helpful.

"We were close by and I just thought I'd help you out with some friendly advice. You've got the wrong guy."

It took just a couple of seconds for his brain to register what she was talking about. And when it did, his expression transitioned through disbelief, irritation and then rage. Oh yeah, she remembered well that Lennox didn't like being told he was wrong. Shame.

"Who the hell do you think?—"

"Look, we were just passing and thought we'd try to help out our fellow colleagues given the details of our own case, but have it your own way," she said, taking a gamble and turning away.

"Hang on. You come in here, where you're about as welcome as a dose of the clap, to help us out?"

She turned back. "It's an easy mistake to make. When a guy says he's done it you'd be an idiot not to consider the validity of the claim. And you'd be an even bigger idiot to just accept it without..."

"You do know you're not talking to a fucking trainee, Stone?" he said as the color in his face deepened. "And someone who doesn't need your fucking help to spot a murderer when he sees one."

"Well, as long as you're sure that he's admitted to enough to satisfy CPS and—"

"You wanna come see what we got?" he challenged.

She shrugged and looked at her watch. "If you like. We've got a few minutes."

He key-coded himself back into the body of the police station, and she followed behind. She sensed rather than saw the smile on Bryant's face.

She followed him to his office, which was next door to the squad room. Pokey as it was she remembered he preferred to spend time away from his team and ventured into the work room primarily for morning and evening briefings.

"Maybe this'll shut you up," he said, clicking on a video clip on his desktop.

He had invited neither of them to sit so they both stood behind him as the clip sprang into life.

She recognized the man immediately. She knew him as Butcher Bill, a homeless guy who had graced the streets of Wolverhampton for decades. No one knew his exact history but he had been so named as he'd slept in the doorway of a butcher's shop for almost twenty years, although he was looking a little cleaner and smarter than she remembered.

Lennox forwarded the footage to a point in time he obviously knew well.

"Dirty bastard had it coming," Butcher Bill said with a smile. He leaned forward across the desk toward Lennox. "I enjoyed every minute."

She watched as Lennox glanced sideways at his colleague as though all his Christmases had come at once.

"You saying you did this, Bill?" he asked.

No hesitation. "Yeah, I did it. Dirty bastard had it coming."

The man raised his right hand and made a slicing motion with his fingers. "Snip, snip," he said before he burst out laughing.

"Bill, I need you to listen carefully to what I'm saying," Lennox said across the desk.

"Snip, snip," he repeated.

"Are you confessing to the murder of Tommy Deeley?"

He nodded. "Snippety snip."

Lennox stopped the recording. "Satisfied?"

"You're taking the words 'snip snip' for proof that he performed the genital mutilation?" Kim asked.

"Wouldn't you?" he asked. "What else could he mean? Those details weren't released to the press."

Kim was saved from any further response as her phone rang. She turned away from the screen.

"Stone."

"It's Jerry at the lab. I'm into that laptop and you might wanna come take a look."

His tone was low and dark. Shit, what the hell had he found?

"On our way," she said, ending the call. She turned to Lennox.

"If you're happy with that as a confession, you're an even bigger prick than I thought," she said before heading back toward the door.

"So, what do you really think, guv?" Bryant asked as they exited the police station.

"What I thought before I went in there. They've definitely got the wrong guy."

CHAPTER 33

Kim had dealt with Jerry before and knew that as a police constable he had not blown anyone away. Eleven years ago, he'd been injured in a riot incident when he had been pushed to the ground and then trampled by one of the horses. His left leg now contained metal plates and screws and he was forced to use a crutch to get around. The police force had retrained him in digital forensics for which he'd appeared to have an aptitude.

"What you got, Jerry?" she asked, pulling over a chair from an empty desk. Bryant stood behind.

"Nothing you're going to like," he said, placing the laptop in front of his own computer and opening the lid.

"This guy certainly knows how to hide stuff. I won't go into detail but I'm not sure I've found everything yet. However, I've found enough to give you some idea of the kind of man he was."

Kim could see the tension in his jaw. Her stomach began to churn in response. He'd been doing this job for a long time and it looked as though Luke Fenton had been hiding this computer in the cooker for good reason.

"Go on," she said.

"Images, Inspector. Indecent images of girls aged anywhere from six to about twelve years of age." He glanced at his notepad. "So far I've located in excess of twelve thousand photos dating back thirteen years. Half of those were transferred from a hard drive."

When he'd bought a new computer, Kim guessed, as the nausea inside grew.

"They're hidden throughout the computer, mainly in system files, and the last batch were downloaded just two weeks ago. Obviously we'll try and use some of the information gathered here to close down these sites, but we all know they'll be back up a day later."

What they'd learned was bad enough but Kim had to know more.

"Any video or images to suggest he was an active abuser?"

For some sicko bastards looking at images was not enough.

"Not really but…"

"I'd have preferred a straight no," Kim said, thinking of the hoodie found beneath his pillow.

"Well, I've got one file that doesn't quite match the others. Everything I've found comes from an array of sources, from innocent photos posted by proud parents to pornography from sources all around the world. There's no logic or organization to the storage of the photos that I can see so far except for one file."

"Go on," Kim said, sitting forward.

He clicked his way around the screen, and a file burst into life. Images of a little girl filled the screen, in the bath, playing with toys, in the park, in pajamas and dressing gown.

"They're all the same girl," Kim noted.

"Exactly. To the naked eye they're quite harmless, unlike most of the other images. But obviously to a pedophile they are photos of a semi-naked girl, so there's nothing innocent about them."

"Bastard," Bryant muttered from behind.

"But the thing that's strange about this folder of images is that they were all taken with the same camera, downloaded direct from the camera. The first batch."

"Sorry?" Kim said, not sure what he meant.

"Okay, the first photo is dated a year ago. A photo of the child in the park. They continue for about four months. Stop for three months in May, June and July and start again in August until November, when the last one of the files is taken."

He scrolled down to the end.

"Why the gap?" Kim asked.

"Not sure, but this is the last photo he took."

Kim took a deep breath, not surprised to see the child wearing a glittery pink hoodie.

This child had been in his home.

CHAPTER 34

Dawson walked into Brierley Hill station and instantly felt as though he was coming home.

"Thought you'd pissed off to Halesowen," Lenny called from the front desk.

"Just visiting," he called back over his shoulder.

Lenny said something in response but Dawson didn't catch it, sliding through the doors as two constables came out.

He took the stairs two at a time and entered his old squad room. He smiled. This was what a CID room was supposed to look like: a dozen desks, overflowing bins, casual dress, wipe boards half written on with Post-it notes and A4 sheets hanging on haphazardly.

His pleasure turned to dismay as he realized his own desk had been turned into a dumping ground for archive boxes taken from storage. Bloody hell, he'd only been gone a couple of days and he hoped to be back once this case was over and his current so-called team disbanded.

"Missed me, folks?" he called out to the handful of detectives present.

"Hey, Dawson," said a couple before returning their attention to their screens. Viv waved halfheartedly from the far corner with a phone glued to her ear.

"Hey, Dawson, boss is out," offered Gary, the chubby guy he'd come to see.

"Hey, Gaz, it's fine. It's you I'm here to see. How are you doing?"

"Better recently, thanks, and you never call me Gaz."

"Need your help, mate," Dawson said, tapping him on the shoulder and pulling over a chair.

Gary was a good kid and liked to help other folks out. He wasn't given to flashes of brilliance but he had a surplus of something in which Dawson knew that he himself was severely lacking. Patience.

The man had tracked down just about every database known to man. From shoe prints to tire tracks. He'd even written his own database to keep track of all the databases he had access to.

Dawson took the print off from his jacket pocket. "Got nails used at a crime scene. This is the chemical composition. Any chance you could track down where they were manufactured?"

Gary stared at the paper.

This made perfect sense to Dawson. If he could trace the manufacturers, he may be able to get a list of who they supplied and take it from there. Some small manufacturers only supplied a few key wholesalers. And if anyone could find out, Gary could.

"So, what do you think, mate?"

"I'm waiting for the punchline," Gary replied.

"Huh?" Dawson asked as a couple of people looked up.

"Well, this has to be some kind of piss-take. You can't be dumb enough to mean this."

"Hey, Gaz, mind your . . ."

"Only you would have the fucking cheek to come back to a team you've finally left in peace to get them to do your fucking job for you."

Dawson was stunned.

Gary continued and now the whole room was listening, and watching.

"You don't get it, do you? We're all glad to see the back of you. No more stealing everyone else's ideas or snaffling the most promising leads or slacking off and expecting everyone else to cover for you. Mate," he said meaningfully. "We couldn't wait to see the back of you." He thrust the piece of paper against Dawson's chest. "So, the answer to your request is fuck off and do the job yourself."

Gary pushed back his chair and headed out of the office.

Dawson looked around the room. No one spoke.

People he'd worked with for years simply lowered their heads and looked away.

By the looks of it, Gary had been speaking for all of them.

He put the sheet back into his pocket and walked out of the office with his head held high.

Now he knew he really was on his own.

CHAPTER 35

Dawson answered on the third ring. She would have preferred the second.

"Whatever you're doing, stop it and head to Luke Fenton's address and speak to the neighbors. Our guy has an unhealthy interest in little girls, one of which is the wearer of the pink hoodie."

"Aww shit."

Possibly the most intelligent thing she'd heard come out of his mouth so far.

"See if any of the neighbors know if he's ever been married; go and find out everything you can."

"Okay, boss."

"And while you're at it, meet Luke's sister, Lisa Bywater, at the morgue to ID the body at 2 p.m. Keats has been informed. Okay, gotta go, Stacey is calling."

She ended the call. "Hey, Stacey," she answered.

"Boss, I know yer said to carry on with the CCTV, but I've been doing a bit of digging and I think I've found something else."

Kim could hear the breathlessness in her voice.

"I got to looking at the method and the planning and the—"

"Spit it out, Stacey," Kim said.

"I've found something similar a month ago. I think our guy must be on a roll."

CHAPTER 36

Warwickshire Constabulary was first established in 1840 and had been part of more amalgamations and absorptions than any other force Kim could think of.

Proposals had been made in 2006 to merge the force with both West Midlands and West Mercia to form a single force for the whole West Midlands, but plans were abandoned due to a public outcry.

In its current state the force was divided into districts and boroughs with thirty-three local policing teams. One of which was located in Rother Street, Stratford-upon-Avon, where Bryant was parking up right now.

"Not sure how keen they're going to be to share," Bryant said, parking beside a BMW X5. Once upon a time this force had combined with their own and West Mercia to form the Central Motorway Police Group but now it was only themselves and West Mercia.

"Well, let's see, shall we?" Kim said pushing open the front door.

Kim approached the desk. "Sergeant Greene?"

"Please," Bryant added from behind. "Is he available?"

The uniformed officer focused his attention on Bryant. "And you are?"

Bryant held up his ID and introduced them both.

The officer picked up a phone. Bryant stepped away.

"Friendly bunch," he said quietly.

"Are you surprised?" she asked. This force had been messed with more than most.

"All doing the same job, guv," he said, as the door to their left opened.

A man of slim build with pasty white arms protruding from his black tee shirt greeted them with a half-smile.

"May I help?"

Kim remained silent. They wanted something from this man and people clearly responded better to her colleague.

Bryant took his cue from her silence.

"Could we have a word about the body you got at Redland Hall?"

His face tightened but he nodded and ushered them through the door he was still holding open.

They followed him ten steps before turning into a small office with no windows and two plastic chairs.

Documents hung off a single noticeboard, sheets pinned on top of each other, causing Kim to wonder at the relevance of the documents at the bottom.

He took the plastic seat nearest the desk. Kim nodded for Bryant to take the other and she stood in the doorway.

"Not sure what I can tell you but..."

"Aren't you heading the murder investigation?" Kim asked. It was his name that had been mentioned.

"Ha, I wish," he said, bitterly. "Attended the scene, got the first look and an identity before the case got handed over."

"To who?" Bryant asked.

"Joint task force; with bloody West Mercia."

Kim had almost forgotten about the most recent merger where an alliance had been made sharing back office facilities, force systems, support teams and staff below the grade of Deputy Chief Constable.

"So, they're running it from Worcester?" Kim asked.

He nodded. "A few of our lot are over there but..." He opened his hands without finishing the sentence. He didn't need to.

West Mercia had pretty much taken over the case. And no one was going to welcome further intrusion from them.

Kim's first priority was in trying to establish if this case was even related to the murder of Luke Fenton. So far she had a lot of similar cases but still only one victim of her own.

"So, what you got?"

He reached for a file on the top of an overcrowded stack of trays.

"That it?" Bryant asked. It looked as though the folder was empty.

"'Fraid so. A total of three hours I had the case."

Kim struggled not to feel annoyed on his behalf. As an Investigator, it took only minutes to make a case your own. It was almost immediate upon arrival. Once you laid eyes on the victim, assessed the body position, wound, circumstances, there was a bond, a connection, not only to the victim but to the killer. It was that instinct; that need to know every detail, to find the person responsible.

To have it whipped away after just a few hours was degrading and soul destroying.

"Victim was a fifty-four-year-old male named Lester Jackson, stabbed multiple times, final wound to the heart."

"Beheaded?" Kim asked.

He shook his head. "Nothing above the collarbone but a bloody mess below."

"Below..." Bryant said, indicating between his legs.

"Oh yeah, the murderer had gone to town there."

So, the only similarity so far was the genital mutilation.

"How was he found?" Kim asked.

"Tatters," he explained. "All checked out and clean from what I understand. The estate was bequeathed to the National Trust a few years ago but they've not got around to doing anything with it. Place has been a source of income to local shits for a while now. The whole site is huge and difficult to secure." He shuddered. "Bloody horrible place." He narrowed his gaze. "You're not thinking of going there, are you?"

"'Course not," she answered. "It's not our case, but just out of interest, where was the body found?"

"Well, that's the thing I found weird; of all the places, rooms and halls, hundreds of them, this guy was killed in a tiny, poky hole concealed under the stairs."

CHAPTER 37

Dawson hoped he was going to have better luck at the next house he tried, but as he moved farther away from Luke Fenton's property he was losing the will to live.

He'd had no luck at Fenton's workplace. The supervisor had said only that the man had kept to himself. He'd attended no Christmas parties, no laddish nights out and barely passed the time of day with his colleagues, all of whom had got the message and left him alone. They had known nothing about the man himself and even less about any women or children in his life. Dawson guessed if they knew the truth about him they'd now like him a whole lot less than they had before.

What he needed right now was one of those nosy neighbors that knew everything about everyone.

He tapped on the door of number 81. No answer but he could hear a radio playing inside.

He tapped again louder and checked his watch. He hadn't got long before heading off to the morgue for the identification of Luke Fenton.

"Hold your horses, I'm coming," called a shrill woman's voice. The door was opened by an elderly lady using a walking frame. Her hair was a shock of white that didn't look as though it had seen a comb in days.

She looked him up and down. "Don't want no windows."

Dawson knew he could suggest that she ring the station and verify his identity but he suspected she would rather slam the door in his face.

"I'm not selling windows but could I ask you a question or two, Mrs...."

"I ay giving yer my name. You'll have my bank account emptied before I've got back to my soup."

Given his current financial situation she probably wasn't far wrong.

"I'm trying to find out a bit of information on the young guy from down the road. Luke Fenton from number 81."

She popped her head out the door as if to remind herself of the occupants of the street.

"You mean grumpy git?"

Dawson couldn't help but smile. From what he'd learned the woman was bang on.

"Yeah, that's the one. You know him well?"

She shook her head. "Never speaks or waves to me in the window. You know when we had all that snow, plenty folks come to see if I needed anything but not him. Never offered anybody anything. Miserable so and so..."

"Do you know if...?"

"And his lady friend was just as bad."

Dawson was realizing that sometimes it was best to just keep quiet. He'd been asking the same questions all morning with no result.

"Always had her head down when she walked past, dragging that little kiddie of hers. Pretty little thing. Don't know what the mother saw in him, though. I mean, she was no looker herself and that birthmark over her left eye didn't help. Maybe she was grateful to any man that'd take her on with a kiddie and that splodge on her face."

Dawson knew he could be politically incorrect at times but this woman couldn't care less.

"I thought she'd seen sense. Disappeared for a few months but then the stupid cow came back again."

Dawson frowned, remembering what the boss had said about this guy being into kids. Had the mother known and left him and if so, why the hell had she come back?

CHAPTER 38

Redland Hall was located two miles out of Stratford-upon-Avon.

"You do recall Sergeant Greene advising us to stay away?" Bryant asked.

"Aww come on, it'd be rude not to take a bit of a peek. I mean it's not like we're going in or anything. It's practically on our way back."

"It actually isn't," Bryant said, turning off the main road onto a tree-lined driveway. "You know, I never even knew this was here."

"You wouldn't, it's never properly been open to the public," she replied. "It was used in the Nineties for some courses and stuff by the previous owners, to inject some cash, but it didn't work. Owners moved into a small cottage in Evesham and left the property to the National Trust, who inherited it two years ago and don't know what to do with it."

She'd been reading about the place since they'd left the station.

"Bloody hell," Bryant said as the building came into view.

He'd taken the words right out of her mouth.

The structure was grand and imposing, stretching up over three stories.

Kim's research in the car told her that the house originated in the thirteenth century.

The driveway led to a moat and bridge that appeared to be newer than the rest of the property.

She got out of the car and surveyed the building with a mixture of wonder and sadness.

Once it would have been a grand property. Two front wings branching off a turreted central entrance, an archway below a double row of windows. There was no pane that hadn't been broken.

The tiles had been nicked leaving the roof beams exposed and three brick structures that would have supported the massive chimneys. Unchecked ivy and moss covered the walls and crept in through the windows.

"Damn shame," Bryant observed, as Kim took a step forward. "Guv, I thought you said…"

"I'll just be a minute. Stay here if you like," she said, heading for the bridge.

From what she could understand the National Trust had attempted to secure the site numerous times with fencing and each time the fencing got nicked too. It looked to her like they'd decided to make do with the "Danger" and "No Entry" signs nailed into the front wall of the building. She already noted that the perimeter of the property that she could see was tree-lined and not fenced or walled, making it impossible to secure and protect.

She guessed that Bryant's hesitation in joining her was due to some kind of decision-making process going on in his mind. A dynamic risk assessment. She wasn't all that surprised when she heard his footsteps behind her.

"Jesus, even the door's gone," he remarked as they stepped into the building that was little more than a shell.

Daylight shone in from the roofless structure through gaps where the floorboards had either been removed, stolen or had rotted away. Rubble and stones littered the ground where the floor tiles had been removed.

Kim couldn't help feeling relieved that the previous owners never got to see it in this condition.

The staircase swept out of what would once have been a grand hallway where the lord and lady of the manor would have greeted their guests and where staff took coats and hats.

Greene had said the body had been found beneath the staircase. She could see where two wooden panels had been removed by the tatters and how the body had been discovered.

She stepped to the side of the staircase.

"It'd be useful if we had…" her words trailed away as the spotlight landed on the area.

The beam came from Bryant's hand.

"A torch," she finished.

"Yeah, nifty little things to keep in your boot."

Ah, so he hadn't been considering whether or not to follow her. He'd been sourcing much-needed equipment.

For some unfathomable reason that pleased her.

"To the left a bit," she said.

"Now to the right."

"Down a bit."

"What's this, *The Golden Shot*?" he asked.

"The what?"

"Clearly a TV program that was before your time."

"Bryant, I don't get this," she said, stepping back. "Take a look."

He moved into her space and looked around, while Kim considered if it was definitely the right spot, as described by Sergeant Greene. The tiny space that went under the staircase was no bigger than a broom cupboard. Possibly six feet square. The bloodstains were evident.

Regardless of whether it was their case or not, the first question she had to ask was why had Lester Jackson been murdered here?

CHAPTER 39

Dawson worked hard to hide just how much he hated visiting the morgue. It wasn't like he thought anything was going to come back to life or that he was in any danger. It wasn't even that he had any issue with the postmortem itself. He didn't mind the tools or the sounds of the process, it was the sight of all the dead flesh just hanging, slack from the bones.

He shook away the thought as he approached a woman wearing an Asda uniform and a pensive expression.

"Lisa Bywater?" he asked, offering his hand.

She nodded and returned the briefest of touch.

He introduced himself and showed his ID.

A flash of impatience flitted across her face. "Can we please just get this over and done with?"

He nodded and led the way through the doors. He'd met few family members that relished this particular task.

"I'd just like to say how sorry I am for your..."

"Don't be," she said, without emotion.

Well, that was an hour of sensitivity training wasted.

Thankfully for this task he didn't have to enter the belly of the morgue. A private viewing room with a second door was available for this process.

Keats appeared from nowhere and gave Dawson the nod to enter.

He guided her into the room that was neutral and without decoration.

He closed the door and pointed to a door in the opposite wall.

"The pathologist will bring your brother through and will await your instruction before revealing his face. If you could just confirm that it is your brother, Luke—"

"I know his name," she said as the door opened.

Dawson noticed a chill pass through her.

For all her bluster, some part of her cared a great deal and was not relishing what she was about to do.

The doors opened and Keats brought the trolley to a halt.

Dawson watched as she stared hard at the sheet-covered figure for a long minute before nodding at Keats.

He gently grasped the top end of the sheet and began to roll it back.

Her hand had moved to her throat and he saw the tremble.

As though realizing she was displaying emotion she lowered the hand back down to her side.

Dawson found himself holding his breath, praying Keats didn't reveal anything below the jawline.

He didn't.

Lisa Bywater's eyes filled with tears, giving Dawson his answer about the identity, but he needed a verbal confirmation.

"Mrs. Bywater, is this your brother, Luke Fenton?"

She nodded.

"Mrs. Bywater, I..."

"Yes, it's him," she said as the tears began to fall from her eyes.

"Okay, thank you, that's all we need you..."

"Just one minute," she said, with a voice full of emotion.

Dawson took a step away. Some relatives wanted to imprint the features of their loved ones into their memory, lifeless or not. Others wanted to say a silent, final goodbye.

Lisa Bywater raised her right hand into the air and punched her brother square in the face.

CHAPTER 40

"She did what?" Kim asked, as Dawson relayed the events at the morgue.

"Punched him, boss. Like she proper meant it. I got her outside, she shrugged me off and left."

Kim recalled the true nature of the man's injuries.

She closed her eyes as she spoke into the phone. "Dawson, don't tell me his head..."

"No, boss, it was attached."

She was silently grateful for small mercies.

But what the hell was that punch about?

"Okay, Dawson, head back to the station and see what you can find out about this woman and child. Someone has to know them."

He agreed and ended the call.

Immediately her phone rang. It was Keats and she absolutely knew what this conversation was going to be about. But she hadn't known the bloody woman was going to punch a corpse.

"Stone," she answered.

"John Doe," he said.

"Sorry?"

"That victim you asked me to look into who was genitally mutilated. It was a John Doe case and remains unsolved to this day. Six years ago and the victim has never been identified."

"Beheaded?" she asked, hopefully.

"No, and I'm sure I would have remembered that small detail and told you yesterday."

"Anything else?"

"A shoe, Inspector, was found in the woods. It was never proven to have had anything to do with the case, but I have one further note of interest."

"Which is?"

"The mutilation was coarse and amateurish and clearly performed by someone who had not done such a thing before."

She remained silent and waited for anything further.

Silence.

"Okay, thanks, Keats. It was good of you to look."

But it had helped her not at all.

She put her phone back in her pocket and realized her colleague was still looking her way.

"She punched him in the face?"

Kim nodded, still not quite believing what she'd heard from Dawson.

"She sure did and now we're gonna go find out why."

CHAPTER 41

Lisa Bywater wiped at her eyes and vowed it would be the last time he would ever make her cry. She had shed enough tears over that bastard but she hadn't been prepared for the emotions it was going to bring back to the surface seeing his dead body.

It had been bad enough when he'd put that one-word post on Facebook, despite her privacy settings and the deliberate misspelling of her last name.

All night she'd been agitated and hadn't even been able to tell Richard why. She had shared nothing of her childhood with her husband. He knew her parents were dead and she had an estranged brother. All true. She hadn't lied but she hadn't told the whole truth either.

When she'd seen his face, she'd been unable to help herself. Even in death he looked smug, victorious.

Well, no more, she vowed, taking out her phone. He would control her life no longer.

She scrolled down to the contact called "Taxi" and keyed in a quick message.

He's dead. You're safe now.

CHAPTER 42

"She actually punched him in the face?" Stacey asked, shocked at the events at the morgue, but even more surprised that her new colleague had struck up a conversation with her of his own accord. "So, what did yer do?"

"Not a lot I could do. It ain't like she hurt him and I could charge her with a crime. Thing is, she burst into tears before she did it so I've got no clue what was going through her mind."

Stacey realized this was turning into an actual conversation.

"So, the boss send you back to help out?" she asked, wondering if she was seeing a change in the man.

He nodded as he switched on his computer.

"Okay, I'm expecting the phone records through for Luke Fenton any minute now and the boss wants me to do some digging on the guy found at Redland Hall."

"Not our case," he said, without interest.

"Yeah, but I've still got to…"

"Sorry, got my own stuff to do. Trying to track down this woman with a kid and a birthmark so…"

His words trailed away, confirming he was going to be no help at all.

CHAPTER 43

Kim found herself back in Bilston for the second time in one day.

"You really think she's going to let us in after pulling that caper?" Bryant asked, as they approached the entrance to the tower block.

"Oh yeah, she'll let us in," Kim said, running for the door as two teenage girls exited.

They made the journey to Lisa's apartment in silence.

Kim had known the woman would not return to work to finish her shift. Despite the strange reaction to the news of her brother's death, there had been enough emotion bottled up inside Lisa Bywater to cause her to punch a corpse, after bursting into tears, and she wouldn't want to take all that baggage back to work.

Bryant pressed the intercom button.

No answer.

He pressed it again.

And again.

She answered.

"DI Stone and DS…"

"I don't want to talk to you."

Bryant continued. "Mrs. Bywater, we really need to speak to you about the events at the morgue."

"Please go away. I have nothing…"

"We're not going anywhere," Kim said, moving closer to the intercom box. "And if that means waiting out here until your husband comes—"

The door opened to reveal Lisa Bywater still dressed in her work uniform.

"Come in," she said, without emotion, as she walked away from the door.

"Mrs. Bywater, your actions at the morgue were peculiar to say the least. Would you care to explain...?"

"I hate him, Inspector. I think I made that clear earlier today."

"Your response to his death wasn't what we've come to expect from a relative; however punching a dead man in the face is an extreme emotional response."

"Not when you hate someone as much as I hate him. If you've been investigating him you must already know he is not a nice man."

"Was," Kim said, feeling the need to remind the woman of the correct tense, despite the fact she'd seen his dead body.

Lisa nodded her acknowledgment of that fact.

"I would like to find the person who did this and shake them by the hand. I'm only sorry it wasn't me."

Kim sat down and Lisa followed.

"I'm assuming that as you weren't close you know nothing of his private life?"

Lisa appeared guarded but shook her head.

"We're trying to trace a woman and child who lived with him for a while. Would you have any idea who they might be?"

Lisa shook her head again.

"The woman had a birthmark over her—"

"Inspector, I have no idea. I've spent my adult life trying to stay away from him."

"Only there were photos of the child on a computer that he made every effort to keep secret."

She said nothing.

"In fact, there were lots of photos on your brother's computer that would lead us to believe that he was a pedophile."

No shock. No surprise. No response.

Kim finally got it. "Mrs. Bywater, this is not news to you, is it?"

The woman shook her head.

Kim lowered her voice to little more than a whisper.

"Lisa, were you your brother's first victim?"

CHAPTER 44

Dawson glanced across at his colleague and had the distinct impression he was in a race.

Stacey had not looked up as her fingers flew across the keyboard as though she was in some kind of hypnotic state.

Personally, he'd never understood police officers who got fired up data mining. To him, being a detective meant being out there, talking to people, reading expressions, voice patterns, looking for little tics that indicated lying or hiding, looking people straight in the eye and making judgments. He had never done his best work from behind a computer.

So far all he'd managed to find out was that the woman who had lived with Luke Fenton was possibly called Hayley and that was after making twenty calls to local shops and businesses that she might have frequented. For the last half an hour he'd been searching social media for a woman with a birthmark called Hayley. Surprisingly he'd had no luck so far.

A small part of him was tempted to ask the woman sitting across from him if she had any ideas as to where to go next, but there was something inside him that kept the question firmly behind his lips.

So far, he'd found himself two lines of inquiry with the nail and the woman and couldn't seem to move forward on either of them. He'd asked for help once and had got more than he'd bargained for and he wasn't going to ask again.

He knew his colleague was working frantically on the background of Lester Jackson while also looking to interrogate the phone records of Luke Fenton. He knew he could offer to help but he didn't like picking up the slack of someone else's work. He preferred to find his own leads and what he needed right now was a flash of inspiration; a shortcut of some kind so he could get ahead of the woman tapping furiously in front of him.

Suddenly, she sat back and stared at her screen as though, somehow, she'd surprised herself.

"Damn, I think I need to call the boss," she said, and Dawson had the feeling that whatever race he was running, he'd just been lapped.

CHAPTER 45

"You mean *the* Marianne Forbes is his niece?" Bryant asked, as they headed toward Dudley.

"So Stacey says. She went to live with him when she was nine years old after her parents died in an avalanche. She was away at boarding school at the time and Lester Jackson was her only living relative, her mother's brother and an ex-minister for the Methodist church."

"Did you see her in the paper last week?"

Kim nodded. It had been a double-page spread about her fourth shelter being opened in the area. This one in Walsall.

The woman was a local legend, fighting every woman's cause imaginable, appearing on local news to discuss any subject that concerned women and children, from domestic abuse to equal pay.

From what Kim had read about her, she had used a chunk of her trust fund to open her first shelter, formed a charity or foundation and was highly skilled in securing donations and free services from local businesses and tradesmen.

Her facilities were located in Dudley, Willenhall, Bilston and the latest in Walsall.

Dudley was the registered address for the charity so they had decided to head there first.

"Am I missing something?" Bryant said, as they reached the end of Furlong Road.

"I'm looking for number 94 and we end at 93."

Kim looked with him as they passed slowly through the road formed of three-story-high Victorian houses.

"Hang on, what's that?" she asked pointing to a double metal gate at the end of the row. The entrance was flanked by a tall, dense conifer hedge that completely hid whatever lay behind. There was no sign, no number, no identity.

"Aah, you see it?" Bryant asked, driving forward.

On the right-hand side of the gate was a brick pillar housing an intercom.

He pulled up alongside it, his bonnet almost touching the gate.

"Not sure it's worth waiting for someone to slip out of here," he observed, referring to their method of entry into the block of flats earlier.

Bryant pressed the buzzer, which was answered with a very deep manly "yes."

Bryant introduced them both for what felt like the hundredth time that day.

"Please hold your identification up to the windscreen."

Bryant fished in his pocket and held it up, as requested.

Kim leaned forward, trying to spot the camera.

"Both of you, please," said the voice.

Kim glanced at Bryant as she followed suit, feeling like the camera was somewhere in the car.

"You have six seconds to drive through," the voice instructed as the gates began to open inward.

"Bloody hell, what are they guarding in here?" Bryant asked, foot on the accelerator ready to zoom through.

"Vulnerable women," Kim answered, not unhappy with the safety precautions.

The timer on the gate was to prevent any forceful and determined husbands or partners tailgating into the premises.

Bryant drove around a sturdy oak tree that obscured the building from the gate.

The space out front was not as sizable as she'd expected and the Victorian house was no more than fifty feet from the gate.

Bryant struggled to find space to park amongst the cars and electricians vans already crammed into the small space. He parked between a Mondeo Estate and a silver Mercedes, which Kim suspected belonged to Marianne herself. Kim didn't begrudge it. The woman had earned it.

Bryant lifted and dropped the heavy door knocker twice.

The door was answered by a man to whom they both had to look up. His girth filled the doorway. He wore black trousers, a navy jumper and an SIA security license on a lanyard around his neck.

She peered at the identification and saw that the voice on the intercom belonged to a brick shithouse of a man called Jason, which didn't suit the bearded guy one bit.

"May I help you?" he asked, pleasantly.

"We'd like to speak to Marianne Forbes if she's free."

"I'm sorry but she's unavailable right now."

"It's about her uncle who…"

"It's okay, Jay, you can let them in," called a voice from the right-hand side of the door.

He stepped aside, and Kim saw that there were two rooms, one on either side of the front door, before a door to the rest of the house could be accessed.

Office to the right. Security room to the left. Both looking out of the front of the house.

Gatekeepers, Kim thought. Again, not unhappy that these women's safety was taken so seriously.

"Please, come in," Marianne said, standing.

Kim noted that she looked just as polished as she had for the newspaper article.

The woman was in her late forties with straw blonde hair pulled back into a simple, tight ponytail with no stray hairs that Kim could see. Just a touch of makeup accented the piercing blue eyes, and high cheekbones. Simple stud earrings adorned her ears and a plain thin chain around her neck was all the jewelry she could see besides a man's watch with an oversize face.

She held out her hand and Kim shook it.

The grip was dry and firm.

"Mrs. Forbes, could we...?"

"Marianne, please," she said, nodding for them both to take a seat.

Jason, the security guard, closed the door to the handsome office that Kim guessed might previously have been a library.

"We'd like to talk to you about your uncle."

Her face tightened slightly and Kim noted that she worked hard to relax herself.

"Isn't the case being dealt with by a different force? I've already spoken to detectives from West Mercia."

Kim suddenly thought of Sergeant Greene, the first officer on the scene. And now it was a West Mercia case.

"We're investigating what we feel might be a similar crime."

"There are two..." she interrupted and then stopped herself.

"Two?" Kim asked.

She shook her head. "Never mind. I haven't seen my uncle for years, as I told the other officers, so I'm not sure exactly how I can help."

"It was a particularly brutal murder, Marianne."

"So I was told but I've had no involvement with my uncle since I was sixteen years old."

"Didn't you live with him after the death of your parents?"

She nodded. "My uncle took me in for his own reasons, some of which were financial. My mother and he came from humble beginnings, but my mother married well. My uncle never did anything to help himself toward a better life and their deaths were quite fortuitous for him."

Kim was surprised at the bluntness of this woman's words.

"But surely there were some people that liked him?" Bryant asked.

"If there were I don't know them. Just as I don't know who would do this to him. I hadn't seen the man for over thirty years."

Kim was sensing a strange dynamic here. What she wanted to find out was whether his murder was in any way connected to her own case, but something in this woman's manner was tinging the alarm bells in her head.

"But weren't you grateful to him for taking you in when you lost?—"

"I am grateful to him for nothing although many people here are," she said, rising from her seat. "Come with me."

Kim was confused but followed anyway.

Marianne led her across the hallway to the security room next door. Of a similar size to Marianne's office, this room would once have been a small drawing room. Marianne's office still held some of the period features of the property but this room was all business.

Jason sat at a curved desk surrounded by computer screens, each showing a quad display. The first covered the outside of the property: front and rear. Kim saw that the camera they had shown their identification to was actually installed within the gate.

The cameras at the rear looked onto a walled garden and were sweeping the entire area.

Marianne stood to the side of her.

"Obviously I'm not going to let you through to the house as that would only unnerve the women but I just want you to see what we do."

She pointed to the kitchen.

"That's Dawn, a student at the catering college, who comes a couple of times each week to show the women how to cook themselves quick, nutritious meals." She pointed to another screen. "That's Nigel in the lounge. He visits two afternoons a week to give the ladies a haircut, to help them feel better about themselves."

Kim saw a slim man wearing tight jeans and a tee shirt with a blonde undercut fringed haircut holding a mirror to the back of a woman's head.

Marianne pointed to another screen.

"That's Louella, a counselor from the Salvation Army, who comes in when needed to offer the women a chance to talk. These people offer their time and services to broken women who have been subjected to physical, sexual and emotional abuse."

The words "broken women" worked their way under her skin. Every woman here had suffered at the hands of someone else, most likely someone close to them, someone they loved or had loved, trusted, relied on. She couldn't help but think of her own mother, someone she should have been able to trust.

She forced the thoughts from her mind and back to the present where it was safe.

"Who's that?" she asked, spying a rare male figure on a pair of stepladders in one of the stairways.

"That's Carl. He and his brother Curt look after the general maintenance in all four facilities." Marianne turned to her. "You seem surprised?"

"I'd have thought having men on site would..."

"We don't encourage the women to hate and avoid all men. We do keep the presence of men to a minimum and only have Carl and Curt here on a regular—"

"Ahem," Jason coughed.

Marianne touched him lightly on the shoulder. "Sorry, Jay. And of course, our team of four security personnel that provide a 24-hour service, headed by Jay here."

He nodded, satisfied, and continued scrolling through the screens.

Kim watched for a moment, her eyes taking in a couple of mothers with their children in a playroom. A few others sitting in a second lounge chatting. A woman in another room reading while her toddler crawled around the floor.

"How many places do you have here?" Kim asked, following Marianne back to her own office across the hall.

"This is our largest home and here we can take up to four mothers with children and twelve singles."

"How long do they stay?" Kim asked, wondering if any of them ever wanted to leave the safe environment created by this woman.

"We normally feel we've done all we can after about six months but it varies. Some women stay for much shorter periods; a few weeks while they decide their long-term options; return to family, move away but we do what we can while they're here with—"

Her words were interrupted by a knock at the door.

"Come in," Marianne called despite their presence. Kim suspected there was little that was more important than being available for the women in her care.

Nigel stepped into the doorway, a pair of scissors and a comb in his hands. "Are you ready for . . . ?"

"Give me five minutes, Nige."

"No probs," he answered brightly. He snapped the scissors open and closed, looking at both her and Bryant. "Anyone else fancy a free trim?"

"We're good, thanks," Kim said, as he backed out of the room.

"And for what it's worth, I pay for mine," Marianne said, once the door was closed.

"Of course," Kim said. She would have expected nothing less. She couldn't help but be impressed by the woman's commitment and drive, though she was bothered by something Marianne had said earlier.

"You said these women had a reason to be grateful to your uncle. Why?"

"It was because of him that I opened this place."

Kim frowned. "I'm sorry but I don't quite understand..."

Her words trailed away as Marianne held her gaze and Kim saw the look in her eyes.

Aah, now she understood.

CHAPTER 46

"Sir, we need that case from West Mercia," Kim repeated.

DCI Woodward shook his head. "And I repeat that we are not going to get it. It would have been one thing trying to get a case handed over from a team in our own borough but from another force entirely…"

"And I still think Tommy Deeley's murder is linked to ours."

He narrowed his gaze. "Even after viewing the taped interview earlier today?"

News traveled fast so there was little point denying it. "Especially after watching the interview," she said. "I was literally passing the door, sir," she explained. "And he offered."

The fact she couldn't get access to that case right now bothered her no end. Her instinct told her the murders were related and until someone with some sense ruled out Butcher Bill it would remain where it was.

But she'd heard of cases being wrestled from other forces before. She had to give it her best shot.

"They're related, sir. Both victims are pedophiles."

"And you know this?"

She nodded. "Our victim sexually abused his sister from when she was nine years old, and Marianne was sexually abused by her uncle when he became her legal guardian after the death of her parents."

He shook his head.

"Both were mutilated at the genitalia."

"Copycat?"

She shook her head. "Wasn't revealed, just like ours."

He shook his head again.

"Sir, it's got to be the same killer."

"I'm not sure I disagree with you, Stone, but we're never going to get the case away from West Mercia and nor should we."

"Huh?"

"It's already been through two police forces: Warwickshire and West Mercia. If we get involved, CPS will never even take it to court. Way too many chain of evidence and procedure loopholes for the defense to drive a truck through."

"But this is like asking me to finish a jigsaw puzzle while keeping half of the pieces in your pocket."

He nodded. "Yes, I'm afraid that does seem to be the case."

If she didn't know better she'd think he was enjoying the challenge he'd laid before her.

"So, Stone, time to see just how creative you and your team can get."

CHAPTER 47

Marianne took a quick look at herself in the rearview mirror before getting out of the car. The hair was Nigel's but the makeup was hers. Not too much and not too bright; a gentle pink lipstick instead of rose red. Enough concealer to disguise the deepening lines beneath her eyes but not cover them completely. Her companion knew exactly how old she was. And just a touch of mascara to frame her blue eyes. He'd always liked it when she wore mascara.

She got out of the car and headed into The Jolly Crispin pub in Upper Gornal, chosen by her, as the small establishment formed of brick and black beams sold exceptional beer. He liked good beer.

She spotted Derek Hodge sitting as far away from the bar as he could at a small table behind the fruit machine, as though hiding.

She smiled as she saw two drinks already on the table.

"Dry white wine still?" he asked, as she approached.

"Of course," she said, taking a seat.

She'd seen photos of him in the press, normally when he opened a new food packaging plant, and the photographer had been kind to him. Twenty years had added roughly that number of pounds to his stomach and more than a smattering of silver strands to his head. Despite that there were still traces of the attractive man she had known.

They'd had a thing in their early twenties, before he'd met Patricia and she'd found her purpose. It hadn't ended so much as fizzled as they'd shared less and less in common. But the sex had been great.

"So, why the call after all this time?" he asked, getting straight to the point.

"Money," she said, matching his directness but with a softening smile.

He threw back his head and laughed. "You never did beat about the bush, did you?"

She shrugged. "If you want something you have to go get it," she said. "Take you, for example, opening your third packing plant in the Midlands in the last five years. That's a lot of plastic containers..."

"Hey, we're as environmentally friendly as we can..."

"Of course," she said, waving away his protestations. Marianne didn't care for the planet as much as she should do. Her priorities lay elsewhere. "I meant that's a lot of food being packaged. Your rate of expansion is pretty impressive."

The laughter left his eyes. "Don't be fooled. My mortgage and loan payments would make you weep."

She didn't doubt it but his last set of filed accounts available to view at Companies House showed a healthy net profit despite the outgoings.

"We are a charity, you know," she said, taking a sip of her wine. She allowed his business brain to analyze the tax implications of that fact.

He hesitated but shook his head. "I can't right now, Marianne. I'd love to help out but I just can't."

"Come on, Derek. It's Christmas. Surely you can spare something. You know it's for a good cause and the women in my care have suffered—"

"Honestly, I can't," he said, cutting her off. No one ever wanted to hear the details.

"Maybe just a small personal donation?" she pushed. She didn't have a reputation for extracting money from stones for nothing.

His expression remained firm. "The kids' school fees are coming up, and Patricia's got her heart set on a new Lotus."

Marianne worked hard to keep the smile on her face. He spoke of private school fees for his three girls and a six-figure car for his wife. She was talking of trying to raise funds for roof repairs and damp proofing not to mention new bedding and towels needed throughout the centers.

She opened her mouth to try again.

"Honestly, Marianne, I can't," he said, holding up his hands. "Please don't ask me again."

She forced the tension from her face and smiled in defeat. "Oh well, you can't win them all."

"Thank you for understanding," he said, taking a sip of his drink.

"So, how are Patricia and the kids?" she asked.

"At a Christmas ice show in town this evening," he replied.

She'd asked how they were, not where they were.

She lifted her gaze slowly to meet the question. And gave him her answer.

Five minutes later she was back in her car.

Oh well, you couldn't win them all, Marianne reasoned with herself. The man had refused her request for financial assistance but he was now following her to a hotel room she'd already booked. She thought of all the women who relied on her for help. Nothing trumped their safety and security.

She glanced again into her rearview mirror to see his Mercedes was parked behind her, waiting. There was nothing she wouldn't do to ensure the safety of her women.

She started up the car. No, you couldn't win them all but you could certainly try.

CHAPTER 48

"Okay, folks, we're not getting the Lester Jackson case from Warwickshire. DCI Wood...Woody has made that perfectly clear," she said, walking back into the squad room.

"But—"

Kim cut Dawson off by raising her hand. "There isn't a but you can come up with that I haven't already tried and it's not happening. He's encouraging us to be creative on that score, which we'll think about tomorrow, but for now let's just recap before we call it a day."

Her gaze remained on Dawson, signaling for him to go first, as she reached for the mug of coffee that had magically appeared on the spare desk.

"Still trying to find this woman and child who lived with Luke Fenton. I have a first name and a vague description, but that's about it."

"And the nail?" Kim said, referring to it for the first time.

"My source didn't come good on that one, boss, but I'm still working on it."

She folded her arms and waited.

Everyone waited and he at least had the good grace to look mildly uncomfortable.

"Nothing from his workplace, either," he added and she was unsure if he was trying to fill the silence or fill his day. The morgue visit had taken no more than an hour from his schedule.

There was nothing further to report.

"Okay, moving on, Stacey?"

"Got the phone records in for our victim and was just about to start."

"Okay, get on with those first thing tomorrow and liaise with the lab about the computer to see if there's anything else there."

"Will do, boss," she answered.

"And great work on finding the Lester Jackson case."

"Thanks, boss."

Kim saw the shadow that passed over Dawson's face and she didn't mind it one little bit.

"Okay, folks, that's enough for tonight. Briefing in the morning at seven."

Stacey and Bryant reached for their belongings, and Dawson glanced her way.

She shook her head and he remained where he was.

*

She waited until the others had left the room before meeting his gaze.

"I think we need to have a little chat."

"I know it doesn't look like I've done much but…"

"Yeah. It's not that kind of chat. It's the type where you listen and I talk."

He closed his mouth.

"I don't know what kind of team you've come from and I don't care. There are things I'll tolerate and things I won't. I like flashes of brilliance and I like initiative. I don't mind confidence that stops short of arrogance but here are the things I won't accept: disinterest and laziness. No one is going to do your job for you and I don't expect you to pick up anyone else's slack if they're not performing, but I do expect you to earn your pay rate."

She paused and nodded toward the door.

"That will remain open at all times. No one is holding you hostage and if you miss your last team so badly, go back or request a transfer elsewhere. Your choice. But if you stay, put your back into it and do your job. End of chat. If you're here tomorrow I'll assume you've listened, if not good luck in your next job."

Kim retrieved her belongings from the bowl and left without another word.

Good chat, she decided as she headed down the stairs.

CHAPTER 49

Dawson stared hard at the computer for just a minute trying to work out how he felt.

Well, at least he'd learned how a chat worked with the boss.

He was honest enough to accept that she was right about his levels of enthusiasm and that he wasn't feeling this team dynamic.

What she didn't know was that the option of returning to his previous team was no longer on the table.

The events from earlier had played over in his mind a few times and as far as he could see there was only one logical explanation. They were jealous. They knew he was a gifted detective and that he was going places. They wanted him out of the way so they could shine more brightly in his absence. Well, let them have their moment in the sunshine. Karma would be a bitch once he was their boss.

Now, he felt better.

So, for now, he was stuck here, literally. He had no bed for the night and asking to transfer to another team after just a couple of days was not going to do his long-term career plans any good.

The boss had made it clear that she expected something from him on the nail front and he could kind of understand why. It was a job he'd gone looking for to prove a point and now he had to prove another one. That he could use the information once he got it.

He turned to the computer and began to search for nail manufacturers. With no database to hand he was going to have to do this the long way.

He began copying and pasting email addresses into his address bar and formulated a standard email including the composition.

An hour later he found himself feeling strangely pleased with himself. He sat back in his chair as though he'd just finished a hearty meal.

In the silence, some of the things the boss had said started to come back to him.

Be creative. Show initiative.

He had an idea how he could manage to do both.

CHAPTER 50

"So, how was day two?" Jenny asked him as he speared a piece of chicken.

"Much like day one," Bryant answered.

"And you didn't say a lot about that either," she noted, raising an eyebrow.

He shrugged.

"Do you even like her?"

"She's not the easiest person to like."

"Bloody hell, husband, speak to me."

"Yeah, I like her," he answered, sensing his wife's impatience. "She's driven, passionate, intelligent..."

"So, just the kind of person you like to work with?"

"I suppose so. It's just..."

"What, spit it out."

"She researched us all."

Jenny put down her knife and fork, folded her arms and waited.

"And?"

"Seems a bit sneaky to me," he said, choosing not to reveal that she had fought his battles for him.

"What? Trying to get some background on the people who form her brand-new team. I suppose she could always have taken you away on a weekend team-building course if that pesky dead body hadn't got in the way."

Bryant chuckled as he cleared his plate. That was one of the things he loved about his wife: if she didn't agree with him she didn't sugar-coat it.

"And you know something else," she continued, "it's not even that that's bothering you. It's all this promotion stuff going around in your head. You should talk to her about it."

He shook his head. "No point. Team might be disbanded at the end of this case."

Jenny shrugged as she collected up the plates. "Well, if you're not going to help yourself…" Her words trailed away. She stopped at the doorway. "But bear in mind, that knowing more about the people you work with is never a bad thing and it can work both ways."

He looked after her for just a second.

There was something in him that didn't want to learn anything about his boss that she wasn't willing to share herself. And yet, a more realistic part of him already knew she wasn't the sharing type.

He grabbed the laptop and fired it up at the dining table.

He was no data miner. He knew that. His idea of police work was following clues and reading people. He'd been brought through the force the old-fashioned way. His best learning had come from walking the beat and getting to know people; how they walked, talked, acted out their guilt or innocence without really knowing it.

He'd been in his mid-twenties when he'd decided he wanted to join CID, and their meeting with Sergeant Greene earlier had resonated with him, and reminded him of a fifteen-year-old girl raped and murdered in Pelsall. His own daughter no more than two years old then.

He had been first on the scene following an anonymous phone call and had been rendered speechless, numbed by the sight before him. Out of that numbness had grown an anger, a rage unlike anything he'd known before. He wanted to find the bastard who had done this, who had brutally raped, murdered and discarded this young girl in a state of undress.

He had worked through every emotion that her parents would feel upon hearing the news, of both her murder and the manner of her death. Their lives would be destroyed forever because of one man. And he'd wanted to be the officer to cuff and caution that bastard.

Forty minutes later CID arrived and dismissed him from the scene pending his statement. After watching over her body and silently assuring her that her murderer would be found, he'd been told to walk away. As he'd trudged back to the squad car he had felt as though he was abandoning her; already breaking the promise he'd made. That he was somehow letting her down.

The following day he'd begun the process to become a detective. The face of Wendy Harrison had driven him all the way.

He shook away the memory and wondered if his boss had any such defining cases, victims who had never left her.

He typed her title into the search bar and got results. He scrolled down to see a collection of news videos and quotes for press statements. There were not as many as he'd thought he'd find. He could have guessed that she was not the type of DI to court either the press or the limelight. He saw a couple of commendations and yet no photos of her receiving them. He smiled. She probably never bothered to turn up to the events.

Two pages of Google results were pretty much the same and told him what he already knew.

He was about to log off, satisfied he could tell Jenny that DI Stone was exactly the kind of officer he'd thought she was.

Then he saw a note at the top of the screen which asked him a question.

Did you mean Kimberly Stone?

He paused. He wasn't sure. Did he?

His hand hovered over the mouse button. To his knowledge the guv had only researched his work achievements and not his personal history or private life. He should offer her the same respect.

He pressed on the link and was immediately presented with a photo of a dozen police officers surrounding a stretcher being carried to an ambulance.

The headline screamed:

Surviving twin critically ill

Bryant tore his eyes away from the narrative while he still could. No way was he going to intrude on her private life to this degree. No way in hell.

But he couldn't help glancing back at the photo where he saw something that he really wished he hadn't.

CHAPTER 51

Kim wasn't one to let the issue of opening hours stop her from going where she wanted to go, and under the cover of darkness she climbed over the metal entrance gate to Powke Lane Cemetery.

Didn't everyone visit dead relatives at 9 p.m.? Well, after a long day at work she certainly did.

It wasn't something she did all the time. Now and again she came to Mikey's grave when the gates were open. The only problem there was that other people were around and sometimes she wanted a private conversation with her brother.

She followed the road as it wound its way to the top of the cemetery, the graves on either side overflowing with wreaths, flowers, reindeers and snowmen. Many of them guilt gifts, already apologizing to the dead for the merriment of Christmas they were about to enjoy. Mikey's grave was empty of adornments. There was nothing of the festive season she intended to enjoy.

She came to a stop right beside the bench. She needed no lamplight to guide her to his headstone. A tall black marble headstone that she had saved for from her sixteenth birthday to replace the temporary marker that had been there for ten years.

It was simple in its inscription. His name and the years in between. Six short years represented by a short dash that mirrored barely any life at all.

Even now she could not hold down the rage at the woman who had done this to them. Their own mother, Patricia Stone, who now resided at Grantley Care, a secure facility for the criminally insane. She tried not to think of the woman, but a visit to Mikey was inextricably linked to the rage button in her soul.

Kim's earliest memory was of her mother advancing toward the two of them with a bread knife in her hand.

Paranoid schizophrenia had been responsible for the woman's conviction that Mikey, her own son, was the devil.

Kim recalled little else from those first six years, other than her numerous attempts to kill him and her own efforts to protect him. Kim had always sensed she was the oldest twin and her innate need to protect him had confirmed it.

But her mother had finally got her way when she'd chained the two of them to a radiator, in the scorching heat of the summer, in the flat from where no one had heard their cries.

A few cream crackers and a half bottle of Coke that she'd fished from under the bed with her foot had been rationed for the first few days, but eventually, soiled, ill and dehydrated, her twin brother had died in her arms.

She had lain next to his body barely conscious for two days before help had finally come and the door had been broken down by police officers.

She remembered little of the two weeks that had followed, where she had been in hospital fighting for her life. By the time she was released the press had lost interest in the story. She had never read a report or looked at a newspaper clipping about the events of her life. She didn't need to: she'd been present the whole time. She'd even heard that a book had been self-published by a money-grabbing journalist trying to make money from her misery. She had been oblivious to it all when she'd been removed from the hospital and delivered to Fairview Children's Home with a half-full bin liner containing her possessions.

What had followed was a succession of foster homes that had each left a mark on her in some way. With the stream of homes had come an equally long line of psychiatrists, psychologists and counselors all trying to crack open her psyche and pour out the contents like a raw egg. Only one had been different; a middle-aged man named Ted who had allowed her to sit silently and watch the fish in his tiny garden pond. She didn't speak during their sessions but she had always felt calmer when she left. In his own quiet, non-invasive way he had tried to get her to talk about her pain, but she had resisted every attempt and had instead chosen to build boxes in her mind where she stored all the bad memories from her past. She didn't open those boxes for fear of what would happen if she did.

Even when she visited her twin brother she tried only to remember his smile when she'd found some kind of treasure in the kitchen or his chuckle when she had tickled his feet. Those were the memories she allowed out of the box.

Those moments were precious to her, evidence of the bond that had existed between them and couldn't even be broken in death.

He was still, and would always be, the other half of her and it was where she would always go when she needed to talk.

She lowered herself and sat down at his headstone.

"So, Mikey, I've got this new team..."

CHAPTER 52

Kevin Dawson reclined the passenger seat in his Ford Escort to the lowest position and lay back. He'd considered trying his mates again to beg a bed for the night but had known that wasn't going to work. His mates didn't mind him kipping on a spare sofa, but the patience of their wives and girlfriends was starting to wear thin. And much as he would have loved to have been bedding down somewhere comfy and warm, he didn't want to place a strain on anyone else's relationship.

He had briefly considered Lou again but the sick feeling from the morning had stayed with him until lunchtime.

He'd considered his parents but they wouldn't leave him alone until he told them what was going on with Ally and he wasn't ready to do that. He didn't even want to think about it, let alone talk it out.

And his overdraft limit prevented him considering a hotel, even a cheap one. The few quid he had would be needed for food and drink, to get him to next payday. But none of that mattered right now.

The discomfort couldn't wipe the smile from his face.

After some gentle persuasion he had something coming that would blow his boss's socks off.

Yeah, Stacey had spent the day pounding the keyboard without stepping out of the office once. And yes, those efforts had yielded some results, he admitted grudgingly, but that wasn't real police work. That was an office job.

And DS Bryant had spent the day following the boss around the outskirts of this case, driving her wherever she wanted to go. That wasn't his idea of the job, either.

He believed in talking to people, using what and who you knew, and he couldn't wait for the following morning to demonstrate to the boss that he really was the star of this show.

CHAPTER 53

"Okay, guys, before we start, I've been told that there are Christmas drinks in the canteen this evening at sixish if anyone is interested."

"A glass of cheap warm wine and a budget mince pie?" Dawson asked.

She thought and then nodded. "Pretty much."

"I'll pass."

"They do know we've got a body, guv?" Bryant asked. "I'd rather be up here working the case."

"Yep, me too," Stacey added.

Dawson nodded as though he wished he'd thought of that response himself.

In her experience the station party was a budgetless directive from above for the purposes of station morale. A couple of plates of portioned sausage rolls, pork pie and a bowl of crisps did not offer the team a sense of value.

The fact that two thirds of her team had immediately prioritized the case they were working over an early finish and a bit of socializing, said much about the two officers concerned. And even more about the remaining one third who hadn't given it a thought.

"Please yourselves. Now, I'm sure you've all taken a look at the boards so I'll talk you through what I've done. We've been getting crumbs of information for two days about cases that might or might not be linked to the murder of Luke Fenton." She pointed to the white board to the left of the door, which had been divided into three columns. "I've noted what we know about each of these cases."

They all looked again at what she'd written.

John Doe (Staffs)
Genitally mutilated
Shoe
Six years ago

Lester Jackson (West Mercia)
Genitally mutilated
Small Space
Sexual Abuser
Four weeks ago

Tommy Deeley (Wolverhampton)
Genitally mutilated
Bell
Six days ago

She gave them a moment and continued. "And on the other board we have what we know of our own victim."

Luke Fenton
Genitally mutilated
Sexual abuser
Beheaded
Packing paper
Two days ago

"So, we have to be careful just how much time we give to the other cases although we can't afford to discard them completely. The beheading of Luke Fenton sets him apart from the other victims. We know he was a pedophile whose first victim appears to have been his sister. We also know that a woman named Hayley with a facial birthmark lived with him for a time with her daughter. There's no evidence to suggest the child was his as the photos began when the child is around nine years old. Incidentally, that's the age his sister was when he began with her."

"Sister did it," Dawson said.

"Not according to her clock card at the supermarket that says she was doing an extra shift on nights to cover annual leave."

"Could have been—"

"Let it go. She's not a suspect," Kim stated.

"We know that he had no friends to speak of and kept everything about himself private."

"Neighbors are just as—"

"Dawson, if you'd like to interrupt me one more time I sure would appreciate it."

"Sorry, boss," he said, not sounding sorry at all.

"And we'll get back to Fenton's neighbors in a minute. But what we don't know about Fenton is whether there are any other victims of his deviant behavior. He's never been charged with an offense and hasn't crossed our radar, why not?" She held up her hand. "It's rhetorical, Dawson. I just want you to give it some thought. If his first act of abuse was to his sister when she was nine and he was fifteen, what about the fourteen years that followed? Why has he never been a person of interest in any intelligence, operation or surveillance?"

Kim knew that the force had achieved great success in uncovering and breaking up pedophile rings both online and physical and yet his name had appeared nowhere.

"Okay, so, Stace, I want you on the phone records and chasing up the lab for anything further."

The constable nodded her understanding.

"Dawson, I want you looking for any links between Luke Fenton, Lester Jackson and Tommy Deeley. There has to be something. And Bryant and I are going back to the neighbors to find out more about this girl."

Dawson's face fell. "Boss, I already..."

"You may have missed something," she said, honestly. He'd spoken to one elderly lady. There were doors he hadn't knocked and this woman and her child needed to be found.

She offered him a warning glance to leave it alone. They all had their instructions and she was hoping to make it out of this briefing without murdering one of her team.

"Boss, can I say something?" Dawson asked.

Or not, she thought as her hands clenched in her pocket.

"Go ahead."

"I have something I'd like you to see," he said, sliding a piece of paper to the edge of his desk. "It's Lester Jackson's postmortem report."

She looked at him before reaching for the piece of paper.

"I know a woman..."

"Dawson," she said, narrowing her gaze.

He shook his head. "Nothing like that. An assistant at the morgue owes me a favor. I gave her son a bit of a talking to when he was making some bad decisions."

She reached for the paperwork. "Not sure how this is going to help us. We know how the man died."

"But we didn't know every injury he'd sustained or how similar the MO was to our case."

She looked over the single sheet of paper that was not the full report but contained the list and sites of injury, marked on a printed drawing of a male body.

Her gaze passed over all the information she already knew.

And then located the fact she didn't already have.

Just like their victim, Lester Jackson had been bashed on the back of the head.

"Note it on the board," she said, sighing heavily.

Everyone watched as Dawson did what she asked.

"Despite the similarities, we have to hope that everyone else is right and we're wrong and that these cases are not related to our own."

"And if they are?" Bryant asked.

"Then what we have on our hands is an escalating serial killer."

CHAPTER 54

Marianne waited for the last page to sputter out of the printer before opening the door.

"Jay, send Carl in when he gets here," she called across the hall before retreating back inside.

She folded the page and closed the envelope on her desk.

It was barely 7:30 a.m. and already she'd cleared her emails from the previous day, designed a new mailshot to send to her list of existing benefactors and written a Christmas newsletter to be circulated around all the shelters.

She knew people marveled at her energy levels. Some of the staff called her The Tornado and it wasn't a nickname she minded. They all knew that everything she did, everything, was born of passion and determination to ensure the safety of the women and children who passed through her doors.

Most of the women who came to her had been beaten to a shadow of their former selves either physically or psychologically. Others were victims of childhood sexual abuse and were still recovering from the trauma. Only last month she'd accepted a twenty-seven-year-old chartered accountant who had recovered memories of childhood abuse by her stepfather. Previously an astute, intelligent, balanced woman leading a charmed life, she had suddenly found herself and her life falling apart around her. Others came because their children had been abused and they needed a place of safety.

She was proud of everything she'd achieved, the number of women she'd helped. The lives she had mended. She asked for nothing in return except their commitment to taking the tools they'd been given and moving forward with their lives.

There was nothing she wouldn't do for the women who came into her care, she thought, as a short, single knock sounded on the door.

"Come in, Carl," she called.

He stepped into the office and closed the door behind him.

She nodded toward the envelope on her desk. "I have another name for you."

He followed her gaze. "Marianne, is it a good idea to carry on?"

She frowned. "You don't believe in what we're doing?"

He shrugged. "You know, with the police coming around. It won't take them long to…"

"It'll be fine, Carl. I promise," she said, surprised at the pensive expression on his face. She had not given the detective inspector another thought once she'd left the building. "But we can't stop now. We have to protect these women. We've come too far." She paused. "We're in this together. You do understand that, don't you?"

He hesitated and then nodded his agreement.

"Good," she said, pushing the envelope toward him. "Everything you need is in there. You know what you have to do."

CHAPTER 55

"Looks like Dawson was right after all," Bryant said, switching on the car engine and the heater. After a week of mild December temperatures the mercury had plummeted by five degrees.

Her colleague had a point. They'd knocked on every door in the street where Luke Fenton had lived and they'd found out no more about this mystery woman and her child.

"You noticed he was wearing the same clothes as yesterday?"

She nodded. She also knew his car hadn't moved from the same spot on the station car park from the day before. She knew nothing of his personal life and she didn't care to, but sleeping at the station and grabbing a quick shower before starting shift was not something she could allow to continue.

"At least he used his brain to get us a copy of that postmortem report," she acknowledged. "Which, regardless of anyone else's opinion, convinces me that it's the same killer."

"Not gonna get us any of the cases though, is it?" Bryant asked.

She shook her head.

"Or help us track down this Hayley woman with her child."

There was no need for her to acknowledge that fact.

"Where to?" he asked, rubbing his hands together.

"Give me a minute," she said, tapping the dashboard with her fingernails.

Think, think, think, she told herself.

The woman had lived here with her daughter. She must have gone to school somewhere but trying to track down where would have them running around in circles. Kim knew of at least seven schools in a mile and a half radius and all they had was the woman's first name, possibly. Same issue for checking with doctor's and dentist surgeries.

But what might her child need? Kim wondered. What else would a mother try to fulfill for her child?

Kim took out her phone and did a quick search of the local area.

"Got it," she said.

"Is it catching?" her colleague asked.

She looked at him sideways. "Was that a joke?"

"Obviously not. Sorry, what have you got, guv?"

"An idea. Take us to the end of the road and turn left."

CHAPTER 56

Dawson looked again at the old plans of Redland Hall and although he was no architect he could see that there was a certain area missing. The place where Lester Jackson's body had been found.

He knew the boss wanted him to look for any possible links between the victims, but just like her he wanted to understand why Lester Jackson had been killed where he had. And looking at these plans had done nothing but stoke his curiosity. The place was vast. By his count it had 117 rooms. He could understand the body being placed there after the fact to hide it from less tenacious looters, but why kill him there?

He'd found the floorplan on the local council's archive website. The National Trust had it listed as only one of their properties along with a brief history of the families that had owned it, but gave no more detail than that. It appeared that no one seemed to know what to do with the rambling old property. He guessed it would take millions upon millions to restore it.

He returned to the National Trust site and vowed to spend no more than a few minutes looking at similar properties for clues. At this rate, he'd be facing his own charge of wasting police time.

He clicked into the link for a place called Baddesley Clinton, a moated manor house, eight miles out of Warwick. The house had been built in the thirteenth century when large areas of the forest of Arden were cleared for farmland.

Dawson had no idea what he was hoping to find but the property bore striking similarities to Redland Hall.

He learned all about the history of the place and was about to click out when something caught his eye. He read it and read it again.

"You ever heard of a priest hole?" he asked Stacey across the desk.

"Huh?" she answered without looking up.

Obviously not, he thought, as his stomach began to react.

He continued reading about the Ferrers of Baddesley Clinton who had remained Roman Catholic after the Reformation.

Many such families had sheltered Catholic priests who would have been killed if discovered.

Special arrangements were made to hide and protect them by building priest holes and secret passages to hide priests when properties were searched by the authorities. Some were hidden by wooden paneling, others in the sewers and some even hidden beneath the stairs.

Dawson sat back and thought for a moment. This was why the tiny space was nowhere to be found on the floorplans. It had either been a secret space or built after the issue of the ancient plans.

The priest hole had to mean something. Of all the space in that house, why had he been killed there?

CHAPTER 57

"Not really much of a playground, though, is it, guv?" Bryant asked, rubbing his hands together. The temperature had risen only two degrees above freezing due to a biting wind.

He wasn't wrong about the park. The space had a see-saw, three swings and a short metal slide.

But it was the nearest playground to Luke Fenton's house, and from what the elderly lady had told Dawson about this Hayley woman walking past the window, she didn't have a car.

Unsurprisingly there were no kids out playing.

"You didn't think she was going to be here, did you?" Bryant asked.

She rolled her eyes. "Yes, Bryant, that's exactly what I thought."

She got out of the car, walked toward the playground and was through it by the time Bryant caught her.

A row of semi-detached houses lay beyond a grass verge on the other side of the space.

She walked along the pavement, looking over fences and hedges as she went. A threadbare silver Christmas tree had been slung into the corner of one garden. No doubt to make way for a brand-new model, possibly with snow-speckled branches or built-in LED or even a pine-smelling real one that lasted barely longer than the goodwill that accompanied the season.

"Err ... guv, what are ...?"

"This one," she said, opening a waist-high gate onto the property.

Bryant's gaze finally found what she had spotted. Two bikes beneath the windowsill.

She knocked on the door, which was quickly answered by a slim woman wearing a jogging suit and an angry expression.

"I'm sorry but I already donate to enough..."

"Police," Kim said, holding up her identification.

Her expression softened. "Sorry, but I've had three callers already today. Time of year but you can't give to everything."

"Understandable," Kim said, as the expression turned pensive as she remembered who they were.

"Is everything okay?"

"Everything's fine, Mrs...."

"Willis, Kate," she said.

"Mrs. Willis, do you use that playground over there?"

"Of course. I have eight- and six-year-old boys," she said, as though it were obvious that the house alone could not contain such levels of energy.

"Have you at any time seen a woman here with a birthmark over her right eye and a little girl..."

"You mean Hayley?"

From the corner of her eye she saw a smile tug at her colleague's features.

"You know her?"

The woman shook her head. "I wouldn't say I knew her. I struck up a conversation with her once, got a name out of her but she wasn't one for conversation. She'd stand over by the bench just watching her little girl play. Lovely little thing named Mia, polite but quiet."

"Any idea how long she'd been coming here?"

"It's been a while, I'd think. A couple of years. I just never bothered to strike up a conversation with her again."

So, she'd been coming to this little park before she moved in with their victim. If she didn't drive then she must have lived close by.

"Is there anything else you can tell us?" Kim asked. Open-ended questions could sometimes yield priceless results.

"Nothing much except that I really felt sorry for her. Not because of the birthmark but she just always seemed so sad and lonely. Staring off into space and not really speaking to anyone both before and after she got with the guy from the council. Didn't seem to make her any happier."

"Guy from the council?" Kim asked as her phone began to ring. She ignored it, and waited for an answer.

The woman continued. "Yeah, I felt pleased that she'd found someone."

"And how do you know he was from the council?"

"Always coming around to check on the playground equipment. Safety and stuff for the kids."

Kim felt the nausea rise in her stomach, remembering all the photos. That had been no maintenance guy for the council. This was where Fenton had found Hayley and her child.

"Okay, thank you for your time," Kim said, moving away and heading back toward the gate.

Bryant seethed behind her. "Bastard was here posing as a..."

His words trailed away as her phone rang again.

"Stone," she answered.

"It's Keats. Are you busy? Actually, scrub that. Don't care. I need you to get to the Wren's Nest estate right now."

CHAPTER 58

Stacey had been through the phone records three times and had thought she'd found Hayley's number; not hard to find as it was listed under her name in his contacts list. She had paused before ringing the boss, because something had not felt right. The last contact between the two phones was too long ago. It was before the six-month absence of the photos.

Of the numbers he'd called or had called him in the three months prior to his death, she had accounted for them all except two.

She'd already fired off an email to the provider requesting content information for all of the numbers, but for these two first. If she'd had the phone itself she felt sure she could have got in and found any text messages.

She got two pieces of paper and wrote down the details for each phone. She wasn't prepared to call the boss unless she was absolutely sure she knew what she was talking about. Her colleague across the desk was doing enough of that for both of them.

And now he was wittering on about something to do with priest holes, or something.

No, she had to be sure she'd got something the boss could use.

Right now, she suspected that one of the numbers belonged to Hayley. And the other one had called him the night of the murder. Could just be some kind of coincidence but she dared wonder if the other one belonged to their killer. Both went straight to voicemail. But the killer had to have got in touch somehow. Luke Fenton had left his Chinese meal to meet someone.

She grabbed a pen and began to make a list.

CHAPTER 59

The Wren's Nest estate was originally all council housing built in the 1930s to rehouse families from town center slum clearances.

By the 1980s the poor quality of housing alongside all forms of crime including antisocial behavior, joyriding and burglary sent the area into decline. Unemployment was above the national average and the decay of the estate seemed irreversible.

In the 1990s the council committed millions to a regeneration project giving properties new boundary walls, double glazing and decent heating. Crime levels fell along with the unemployment rate and the estate continually walked a tentative line dictated by socioeconomic factors.

The residents were served by schools, shops and the Summer Road Chippy, in front of which Bryant was trying to park right now.

"Do you think he does this a lot?" Bryant asked, blocking in a couple of squad cars. "You know, just ring up and demand attendance somewhere?"

"Not sure he's gonna get to do it again," she answered, getting out of the car.

She began the walk around the building to a row of bins and a collection of high-visibility jackets.

Yes, maybe a quiet word with Keats would be required. She didn't appreciate being summoned to a location with no explanation.

"Excuse me," she said, walking through two constables trying to find somewhere to tie the cordon tape.

"Okay, Keats, what the hell...?"

She stopped speaking as Keats silently stepped aside to reveal the figure on the ground.

Her gaze began at the bony feet, bare, with shoes kicked to the side. A bird tattoo on the ankle peeped out from beneath dark, worn jeans that hung loose from the body. An open denim jacket revealed a striped, woolen jumper underneath.

Her gaze continued to travel up to the carnage at the neck where the head had been severed from the body.

The ringing of her phone shattered the silence.

She took it from her pocket and pressed the answer button without looking away from the body.

"Go ahead, Stace," she said, quietly.

"Boss, I think I've got the correct phone number for our girl, Hayley."

Kim's gaze finally rested on the birthmark covering the left eye.

"Never mind, Stace, I'm looking at her right now."

CHAPTER 60

Dawson walked into the Black Country Museum, which he barely recognized from his only visit when he was around ten years old.

The museum entrance now doubled as a gift shop displaying souvenirs, traditional homeware, local history books and artists' prints and canvases from around the area.

The site had originally opened to the public in 1978 and had since added more than fifty shops, houses and other industrial buildings that had been relocated from their original sites around the Black Country and had been used as a filming location for many films and TV series including *Peaky Blinders*.

Dawson hadn't realized how much the place had grown since his one visit, but right now, he was here to meet a man named Arthur who supposedly could help him.

One of the contacts he'd emailed regarding the nail composition had replied to say the nail was like nothing he'd worked with as it consisted mainly of wrought iron. He had suggested a meeting with someone from the museum who would perhaps know more about where in the area these nails were being produced.

Dawson thought he was on a highway to nothing but he'd taken this lead and now had to run with it. He was beginning to wish he hadn't when Arthur Nugent offered his hand across the reception desk.

"You're the police officer that called?" he asked, lifting the glasses from their resting position against a check jumper and placed them on his nose.

"I am Detective Sergeant Dawson."

"Okay, well, let's see it," he said expectantly.

Dawson raised his hands. "I don't have it."

Arthur frowned. "You want me to look at a nail that you don't have?"

He took the sheet of paper from his pocket.

"I have this."

Arthur looked at it and humphed around the reception.

Dawson followed him past life-size photo boards with brief histories of prominent industrial figures from the area.

Dawson was about to ask where he was being led when Arthur stopped abruptly at a waist-high cabinet full of nails.

"Okay, which one of these does it most resemble?" Arthur asked him.

Dawson ran a hand through his hair. "Jeez, I've got no . . ."

"Lad, have you even seen this nail?"

Dawson put aside his resentment at being called "lad" as he knew the man was just trying to help.

"Yeah, I've seen it, briefly."

"Well, take a closer look. They're all very different."

A nail was a bloody nail as far as he was concerned. You picked up a box from a hardware shop and hammered stuff into a wall. All he wanted to know was which bloody hardware store this particular nail had come from.

To pacify the man he took a closer look, thinking back to the ones he had seen at the crime scene.

Arthur talked as he looked.

"Nails date back at least to Ancient Egypt, even as far back as 3400 BC. Trust me, they're not all the same."

He looked hard and realized the man had a point.

"That one," he said, resting his finger on the glass. "Or the one beside it."

"Well, make up your...oh, yes, they are quite similar. Those, my boy, are not your standard mass-produced nails we have today. In fact, they're not even from this century, or the last, or even the one before."

"Go on," Dawson said, his interest piqued.

"Those nails were made by hand, as was usual up until around the early 1800s. Do you see those marks on the side?"

Dawson nodded. That's what he'd remembered from the one he'd seen.

"They're slitters' marks. From the late sixteenth century, workmen called slitters cut up iron bars to a suitable size for nailers to work on. But over time manual slitters disappeared due to slitting mills."

"So, you're saying it could be from the sixteenth century?" he confirmed.

"If it looks like that, yes."

Dawson thanked him for his time and walked away.

He now had undeniable proof that those two murders were linked.

CHAPTER 61

Kim was reminded of scenes from cheap horror movies as she looked again at the separation of the head from the body. Only this wasn't latex and paint or tomato ketchup. This was flesh, muscle, skin and veins all cut crudely, hacked and chopped after the killer cut.

Kim knew she was projecting when she sensed a sadness in the eyes that stared up to the sky. She knew that the muscles relaxed and that any emotions drained away from the eyes.

She knew it was her own sadness she saw reflected there; sadness that this young woman's life had been taken, but more because they hadn't been able to find her in time.

In truth, she had wondered if Hayley had been responsible for the murder of Luke Fenton, though her mind had been unable to link her to the murder at Redland Hall. But now she didn't have to find that link. Because clearly someone had hated both Hayley and Luke.

"Who found her?" Kim asked.

Keats nodded toward a male in his seventies sitting on the pavement with a Jack Russell on his left and a small black bag to his right.

Kim glanced at Bryant, who got the message and headed over.

"Same as before?" she asked Keats.

"Similar," he said. "But the knife wound to the throat that killed her looks proportionately shorter than the first. Decapitated post mortem. And with a lot less finesse."

"Go on," Kim said, stepping closer. Every action of the killer told her something.

He pointed to different spots across the opening. "Clumsier than the first. More hacks."

"In a hurry?" she asked.

He shrugged. "Not for me to say."

If their killer had been in a rush, why bother with the beheading at all? The girl was dead from the cut throat.

What the hell was the message in cutting off the head?

"And you'll have noticed the absence of—"

"The genital mutilation," she finished for him. Her jeans were intact and there was no obvious staining to the fabric.

"Bang to the head?" she asked.

"Haven't moved her properly to look yet," he answered, as Bryant appeared beside her.

"Albert Thomas," he said of the man being helped to his feet by a PC. "Seventy-six years of age. Walks his dog this way every day and approached the bin to dispose of Buster's poo bag."

Kim glanced over at the tiny dog.

"Buster?" she asked, raising an eyebrow.

"Aspirational, guv," he answered. "Got all his details but I don't think he's our guy. With the arthritis in that guy's hands he'd struggle to cut a loaf of bread, never mind someone's throat."

Yeah, but they'd still check him out anyway.

She turned her attention back to Keats, as Roy approached with evidence bags.

"Time?"

"Almost eleven o'clock, Inspector," he said, looking at his watch.

"Of death," she clarified.

"Sometime before ten fifteen, which was the time I got here." She said nothing and waited.

He shook his head at her lack of humor. "I'd say between seven and twelve last night."

"Thank you. And when will you be...?"

"I'll see you at 4 p.m."

"So soon?"

"Slow day on the suspicious deaths front but of course if that's..."

"We'll be there," she said, turning to Roy.

He held up three bags.

"Debit card, phone and a five pound note."

Kim took all the bags and looked them over.

She handed two back. "I'm keeping this," she said, holding up the phone.

"But, it needs to come to the—"

"It's coming with me," she said, turning on her heel and heading back toward the car.

"Guv, I've got a question," Bryant said, catching up with her.

"You don't have to warn me of that fact. Just ask it."

"Where does she live? Where are the keys to her home?"

That wasn't the most urgent thought in her head. It wasn't even her first question. There was something far more precious that Hayley had taken with her everywhere. And that now had to take priority above all else.

"Not the only thing missing, is it, Bryant? Where is her nine-year-old daughter?"

CHAPTER 62

I knew I would find you, my Queen. And your death matches that of your King. Your reign of terror is over forever and that child will not know the fear you inflicted on her ever again.

From the very beginning I knew that my actions were right and just. I knew I had approval from above. That if there is a God He is watching, waiting for your soul to be dispatched so He can give you your final judgment and send you to Hell for eternity.

It's His way of saying sorry for letting me down despite all my prayers.

Oh no, it's not happening again. I won't go back there. I refuse to relive that pain. I have my proof and that is enough for me.

It's time to mark it done.

I take out the book and the thick black marker pen. I can now put a line through the page. I can mark the duo as complete.

I hesitate and wonder why I'm not filled with the same elation and triumph at your death that I felt with the King.

I wonder if it's due to the circumstances of the kill. I had no time to prepare as I've done with all the rest, but when God presented you to me like a mirage of an oasis in the desert there was no choice but to get it done.

No, it's not that. I had time to make my plan while I watched you eat, while you talked to me as you already had when we first met. I knew where I was going to take you, where I could leave my message. You talked of Mia and the actions you'd finally taken to ensure her safety. Too little too late.

You spoke to me of a cryptic message you'd received and that your fear had not been only from Luke. I kept the smile to myself at the knowledge that the threat was sitting right in front of you.

You got into my car with trust. You accepted the meal I offered easily. You got back into my car with the promise of a bed for the night, somewhere to get your head together, excuse the pun.

I began to anticipate your fear once you realized that I was the one you'd been running from.

I parked the car and turned to you, my true feelings for your actions showing on my face and you finally understood.

A slight sad nod of acceptance.

You had given up. You had no fight.

I understand that your life had been hard, that you had been a victim. Maybe you had suffered like me as you'd bounced around the care system. But you did something unforgivable. You went back to the bastard who was abusing your child. You were her mother. And you had to die.

And now I know why your death did not satisfy me. You did nothing to fight me back. There was no effort at self-preservation. You had no fear. You no longer cared for your life and were not fearful of losing it. Your gaze was devoid of all emotion as you stared up at me. You welcomed the end.

"Do it and make it quick," you said.

I told you I would linger and make you suffer. You shrugged your shoulders. Even that didn't bring forth a response. You wanted death too much to be scared. You knew that however long I took your end was in your sight.

I put my hands around your throat and pressed hard. Still no fear. Your eyes begged me to do it. You welcomed it.

I slapped you. I screamed in your face and still you lay there defeated.

"I'll get your daughter," I threatened. "Fight for your life or I'll find her and kill her."

A sad smile spread over your face. "You won't find her," you said. "And you won't hurt her."

How did you know that? I was about to take your life and somehow you knew that.

But now I'm angry. You robbed me, my Queen. I wanted your fear. I wanted to see the terror in your eyes so you would feel as Mia had.

I promise myself that from the next one I will get the fear.

CHAPTER 63

With Hayley's full name Stacey felt as though she was being spoiled.

Within minutes of the boss's call she'd managed to cobble together a brief history of the woman's life. Nothing yet that would help track down nine-year-old Mia, which was the information the boss wanted. Pronto.

Hayley Smart was born in 1987 and placed into the care system at two months old by her sixteen-year-old mother. Stacey had seen no evidence to suggest that the relationship had ever been rekindled.

There followed a succession of foster homes and children's homes until she left the system at the same age her own mother had left her there.

Stacey couldn't help the sadness that engulfed her as she learned more about the woman.

Having grown up as an only child with both parents and part of the wider Nigerian community in and around Dudley, she had felt nothing but love and security. Even at school when her color had brought her first brushes with cruelty and isolation she had known she would return to the loving, reassuring embrace of her family.

As she read about Hayley Smart she found herself wishing for the happy ending. In films and TV dramas, no matter what the hardship, most folks got their happy ending. She kept hoping that each foster home would be the last, that the girl had finally found somewhere to feel safe and loved.

But now she'd met her end and there'd been nothing happy about it at all.

Hayley had first come to the attention of the police at the age of seventeen for shoplifting. The charges hadn't stopped there and for the next few years she'd been brought in a total of seven times on crimes ranging from petty assault to burglary, resulting in some decent stretches of prison time.

Stacey kicked herself for not searching their own system with nothing more than a first name and the birthmark, though she wasn't sure how effective the search would have been or if the boss would have felt it a good use of her time. This week was turning into the biggest learning curve of her life, she thought, as she continued to read.

For a couple of years Hayley had disappeared from the radar and a simple calculation told Stacey it was when she first had her daughter. And the crimes were back down to petty theft.

Personally, Stacey had never been a believer in victimless crime. Someone, somewhere always suffered or felt the repercussions whether it be through violence, fear, loss or a stock-take that didn't add up at the end of the day. Someone lost something.

But she did believe in survivor crime. Desperate people carrying out criminal acts to get by. They weren't trying to hurt anyone or take more than they needed, they were simply trying to survive.

And that's what Hayley appeared to have been trying to do.

Once she had a child only three short prison sentences had occurred, the last one being less than a year ago.

Stacey noted that on each of those three occasions her address given was completely different. Had this woman never had a proper home?

The boss had told her the priority was finding where the woman had lived. Little Mia could be there all alone. They had to find her. Was she safe? Had she been with Hayley at the time of the murder? Did the murderer still have her? And the worst question of all. Was she still alive?

She pushed the thoughts away, noting all three addresses listed on Hayley's record.

Stacey prayed Mia was safe and sound at one of them.

CHAPTER 64

The ringing of her phone took just a couple more minutes than she'd expected.

"Stone, turn the car around and head back to the scene. Now," Woody instructed.

"For what, sir? We're miles away from Wren's Nest now."

That wasn't a lie but she was careful not to state exactly where they were or this conversation would be taking place in person, and with a missing nine-year-old girl she wasn't going to waste the time.

"You know full well why. That phone needs to go to the lab."

"Sir, I beg to differ. I have a person sitting…"

"Stone, are you arguing with me?" he asked as Bryant parked the car.

She got out and started walking as she continued to talk. "I firmly believe that my detective constable will be able to access anything of value," she said, taking the steps two at a time.

Woody continued arguing as she entered the squad room and placed a finger to her lips.

Stacey was just hanging up the phone.

Kim handed her the evidence bag.

She looked at it and smiled widely before scribbling something on a sheet of paper and pushing it toward her.

Kim read it, took it and nodded her understanding before heading back out of the office.

"But, sir," she said, heading back down the stairs, "if that phone goes to the lab it will sit in a queue of jobs that may or may not get actioned in the next few days. Our killer appears to be on some kind of rampage and right now every second counts," she said, getting into the car. She handed Bryant the piece of paper and pointed at the last item.

He nodded and started the car.

"Sir, I can assure you that the chain of evidence will be preserved and that no prosecution will be compromised."

"Stone, you're dealing with a very young, inexperience..." His words trailed away for a second. "Stone, is that you driving off the station car park?"

She said nothing.

"You've already handed it to her, haven't you?"

"Err... kind of," she admitted.

"Debrief, my office. Six o'clock," he barked, before ending the call.

CHAPTER 65

"Bloody hell, guv, I heard him shout from here," Bryant said. "So, I guess we'd best not be late back for tea."

"You're right there. By which time I'm hoping we've found Mia, whose safety comes way before my bollocking. And it gives me a few hours to practice my sorry face."

Bryant laughed out loud, surprising her. She hadn't been joking.

"I'm assuming these are Hayley's last known addresses and that she was pretty known to us."

"Appears that way," Kim said, glancing at the note that said the bottom address was only one month old. If Mia was going to be alone waiting for her mother's return, surely that's where she would be.

In one way Kim hoped they were going to find a little girl there safe and sound, and in another way, she hoped the girl was already safe. She'd called it into the station before they'd left the crime scene and she knew that officers were already out looking. Nothing in this case was moving forward until they knew what had happened to Hayley's child. Kim just prayed she had not been with her mother when the murderer had caught her. If so she could only hope that the murderer valued a child's life higher than he'd valued Hayley's.

It took only a few minutes to reach the council house in Colley Gate a couple of miles out of Halesowen town center, and Kim found herself itching to jump out of the car while it was still moving, run up to the house, break a window and see if Mia was in there.

"That's the one," Bryant said, nodding toward an end terrace with a wrap-around garden.

Kim's stomach dropped a little as she saw that the property was empty. Windowless curtains revealed the dark space of emptiness beyond. Some kind of notice had been taped to the front door.

"Damn," Kim said, heading up the path of the house next door.

She knocked hard to penetrate the loud rock music being played.

No answer.

She moved along to the front window and banged even harder. Her frustration at one dead end after another. And yes, she expected everyone to know there was a child missing.

The music died suddenly, and the door was thrust open by a man she had to look up to.

"Police," she informed him immediately.

The aggression dropped from his face.

"It weren't that loud and next door's empty anyway."

"You sure about that?" Kim asked.

He nodded. "Been gone for weeks."

Kim felt the irritation building within her. She knew that Mia was not in there and this was the most recent address she had. She had to hope this man could tell her something that would help locate the child.

"Did you know Hayley well?"

A slow smile spread across his face. "Tried to, if you know what I mean."

"Yeah, I think I get you," Kim answered, trying not to react to the filthy look on his face.

"When did she move out?" Kim asked. This address was barely a month old.

He shrugged. "Not sure she really did."

She looked to the property. Maybe she'd been wrong. "You mean..."

"Nah, she's gone all right but she didn't take a lot with her. Saw the council removing it all. Tried to get what I could but council wouldn't let me. Tight bastards. Probably having it themselves for—"

"What kind of stuff?" Kim asked. She didn't have this kind of time to waste.

"Furniture, kitchen stuff, kid's stuff, toys. Wasn't interested in the clothes, of course."

"She left her clothes?" Kim clarified.

He nodded vigorously as though he was now enjoying being helpful.

"That's what I'm trying to tell you. Looked like she didn't take a bloody thing."

"Okay, thanks," Kim said, walking away with a frown and two questions on her mind.

What had driven Hayley to flee without her possessions and where the hell was her child?

CHAPTER 66

Stacey smiled widely as she finally cracked the code into Hayley's mobile phone. She had needed to visit some rather questionable websites to do it, which she'd done on her own phone, but she was in.

"Yessss," she said, punching the air and then bringing her arm back down quickly as a figure appeared in the doorway.

Stacey felt the heat flood her cheeks but the uniformed officer was too busy looking around, as though checking he was in the right place.

"CID, mate," she said, although there was a brass plate stating as much on the door.

A frisson of pride had surged through her as she'd said it.

"PC Chalmers," he said, stepping over the threshold and into the squad room as though it was a fresh new world or alternate universe.

He looked at the photos on the wall. He swallowed and looked away.

Stacey guessed he was early twenties. His blonde hair appeared to be held down with some sort of lotion.

"And may I help you?" she asked, hoping to prompt him into his reason for coming.

"Saw the briefing. The one about the little girl."

"Mia Smart?" she asked, hopefully.

He nodded and the phone records on her desk were momentarily forgotten.

"You know the little girl?"

He shook his head.

Her hopes began to plummet.

"So, you're here…"

"I don't know her but I can definitely tell you where she is."

CHAPTER 67

Kim felt the relief flood through her as Stacey spoke.

"So, you're saying that Hayley voluntarily gave Mia up to the state temporarily when going to prison that last time?"

"Apparently, she has no one she could leave the child with. Mia was handed over three times altogether."

"But she's been out of prison for a month. Why didn't she get Mia back?" Kim asked.

"Not sure how easy it is to keep putting your child in and out of care, boss," Stacey said. "Maybe Child Services weren't letting her go quite so easily until Hayley could prove she was back on her feet."

"And this police officer?"

"Was there when Mia was taken to a foster home. Some concern for her safety so the Social Worker requested an escort."

"So, you have..."

"The address of the foster home right here."

"Stacey, bloody good..."

"To be fair, boss, the officer came to me but I'm hoping to have something more for yer later."

Intelligent and self-effacing. Kim liked that. Kim ended the call and checked her watch.

She waited for her phone to ding receipt of the text message giving her Mia's foster parents' address.

She read it out to Bryant before scrolling through her contact list.

He picked up on the second ring.

"Dawson, what you got?"

"Boss, I'm just looking into this thing about the location of Lester Jackson's body. About the nails used at the first crime scene. They…"

"Were old nails, made of wrought iron and most likely came from a place like Redland Hall?"

Silence.

She continued. "Said the report that came through from the lab about an hour ago."

She let that sink in for a minute.

"Let other people do their jobs and stop trying to get the gold star. I don't give 'em out. You found any more links between Luke Fenton and the other victims?"

"Nothing yet, boss, but I'm still on it."

Kim wondered how hard he was working on the job that she'd tasked him with versus the lead he had found on his own.

"Drop everything and get to the morgue by four. It's Hayley's postmortem and we're not going to make it."

She hung up the phone before he had chance to argue.

"You sure you want to do this?" Bryant asked. "I'm not sure DCI Woodward would…Jeez, that's hard to say."

"Yeah, in my head he's now Woody. I'm pretty sure I've got a bollocking coming at six anyway and I'm all for a buy one get one free."

Silence fell between them.

"Guv, was that a joke?"

She thought about his earlier attempt at humor.

"You know, Bryant, if we're going to spend much more time in this car together we are gonna have to learn each other's humor. And to answer your question, yes, it is a good idea to try and speak to Mia because we could learn an awful lot by talking to that nine-year-old girl."

"And her foster parent will allow it, do you think?"

Kim was genuinely surprised. "To help us catch a murderer, I'd think so."

"Hmm...you don't have children, do you, guv?"

"I'm not sure what that..."

"Never mind," he said, pulling off the main road onto the Caledonia housing estate in Brierley Hill. He followed the road around until he came to a small cul-de-sac of semi-detached houses.

"It's the one with the dormer," he said, pulling up in front of the drive.

A Ford Fiesta was parked to the far left of the tarmac showing that another car shared the drive.

Kim thought about the address they'd just come from and what they'd learned about Hayley so far. The last thing Mia had experienced in her life was stability and routine. And now her mother was dead. For this poor kid, the hits just kept on coming.

The door opened before they'd even knocked.

A small, unobtrusive camera was fitted to the corner of the house. A recent addition by the looks of a small pile of plaster on the ground.

The woman holding the door was around five foot four with freckles and a mass of red curls that were being left to do as they pleased.

Kim held up her identification and introduced them both.

"May we come in?"

The woman's face remained creased in suspicion and she didn't move an inch.

"Mrs. Roberts, it's regarding Mia, and her mother."

Still the woman hesitated but she moved aside.

Kim stepped into a hallway that was littered with coats, scarves, wellington boots. Three different sizes, she noted, and a lot of pink.

"Please come through," she said, leading them to a conservatory at the back of the house.

A cup of coffee sat beside an open crossword puzzle book.

"A little time to myself before fetching the girls."

"And how many girls do you have?" Kim asked.

"Three including Mia," she said, taking a seat on the single wicker chair.

Both Kim and Bryant sat on the two-seater opposite looking out onto a garden that although not huge managed to accommodate a small patio area, a square of lawn, a slide, trampoline and cozy summer house right at the end.

Kim already liked the way the woman had included Mia in her list of children.

"I'm afraid I have some bad news that I must ask you to keep to yourself."

"Okay," she said, sitting forward.

"Hayley Smart is dead."

The woman's hand rose straight to her open mouth which mirrored the roundness of her eyes.

"Oh my God, how, where? I mean. Are you sure?"

Kim nodded. "I'm afraid so. I can't divulge much detail but she was murdered sometime last night."

The woman started to shake her head, and Kim noticed a slight tremble to her hand as she pushed an errant curl behind her ear.

"We'd really like an opportunity to speak to Mia if—"

"Absolutely not," the woman said, straightening. "That child has been through enough. I'll explain about her mother but I'm not letting you anywhere near her."

Kim hadn't considered this. Whereas Bryant clearly had when he'd made that crack about not having kids. For a foster parent Mrs. Roberts seemed very protective of her charge.

Kim couldn't help remembering some of her own foster families, who had taken in kids for many different reasons, very few of them altruistic, and would have let her speak to anyone.

Except for Keith and Erica, who would have protected her with their lives.

"I understand that you want to safeguard your charge," Kim said, offering a gentle reminder.

"Please don't call her that," she said with distaste. "This is the third time Mia has been with us. The previous two times were due to her mother serving prison time. She was with us for four months when she was seven years old. She didn't speak for the first three of those months and we didn't try to force her. She was behind in all her school subjects and was placed into a lower year at school. Just when we thought we were making progress her mother was released and Mia was returned to her. I won't lie, Inspector. It all but broke my heart."

"And the second time?" Kim asked.

"About a year later and Mia had regressed even further. Wetting the bed, silent, totally withdrawn and at times hostile. On that occasion, we never heard her speak once."

"And you took her a third time?" Kim asked.

"Of course," she said, as though it was a no-brainer. "She's a child. A sad, damaged, confused child. None of this is her fault. Whatever's happened to her is not..."

"And do you know what's happened to her?" Kim asked, remembering the photos on Fenton's computer.

"We have a good idea and there are many reasons to hate her mother except one."

"Many reasons?"

"Not taking proper care of her, allowing her to fall behind, moving her from one unstable situation to another. I'm sorry she's dead but I can't forgive her for what she's done to this child."

Kim heard the emotion gathering in her throat.

Regardless, Kim felt she had to give it another shot.

"But, Mrs. Roberts, Mia might be able to help—"

"Last night, Inspector, out of nowhere Mia walked over to me, silently, and got onto my lap. She said nothing and stayed only for a few minutes, but if that child is beginning to put even an ounce of trust in me to protect her, there is not one thing you can say to convince me to let you anywhere near her. You are not what she needs right now and that is my one and only priority."

Kim knew this battle was lost. The woman could not have been more protective if Mia had been her own child. Another pang shot through her. She had known this kind of love, for a short time, but she had known it.

Kim knew there was nothing she could say that would convince her to change her mind.

But she suddenly remembered something Mrs. Roberts had said earlier.

"You said there were many reasons to hate Hayley Smart except for one. What did you mean?"

"That the woman had finally had the good grace to do the right thing."

"Which was?"

"This time she had given Mia up for good."

CHAPTER 68

Stacey had made a mental list for interrogating the phone of Hayley Smart. First, she would tackle the call register, then the text messages and then look for any deleted data.

But first she took a moment to absorb her current surroundings and situation. She could almost feel guilty for calling what she was doing work, when she was feeling for the first time in her life that she'd found her purpose.

Not that she'd hand back her pay at the end of the month. She had bills to pay like everyone else, but right now she was contributing toward the efforts to find a serial killer and she couldn't help feeling she was finally where she was meant to be.

Yeah, it got a bit quiet and lonely in the office sometimes but she was beginning to realize this was where her skill-set lay.

She felt immensely proud that the boss had seen fit to trust her with Hayley's phone instead of sending it to the lab and they were only on day three.

She rolled her eyes and decided it was time to stop congratulating herself, but oh, if those girls that had called her names and bullied her throughout her school years could see her now.

Enough, she told herself as she began to scroll through the actual contact list, which was painfully short.

Stacey had few friends but her contact list at least held a few friends and family.

There was a contact for "school," "Pro Officer" and "Taxi."

She moved straight on to the call register and was surprised to see that pretty much every call Hayley had received in the last few weeks had been missed and very few people had been called.

"Where the hell were you, Hayley?" she said out loud. "And why day yer want to speak?"

Stacey knew that the only way to find anything out was to start calling these numbers and try to find out who they were. She hoped the boss wasn't expecting a quick result on this one.

She decided to start with the number that had called Hayley the most, but as she reached for the phone her eyes caught one of the numbers farther down the list. It was a number she had seen before.

She remembered that the number had ended with three ones, which had made her think of the NHS phone helpline.

Stacey immediately ruled out Luke Fenton. It wasn't a number she had studied or called. It was a number that she'd seen in passing, but she couldn't remember where.

She put the phone to the side for a minute and began searching through the paperwork on her desk.

Her gut had reacted immediately because it proved one thing.

Hayley Smart had been in contact with someone else involved in the investigation.

And she had to find out who.

CHAPTER 69

Dawson couldn't help wondering if the boss was doing this to him on purpose. Had he somehow communicated to her just how much he hated the morgue or had she just guessed? There was no other explanation for him visiting the place twice in two days.

"You again?" Keats asked.

"Yeah, I'm as thrilled as you are."

"Ooh, someone appears to have adopted their boss's sour mood already."

He grunted in response, wishing the pathologist would just get on with it.

"Well, you'll be pleased to know that I've already carried out the postmortem, so I won't have to keep you long."

Dawson felt himself cheer right up, as a message dinged to his phone.

He was sorely tempted to take it out and read it, hoping it was a response to his queries. He was desperate to take the attention from his younger, lower-ranking colleague.

"So obviously all weights and measurements will be listed on my official report as will the following: this young lady was severely undernourished and around seven pounds lighter than the lowest weight recommended for her height. However, her last meal, consumed only an hour or two before her death, was a burger and fries. And had she been eating meals like that on a regular basis her weight would more likely have been within the recommended parameters. Neither her nails nor her hair were particularly clean and attention to personal hygiene had been somewhat lacking."

Dawson wondered why he was having to stand and listen to the details when the report would follow later.

"I would place the time of death somewhere between seven and twelve last night as already noted to your inspector."

What he really wanted to do was take out his phone and see who had sent him a message. For all he knew, the smoking gun to blow the case wide open was now sitting in an email in his pocket.

"I can confirm that in my opinion the same knife was used on both victims; however, the severing of the head from the body appears to have been more coarsely done than the first."

"But wouldn't Luke Fenton's neck have been harder to cut?" he asked. "More flesh, thicker neck?"

"Aah, finally a question that shows you are present. Yes, it should have been much harder to behead the male."

"So..." Dawson asked, awaiting a better explanation.

"That's for you to answer, Sergeant. I can tell you that it was and you have to find out why."

Dawson worked hard to control his expression.

"Anything else?" he asked.

"Of course. I can confirm that there was no blunt force trauma to the back of the head, unlike the first victim, which is also a question for you..."

"To answer," Dawson finished for him. Yeah, he got it.

"So, in the face of your boredom is there anything you'd like to ask me ahead of the full report that will be sent later today?"

Dawson thought about the message that had dinged to his phone.

"Nope, nothing," he said, heading for the exit. This had gone so much better than he'd thought.

"Of course, you should know that was the wrong answer," Keats offered as he reached the door.

"There is one question you should always ask before leaving..."

Dawson thought for a moment; one more question. Something that would cover everything.

He got it.

"Is there anything else I need to know?"

"Correct and yes," he said, walking over to the desk in the corner.

He held up an evidence bag.

"This was found in the waistband of her jeans."

Dawson took a few steps toward it.

"What is it?" he said.

The item was red in color and an inch wide.

"No idea."

Dawson took a closer look at the plastic object.

"Some kind of knob or top from something?"

"My thoughts too."

Dawson took out his phone and photographed it from every angle.

When he'd finished he turned once again to the pathologist. He rarely needed to be told anything twice.

"Is there anything else I need to know?"

Keats smiled. "No, that'll do for now."

CHAPTER 70

"You know those dreams where your brain is running but your feet won't keep up and you can't escape a certain area?" Kim asked, as they got out of the lift.

"I know the ones, guv."

"Well, that's me and this place right about now."

"I get you," he said, knocking on the door.

This resident already knew they were coming.

Lisa Bywater opened the door minus the green uniform.

"Come in but be quick."

Kim wondered why the woman's past was such a secret from her husband, but she supposed it was her choice and that wasn't the question she wanted answering.

"You know why we're here?"

Lisa shook her head and Kim knew she was lying.

"You made a call to Hayley Smart, the ex-girlfriend of your pedophile brother, which lasted for three seconds, and I think you need to explain it to us."

Lisa's body seemed to wither before her eyes as she folded into the nearest kitchen chair.

"I knew you'd find it. She's dead, isn't she? She's the body on the news?"

Kim knew the news of another murder had broken; however until they established there were no next of kin, her identity would be withheld.

"Is Mia okay?" Lisa asked.

"How do you know them?" Kim asked, unwilling to offer the woman anything until she got answers. She'd had no contact with her brother and appeared to actively hide from him and yet she had the phone number of the woman they'd been trying to find.

She took a deep breath, and Kim took a seat.

"I saw them, together. At my bloody supermarket of all places. I hadn't seen Luke in years. Last I heard he'd moved north, Yorkshire, I was told. So when I saw him I was scared to death. I ran into the back and feigned illness until I was sure they'd gone. It was only later, once I was safely back here, that I remembered there had been a child holding the woman's hand."

"So, what did you do?"

"Nothing at first. You have to understand how hard it's been to get him out of my head. That one sighting brought it all back. I couldn't eat, I couldn't sleep and suddenly I was seeing him everywhere. The nightmares returned and then they changed. I was no longer seeing Luke's face but the face of that child."

"So?"

"I tracked him down, found his address and waited for her to come out alone."

"And?"

"I tried to tell her what he was like, that he was into kids, but she wouldn't listen. Said he loved her child like his own. I talked until I was blue in the face, hoping that something I was saying was going in, but she just stormed away. I saw her again when I was at work and I tried once more, insisting she take my phone number in case she ever needed anything. I left it there at that time as there was nothing I could do except hope she started looking for signs or talk directly to Mia."

Kim couldn't help a growing respect for this young woman who had voluntarily involved herself in a situation that brought her closer to a man who frightened her to death.

"And did you hear from her?"

She nodded. "About a month later when she called me to say that she had suspicions and that she was leaving him."

"But she went back?" Kim asked, trying not to judge but still wondering how a mother could do that.

"He found her and she had nowhere else to go. I don't think her life has been easy but I still tried to talk her out of going back. She told me that it was just until she got sorted and she would make sure nothing happened to Mia."

"And was that the last you heard from her?" Kim asked, wondering about the recent call.

She shook her head. "She texted me from a new number and told me she'd left and he wouldn't find either of them again."

"Did you offer her a place to stay?" Kim asked, unable to help herself. Knowing what she knew about her brother, Kim would have thought this woman would have been the first to step forward and offer assistance.

Lisa looked at her as though she'd lost her mind. "Firstly, officer, my husband knows nothing of my past and it's something I've chosen not to share with him. I'm entitled to make that call."

Kim nodded her acceptance of the fact. There was much of her own past that she chose to share with no one.

There were other ways. Lisa wouldn't have needed to divulge Hayley's true identity to give her a bed for a night or two. "But surely you could have—"

"You don't get it, do you?" she said, licking her lower lip nervously. "Even talking about him puts my nerves on edge and I know the bastard is dead. It doesn't matter, I'm still scared of his power. Having Hayley in my home would only have been one step removed from inviting Luke back into my life, when I've done everything I can to escape him. If you don't understand the fear I can't explain it. I had a full-blown panic attack when I received a text message from her giving me her new number."

"Was this about a month ago?" Kim asked, leaving the subject alone. She didn't blame Lisa for Hayley's death, but she would remain convinced that Lisa could have done more.

"Yes."

When Hayley put Mia into the custody of the state and had clearly gone into hiding herself, Kim realized.

"So, when you knew your brother was dead..."

"I just wanted to let her know it was safe to come out. I just wish Mia..."

"Mia is safe with a foster family who loves her very much," Kim said, thankful that Hayley had finally done the right thing by her child.

"Oh, thank God," she said.

"And do you have any idea at all where she was hiding?" Kim asked. Because as soon as she'd lost that safety she had also lost her life: clearly there had been more than one man looking for her.

"Not this time, no. She didn't want anyone to know."

"But the last time?" Kim asked.

She had eluded him for six months previously so maybe she'd used the same hidey hole twice.

"Oh yeah, I know where she was the first time, when she was gone for six months."

"And you didn't think to share this information?" Kim asked.

Lisa shrugged. "You never asked."

"Go on," Kim urged, biting her tongue.

"She was staying at some shelter in Dudley."

CHAPTER 71

Kim stepped back into the squad room to three expectant faces, following her meeting with Woody.

She considered debriefing the team right now and continuing with the leads they'd found, but it was already after seven at the end of another twelve-hour day.

As explained to Bryant she had adopted her sorry face, which Woody must have found suitably repentant, as it was difficult to continue telling someone off if they were choosing not to argue back.

"Okay, folks, we'll debrief in the morning. Get some rest."

She'd swear that three disappointed faces looked right back at her. As what seemed to be developing into the norm, she indicated for Dawson to stay back. Kim watched as his younger, less experienced colleague threw her satchel diagonally across her front before nodding her goodbyes and following Bryant out of the door. She couldn't help comparing the efforts of the greenest officer on the team to the one left sitting in front of her now. Again. Stacey had begun the week keen as mustard to work hard and learn. She had carried out every instruction she'd been given efficiently and enthusiastically. She'd used her initiative and followed up leads. There were moments that Kim forgot just how inexperienced she was and could already see the potential for further development. It was unfortunate that she didn't feel the same way about DS Dawson.

So far this week he'd tested her. He'd tried to challenge her, he'd ignored her instructions, and right now she was a hair's breadth away from having him removed from her team.

But not quite.

"And again I'm keeping you back," she said, folding her arms and feeling like a teacher reprimanding an errant pupil at detention.

His expression told her that he was searching his brain for whatever else he'd done wrong.

"You slept in your car on the station car park last night," she stated.

He opened his mouth to say something and then changed his mind.

"I don't know and nor do I care what's going on in your private life or why you did that, but it will not happen again. Is that clear?"

Again, with the schoolmarm posture and speech. She wondered why the hell this detective brought that out in her.

"Of course, boss," he said, as a flash of panic entered his eyes, causing her to wonder if he'd been planning to do it again tonight. "I'll find somewhere..."

"There's a room booked at the Travelodge down the road in your name. One night, now sort yourself out and get the fuck on board with this team," she said, before heading into the bowl.

She glanced back and was rewarded by the look of confusion on his face as he collected together his things.

It wasn't an act of kindness on her part. It was a calculated plan. He reminded her of a tired, angry puppy. Constantly distracted and trying to get the upper hand.

And sometimes all an errant puppy needed to refocus its addled little brain was a good night's sleep.

And if that didn't work he would be off the team for good.

CHAPTER 72

Stacey wandered into the kitchen, took off her coat and resisted the urge to reach into her satchel for her phone. She was a grown-up now. She had her own flat, a new job and she had to deal with her feelings and doubts by herself.

During the chaos of the day it was easier to push the thoughts away. Her mind was diverted by the murder investigation: thinking, working, trawling, mining, more thinking.

She had already cursed herself many times for not trying to find Hayley on the system sooner by using just her first name and the knowledge of the birthmark. Maybe it was a life she could have helped save.

The logical part of her screamed out that the information on the system had done nothing to help them anyway but that wasn't the point. She hadn't had the thought to check. She couldn't help wondering if the boss was thinking the exact same thing.

It hadn't taken her long to work out that the boss didn't dispense compliments like sweeties, but even her expression was difficult to analyze so Stacey was getting no clues there.

She sighed heavily as she took a cottage pie from the fridge and popped it into the microwave. If she'd still been living with her parents she would have returned to a home-cooked meal, maybe Ogbono soup, a Nigerian recipe with a hearty mixture of beef, fish and spinach. Or equally a plate of egg and chips with bread and butter. Her mother wasn't faithful to one cuisine and liked to mix it up depending on her mood. But a home-cooked meal wasn't all she'd have got at home. Immediately upon entering the three-bed semi she would have been assaulted by the cooking smells she'd grown up with, sparkly Christmas decorations hanging from every hook in the house, tinsel arching every doorway. Her mother welcomed the festive season into the house from the last week of November.

Stacey had been meaning to get a tree for a couple of weeks but she'd just kept putting it off. Her only concession to Christmas were the family and friends' Christmas cards on the mantelpiece in the lounge, which she dared not divulge to her mum.

But it wasn't even the homely, festive comfort she was seeking. Her mother would have known straight away that there was something on her mind. She would have pumped, cajoled and threatened her until she'd bared her soul. Her mum would have listened, nodded, snorted occasionally and then offered her reassurance and a soundbite. Her mum had a knack with short sentences that stuck in her head and made her see everything differently. There were no long speeches with her; she just thought it over, considered the problem fully and then offered a few words of wisdom.

Her hand reached for the phone once more, but she snatched it back.

She was a big girl now. She was adulting as they said. She had to find her own soundbites.

It was time for her to grow up.

CHAPTER 73

Dawson walked into the supermarket with the same vague sickness that had blighted him after his night with Lou. He wasn't sure of the cause but it wasn't a sensation he was enjoying all that much.

He liked to think he knew and understood people. He'd expected many things from this new boss: another bollocking, another of those one-sided chats, threat of removal from the team. He certainly hadn't been expecting a bed for the night.

He stood in front of the sandwich fridge surveying the last few offerings available. Most of which had probably been picked up, turned around and then rejected at different points throughout the day.

He pictured Ally at home. She'd probably be preparing something nutritious, healthy and bloody tasty. He didn't know how she did it but how she worked full-time as an Accounts Assistant and still managed to cook so well had been a mystery to him.

And he was here looking to get the best value for his meal deal. A sandwich, crisps and a cold drink that would tide him over until tomorrow.

He knew which he preferred, but he couldn't go home yet. Or at all. He knew what she expected from him and the pressure was just driving him further away.

He pushed the thought away and settled for an egg triple sandwich—at least he got three slices of bread, even if it was brown—a packet of chicken crisps and a bottle of Diet Coke.

As he reached for the red-topped bottle he remembered the photo of the item found in Hayley Smart's waistband.

At first, he'd wondered if it meant anything at all. The woman had been found by a row of bins behind a chip shop. Surely it would have been more unusual if some kind of debris hadn't worked its way into the crime scene.

Although nothing else had, a small voice said inside his head. And for it to actually have worked its way into her clothing and not just beneath her niggled at him.

But what the hell was it? he wondered.

He took out his phone and scrolled to the photos he'd taken at the morgue. He put his meal deal back in the fridge and began walking the aisles of the supermarket.

He quickly ruled out the electrical, clothing and magazine sections and moved quickly past the fruit and vegetables.

No joy around the tinned goods or the chilled and frozen.

He was considering asking one of the shop assistants he'd passed if they recognized it when he reached the condiments.

Something in his brain snapped a flash of recognition from his childhood, of Friday night tea when his mum didn't feel like cooking and his dad came home with a steaming carrier bag.

His eyes scoured the shelves until he found what he was looking for.

He lifted up the object with a red top and took out his phone.

This red top, found in the waistband of Hayley Smart's jeans, had come from a bottle of vinegar.

CHAPTER 74

"Okay, guys, let's get to it," Kim said, taking what was becoming her usual spot perched on the edge of the spare desk.

She reached for one of the coffees in the cardboard carrier.

"Thanks, Bryant, but I've already told you..."

"Wasn't me, guv," he said as Dawson raised his hand.

Kim nodded her thanks for the gesture, given what appeared to be a dire financial situation.

She looked across the wipe boards trying to focus on the information they had rather than the gaps that were smacking her in the face. If only she had access to all of these damned cases.

The first genital mutilation had occurred six years earlier, to someone who remained unidentified. The second victim had been Lester Jackson, at Redland Hall, a month ago. Next had been Tommy Deeley in Wolverhampton almost a week ago, followed by their own victim: Luke Fenton, who was found on Monday. And now they had Hayley Smart too.

"Okay, so we have either our second or fifth victim, Hayley Smart, the ex-girlfriend of Luke Fenton. We know from his sister and the photos on the computer that she left him and then went back. There was no genital mutilation so what does that tell us?"

"That our killer is pissed off with her but not as much as he is with the others," Dawson offered.

"Why?" she asked.

He thought for a second. "Because Hayley didn't actually abuse anyone but she put her daughter back in a position to be abused."

"My thoughts too," Kim said. "I think Hayley has paid the ultimate price for going back to Fenton after her time at the shelter."

"The sister?" Stacey asked. "I mean she did punch her dead brother in the face, so she's still pretty angry."

Kim had been thinking the same thing. The voicemail left on Hayley's phone could have been deliberate to draw her out. In addition, after reading Keats's full report first thing she'd found it odd that Hayley had consumed her first proper meal just hours before she'd been murdered. Had someone else bought her that meal, and given that she'd been hiding, who did she trust? She knew and trusted Luke's sister enough to give her her new phone number.

"Can't see any link between Lisa Bywater and any other victim, but she's definitely a person of interest," she said. And even more so if they ruled out the other incidents like people wanted them to, because then Lisa was the only person they'd encountered who knew them both. Except, she wasn't yet prepared to accept that three other deaths had nothing to do with the cases of the two victims that were on her desk.

She nodded toward Stacey. "Start checking out ViSOR and see what you can find. The two victims we know anything about were both pedophiles."

"Will do."

They all knew that ViSOR was the database of those required to register with the police under the Sexual Offenses Act 2003, which included persons jailed for more than twelve months for violent offenses and un-convicted people thought to be at risk of offending. Commonly referred to as the sex offenders' register, it was accessed by Police, National Probation Service and HM Prison Service personnel.

"Boss, I found something else out last night," Dawson offered, taking his phone from his pocket. "That bottle top found in Hayley Smart's clothing. It came from a bottle of vinegar. You know, the old-fashioned Sarson's bottle that..."

"I saw the picture," she said, and although the shape had looked familiar, part of her had wondered if it was just crap from the nearby chip shop bins.

"I'm just wondering if it means anything, boss. These small things we're overlooking at the crime scenes like the priest hole, the bell, the shoe. I wouldn't mind looking into them further."

A sound and reasonable argument presented as a request. A startling change from the beginning of the week.

"Okay, Dawson, get into it."

He nodded his understanding.

"Okay, folks. Time to get to work," she said, finishing her drink.

Kim knew her first visit of the day was straight back to the shelter in Dudley.

CHAPTER 75

Stacey breathed a sigh of relief as Dawson headed off to the canteen for coffee the minute the boss was out the door, as she wasn't quite sure how she felt about having him sitting opposite.

She had kind of got used to everyone departing after the morning briefing and leaving her alone. She also wasn't sure how she felt about the can of Diet Coke he'd brought in for her this morning. She'd written him off as a colleague to be ignored at worst and tolerated at best. He'd been a total arse all week but one act of kindness and she was ready to give him the benefit of the doubt. Yep, people pleaser all the way, she acknowledged to herself. She resolved to respond if he spoke to her, but no more trying to make him like her. She was over it.

She bent down to retrieve her satchel from the floor and started when she raised her head at the figure who had appeared soundlessly in the doorway.

"Boss?" she questioned. Her colleague had been subjected to a couple of one-on-one conversations this week but she'd escaped unharmed. Her hand trembled on the fastener catch of the bag. What had she done wrong? Was it the Hayley Smart thing she'd been worrying about all night?

"You know, Stace, just in case you were wondering, you're doing a cracking job. Keep it up."

"Th-thanks, boss," she said, feeling the heat rush into her cheeks. Strangely, compliments were harder for her to take than reprimands. She knew what to do with one of those; try harder.

The boss turned and left as the smile found its way to her lips. Not only had the boss complimented her, she had nipped back to the office to do it. Had the boss been in her flat last night or more importantly had she been in her head? Either way Stacey was grateful for the shortest pep talk she'd ever received.

She sat up straight and took out the notebook that had accompanied her on every training course she'd attended in the last two years. Hardcover pink with the words "You got this" scrawled across the front in purple. A present from her father when she'd started detective training.

If she recalled correctly, her notes on accessing and using ViSOR were pretty near to the front.

Most people, herself included at one point, thought the register was a long list of names, date of birth and address of known sex offenders. She now knew it was a management tool used by Law Enforcement, National Offender Management Service and other agencies to manage registerable sexual offenders, other sexual offenders, violent offenders, dangerous offenders, terrorist offenders and potentially dangerous persons; it enabled each agency to share information.

There were different levels of training, and she'd received the Basic Level Access Learning Program, which was designed for people to access information and intelligence but did not give access or responsibility to update the system.

"Ah, there you are," she said out loud.

"Yep, I haven't moved," Dawson responded, startling her. Yes, she really had forgotten he was still sitting there.

She ignored him and glanced at the information on the board. All of the victims.

She couldn't search out anything for the six years' dead victim highlighted by Keats so she put a line through that name.

She was unsurprised to see Lester Jackson's name on ViSOR. They knew for a fact he'd sexually abused his niece. She was even less surprised to see Luke Fenton's name on it, so there was one more name left to try.

She typed in the name of the homeless man, Thomas Deeley, murdered in Wolverhampton just under a week ago.

Stacey let out a long breath.

Yes, he was there as well.

A link to all three male victims.

Was the killer taking his victims from ViSOR?

Stacey was aware of the Child Sex Offender Disclosure Scheme; commonly known as Sarah's Law, it allowed anyone to ask the police in England and Wales if someone with access to a child has a record for child sexual offenses. But she also knew that Joe Public couldn't just type in a name and get a result.

So, if he wasn't getting details from ViSOR, how the hell was he getting access to information about these victims?

CHAPTER 76

Kim tapped her fingers impatiently as she waited for the gates to open. Three of the deaths on the boards back in the squad room could be linked back to this shelter in one way or another and today she wanted answers.

Someone inside these gates knew something and she wasn't leaving until she'd found out who and what.

The door was opened by Jay, who nodded and stepped aside.

Kim headed straight into the office of Marianne, who although as smart and groomed as she had been the last time they'd met, appeared pale. The light makeup she wore did nothing to conceal the dark circles beneath her eyes.

"You've heard, I take it?" Kim asked.

"Not officially but I assume it's true, that the woman found is Hayley?"

Kim nodded. "You understand that we need to talk to people here. I need a list of names of staff and residents who knew her."

"I can get you that. There are only a couple of the ladies who were here with Hayley, and I'll explain to the staff that they need to be open and cooperative."

Kim glanced across the hall.

"I'd like to start with Jay."

"Feel free to speak to him in the CCTV room while I brief the rest of the staff."

Kim headed toward the door, but Marianne's voice stopped her.

"She might have made some bad decisions but she didn't deserve that."

"You mean going back to Luke Fenton?"

"Yes."

Kim had a sudden thought. Yes, they knew Hayley had gone back to a man who was possibly abusing her daughter but they hadn't yet examined why.

"But why was that, Marianne?" Kim asked, recalling the maximum length of time the women were allowed to stay in the shelter. "Was her time here at an end?"

"Yes, we had to let her go. There was no room. There were urgent cases. Her stay here had—"

"Okay, thank you," Kim said, shortly, and headed across the hall.

This woman had thrown her out when she had nowhere else to go. From what Stacey had uncovered about Hayley her life had been anything but joyful. She'd thought she'd found someone to love her in Luke Fenton but had eventually found the courage to leave him. For six months she'd been safe here, but for Hayley six months had not been enough to get her life back on track. Years of abuse, isolation, loneliness and crime had not been erased by a couple of courses and a polished CV. Hayley would have needed years of help, support and encouragement to get her life back on track.

And in that respect, Marianne had failed her. Badly.

CHAPTER 77

Marianne had seen the look on the police officer's face when she'd tried to explain about the six-month time limit on placements at the shelter. Yes, she could have quoted statistics at the detective; that for every woman she accepted she had to turn five away and none were more deserving than the next. Every woman referred her way had suffered and try as she might she couldn't save them all.

She knew this time of year brought reflection from people. Occasionally she wondered if she should have married, had children, taken more holidays, but in truth she was married to the shelters and the women were like her children. Her only reflection was whether she'd done enough to secure as many futures as she could. The festive communication to past benefactors was her own way of making that last effort at a time of year when people were more in touch with their own generosity.

She started combing through the responses to her mailshot. She hated to think of them as begging letters for more money but in effect that's what they were. There were stories of all the good work and the statistics and the success stories over the last six months, evidence of their charitable pounds at work. And then at the bottom a list of jobs and goals yet to achieve. Not least the computer suite that would mean that more women could be online applying for jobs or updating their CVs at one time rather than the hourly time slots they currently allocated to share the resources of the two computers fairly.

The mailshot had been emailed to seventy-six recipients. She accessed the statistics of the email. Of those seventy-six recipients, seventy-five had bothered to open the email, which brought a smile to her face. Of the seventy-five engagements, she'd received twenty-seven responses. Less than half, despite the season of goodwill.

Marianne's agitation increased when she returned to the only person who hadn't even bothered to open the email. Probably the wealthiest person on the list and someone who had been extremely generous in the past.

She would consider devising some kind of reminder; a prompt that would encourage him to reconsider.

She scrolled through the replies she'd received. She only needed to read the first line, in some cases just the first word, before moving on to the next.

> *Sorry but times are hard…*
> *It's been a bad year…*
> *We've had to restructure…*
> *Due to stiff competition…*
> *Unfortunately…*

Marianne cared nothing for the excuses. All she saw was the word "NO."

At the bottom of her inbox was a message from Derek Hodge. The message header simply said "Mistake." She clicked into it and read.

> *Dear Marianne, having thought more about your recent request for assistance, it would appear that my refusal to donate to such a worthy cause may have been both churlish and hasty. After taking time to reconsider I have decided that*

> *a suitable contribution will be transferred by BACS payment*
> *directly to your account later today.*
>   *Best regards*
>   *Derek*

Marianne clapped her hands with glee. Perfect. Maybe the computer suite was not such a distant dream after all. With some of the residents they had to settle for helping them become computer literate as opposed to basic reading and writing.

Hayley Smart had been one of those girls.

Her thoughts returned once more to the unfortunate woman with the birthmark. That final look of desperation mixed with helplessness, the defeated slump of the shoulders. The revelation of what she'd finally done with Mia. The begging, the pleading that had come from her mouth. All to no avail.

Yes, DI Stone had been unable to hide her disgust that the girl had been made to leave after the maximum period. Marianne couldn't help wondering what the detective would say when she found out what she'd really done with Hayley.

CHAPTER 78

Dawson stared at the wipe boards on the wall where bullet points were written beneath the names of all five victims.

Two of the five victims had been hit on the back of the head.

Four of the victims had had their genitals mutilated.

Two of the victims were known abusers.

They were all poring over phone records and witnesses and links between two or four of the victims, but he was beginning to wonder if something linked all five, and if the answer lay elsewhere.

There were things about the crime scene that mattered. He got that. Time of death, Forensics, MO. They all counted. And also, there were things that mattered less, or did they?

What was the constant here between all five victims?

Gender—no.

Manner of death—no.

Time of death—no.

Genital mutilation—no.

While they had uncovered links between one or two victims, there was no single connection between them all. Or was there, he began to wonder, tapping the pen against his lip.

John Doe: an abandoned shoe had been found near the body. Why?

Lester Jackson had been murdered in a priest hole. Why?

Tommy Deeley had a small bell in his pocket. Why?

Luke Fenton had a tiny piece of brown packing paper left on his body. Why?

Hayley Smart's crime scene had included the top from a vinegar bottle. Why?

Dawson turned to his computer and began to search for something that could provide a link between all five victims through the small things found near them or on their person, the five anomalies: could he find something that made the connection?

He scrolled through the results and could find nothing that made any sense using all five items included in the search term.

On the second page of results, Google had decided he had lost his mind and was putting a blue line through two of his criteria, as though he didn't know what he was searching for.

He smiled when he saw some of the results he'd been offered.

But as he looked more closely the smile died on his face and he began to read.

CHAPTER 79

Kim took the seat in the viewing room that meant she could see the screens as they talked to the security guard.

Half of her mind was still on the information Stacey had relayed by phone. That Tommy Deeley had been a registered sex offender too. She thought back to the interview she'd seen with Butcher Bill when he'd called the victim a dirty bastard. Had he known about Tommy Deeley's past? Had he known that the man had been jailed twenty years ago for sexually assaulting a twelve-year-old girl when he'd been a volunteer at a Wednesfield youth club? She briefly wondered if Butcher Bill was responsible for all the murders, but quickly dismissed the thought. The man could barely remain sober long enough to tie his own shoelaces.

There was still something inside her that said all the murders were linked. A similar voice in her head whispered that someone from this shelter was somehow involved, but how those two voices could come together in harmony she had not the faintest idea.

She put the thoughts out of her mind and tried to focus on the cases that were officially hers.

She turned her attention on the security guard. "So, Jason, you've been here...?"

"Three and a half years. Used to be a doorman but it all got a bit crazy out there. Too many drugs and too many knives."

Kim understood. Knife crime was continually on the increase and if you weren't a police officer it wasn't what you expected to deal with when you put your uniform on for a night shift.

He was a big man, though that didn't automatically mean he relished conflict.

"So, you've seen quite a few of these women come and go in that time," she said, nodding toward the screens.

While he considered her question she took a moment to look at what was currently on offer. The scenes were not dissimilar to those she'd seen two days ago.

Dawn, the nutritionist, had a group of ladies in the kitchen; a couple of women were waiting in line for a haircut. Curt or Carl was up a ladder in an upstairs corridor and the other twin was talking to one of the women while he changed a plug on a lamp in the dining room.

"Yeah, I've seen a fair few come and go but don't get involved with them," he offered, which seemed to be more answer than she'd requested.

"I hadn't thought that you did, Jason."

He looked forward to the gate and then back to the screens. "I sit here. My job is at the front of the building, making sure no one gets in. I rarely go back there," he said, nodding toward the door that led to the body of the building.

"How well did you know Hayley Smart?" Kim asked.

"Not very. She was the sort who just kept to herself. She chatted with a couple of the ladies but mainly just played with her kid."

"Did Luke Fenton ever come here?" Kim asked. It wasn't uncommon for boyfriends and husbands to turn up at shelters and make a scene.

He nodded. "One time he turned up. Didn't get past the gate. Called the police, but he disappeared so I canceled 'em, and one of the boys went out and made sure he'd gone."

"The boys?" she asked.

"Twins," he said, nodding toward the screen. "Not sure which one it was now," he said with a wide smile.

Kim glanced back at the screens.

The group in the kitchen had all moved away and Dawn was washing up.

A different woman was sitting in the salon chair being tended by Nigel. And Curtis's or Carl's ladder was in a different part of the house.

The other twin was still changing a plug.

CHAPTER 80

"Bloody nursery rhymes," Dawson cried out, once he'd finished reading.

"Huh?" Stacey said, barely looking up.

"Listen," he said, wanting her full attention.

She looked up properly.

"The small things that have been overlooked. The vinegar and brown paper that links Luke Fenton to Hayley Smart."

His colleague appeared both interested and yet disbelieving at the same time.

"But they're just harmless little rhymes to entertain kids. To send 'em to sleep, or something."

"And that's where you're totally wrong, I'm afraid. Most nursery rhymes appear to have darker meanings in their past. At the least they are cautionary tales."

"Go on," Stacey said, dropping the frown but leaving the interest behind.

" 'Little Bo Peep,' for example, is a harmless ditty about lost sheep?"

"Err...yeah," she answered.

"Wrong. It's about falling asleep on the job and someone getting killed as a result."

"But it's for kids," Stacey argued.

"And back in the day, kids were workers too. There were no child labor laws back when every hand in the family was needed to survive."

"Dawson, I ay sure…"

"Okay, listen to this. 'Goosey, Goosey, Gander where shall I wander, upstairs, downstairs and in my lady's chamber. There I met an old man who wouldn't say his prayers. I took him by the left leg and threw him down the stairs.'"

"Yeah, I know it. To teach kids to say their prayers," she said.

"You'd think, wouldn't you? The origins of the rhyme date back to the sixteenth century. It's talking about the need for Catholic priests to hide in priest holes to avoid persecution from Protestants. If they were caught then the priest and the family were executed. The moral implies that something unpleasant would happen to anyone failing to say their prayers correctly. And by correctly it means Protestant prayers said in English and not Catholic prayers said in Latin."

"So, you're making this whole assumption because Lester Jackson was found in a priest hole?" Stacey asked.

"When he could have been killed anywhere in a hundred or more rooms, then yeah, I'm thinking it has to mean something, but you haven't heard the best bit."

"Oh, do continue cos it's not like I ay got any work of my own to do."

He paused. Was that sarcasm from his meek and mild young colleague? Hmm…so there was a bit of spirit in there just dying to come out.

He continued anyway, unable to ignore the burning in his gut. "'Jack and Jill went up the hill to fetch a pail of water. Jack fell down and broke his crown and Jill came tumbling after. Up Jack got and home did trot as fast as he could caper. He went to bed and bound his head with vinegar and brown paper.'"

"I have no idea what that's about," Stacey offered but her gaze did move over the wipe boards.

"Jack and Jill are said to be King Louis XVI, of France, and his consort, Queen Marie Antoinette, who were both beheaded.

The words were made more acceptable for children by providing a happy ending. They were beheaded for treason during the reign of terror in 1793, so I'm wondering…"

"If that's symbolic of Fenton and Hayley Smart for what they did to Mia?"

"They both made her suffer. Him with the actual abuse and Hayley for going back after being free of him for six months."

Stacey was again looking at the board. At the details that had as yet remained unexplained.

"What about Keats's John Doe. An old shoe or something?" Stacey asked.

"I was just coming to that one and I just found this. Listen, 'There was an old woman who lived in a shoe. She had so many children, she didn't know what to do. She gave them some broth without any bread; and whipped them all soundly and put them to bed.'"

Stacey waited.

"The origins of the rhyme are based in child abuse."

"Jeez, I'd never even considered…"

"And listen to this. Tommy Deeley was found with a small silver bell in his pocket, which could refer to the bell mentioned in 'Mary, Mary, Quite Contrary,' which continues 'how does your garden grow? With silver bells and cockleshells and pretty maids all in a row.' Goes back to Queen Mary I, whose torture techniques earned her the nickname 'Bloody Mary.' But both silver bells and cockleshells were not innocent items, they were torture devices."

"Bloody hell, Dawson," she said, still looking at the board.

"So, what do you think now?" he asked.

"I think it's time for yer to call the boss."

CHAPTER 81

Kim glanced at her watch before opening the door of Marianne's office. The woman had kindly offered her own working space to enable them to speak to the staff.

"Hey, Jay, Curt does know we want to speak to him today, doesn't he?"

"I told him straight away but I think he's just gone into the mess room."

"Mess room?"

"Sorry, small storeroom next to the kitchen with a couple of lockers and toolboxes. So called cos the place is a bit of a…"

"Mess, yeah, got it," Kim answered for him. "Buzz us through, Jay. I'm not waiting any longer."

He hesitated.

"Marianne knows we need to speak to people."

He pressed a button and the door clicked open. Bryant followed her through and pushed the door closed behind him.

If she remembered correctly from the computer screens the kitchen was at the rear of the house beyond the smaller lounge used as the salon.

Kim felt a strange sense of calm as she moved along the hallway. She could hear voices coming from each room that she passed, an occasional laugh against the Christmas carols playing somewhere in the background.

Colorful, handmade decorations mixed with strands of tinsel framed every doorway. A generous tree sparkled multicolored lights from the main lounge.

The aroma of cooking, either late breakfast or early lunch, hanging below the scent of cinnamon guided her forward.

If you were going to be in a women's refuge over Christmas, this was definitely the place to be, she thought, remembering her Christmases at Fairview Children's Home.

An ancient battered tree had been retrieved from the storeroom each year, held together only by dust. One crisp box held all the decorations, which grew less each year with breakages. Two members of staff decorated it halfheartedly, just to say it was done right, before they were all brought together into the dining room on Christmas Eve. Not for a special meal or present giving but to be ready for the annual visit from the Salvation Army. It was the same every year where the kids were told to behave and "look grateful." Christmas morning two plates of mince pies were handed around by whichever staff members had drawn the short straw on the rota. A chicken dinner was served before business returned to normal for the rest of the day. It wasn't *Oliver Twist* and it was no Hallmark movie either. It was just another day.

Kim shook away the thoughts of Christmas past as she headed through the small lounge. Two women eyed them suspiciously as they awaited their turn in the salon chair. Two little girls and a boy were holding hands, singing and dancing around in the middle of the room.

"Come for your free haircut, officer?" Nigel asked, reaching over and turning up the radio as the Band Aid Christmas song came on. "Sorry, kiddies, love this one."

"I'm still good, Nigel," she said, continuing her journey through to the mess room.

"Hi, Curt, you forget about us or something?" she asked, folding her arms in the doorway.

"Nah, just making me a cuppa first," he said, holding up a steaming mug.

"Only, it's not like we've got a murderer to catch or anything," she said, pulling out a thin metal chair from beneath the battered bistro-sized table.

Bryant positioned himself leaning against the door frame.

Kim tried to fight her growing dislike for Curt Wickes but there was something lazily aggressive in his posture as he threw himself down into the other metal seat opposite.

"So, Curt, I assume you know that Hayley Smart has been murdered."

He shrugged. "Yeah, we all know."

"Did you know her well?"

He shook his head immediately.

"Don't really know any of the ladies here very well. We're not encouraged to be too friendly with the residents for obvious reasons."

"Which are?"

He shrugged. "You know. They've all had bad experiences with men either beating them up, abusing them or the kids. We come in, follow our work sheet and go home again. Mind our own business and get on with the job."

From what she'd seen on camera his brother Carl didn't take the guidelines quite as seriously. It had taken him an awfully long time to change a plug.

"You worked for the shelter for long?"

"Two years and seven months. Since we qualified as electricians and started up our own business."

"How'd it come about?" she asked.

"Marianne gave us a chance to prove ourselves. She's a generous woman."

Kim didn't doubt it. Not one person that she could think of had done more for abused women in the area.

"You work at all the shelters?"

He nodded.

"Anywhere else?" she asked.

"Not too much. We're kept pretty busy by Marianne. Always something that needs doing, decorating a room, electrical problems, shelving, well, everything really."

Kim couldn't help herself thinking that was an awful lot of vulnerable women these guys had access to.

"Did you ever notice anything particular about Hayley? Any good friends or particular enemies. I mean, surely not all the women here get on."

He looked up and to the left.

"To be honest I don't remember her having any of either. I just don't know what to tell you. I don't mean to be rude but she wasn't all that memorable. She came for a few months and left again, like all the rest of them."

Kim found that hard to believe bearing in mind the birthmark, which immediately made her hard to forget.

"So, there were no incidents here with her at all?"

Another shrug and a shake of the head.

"I was told that Luke Fenton turned up here one day; made a bit of a nuisance of himself and that you went outside to check that he'd gone."

"Nah, not me. Must have been Carl."

As her phone began to ring Kim had the distinct feeling she was talking to the wrong brother.

CHAPTER 82

"What the hell was that all about?" Bryant asked.

She ended the call as they entered Marianne's office to continue the staff interviews.

Kim frowned. "I'm still trying to work it out. Something about the real meanings behind bloody nursery rhymes."

"Guv, I don't like to say but..."

"Yeah, yeah, I know," she interrupted. Dawson's time-wasting activities had reached a whole new level. She'd speak to Woody this evening and have him replaced by the morning.

"We've got Louella Atkins next. I asked for Carl, but apparently the counselor needs to get off urgently."

Kim swallowed down her annoyance. There was something not sitting well with these two brothers and she wanted to find out what it was.

But Carl would just have to wait, she thought, as a gentle tap sounded on the door.

"Come in," Bryant called out.

The woman who entered was in her mid-thirties with a short, severe haircut that tapered into the back of her neck. The blunt fringe instantly drew attention to the hazel eyes. She wore no makeup to cover two deep acne scars on her cheek.

She offered a smile as she sat in the empty chair.

"We'll try not to keep you too long, Ms. Atkins," she offered.

"Louella, please," she offered. "And anything I can do to help."

Except change your appointment and wait in line, Kim thought.

"You counseled Hayley Smart when she was here?"

"I did the best I could, Inspector, but Hayley wasn't a natural confider."

Kim began to wonder just who Hayley had ever talked to other than her child. She was piecing together a solitary existence for the young woman with no family and friends.

"And she was here for the full six months?"

"She was indeed."

"Would you like to tell me anything about your conversations?" Kim pushed.

"She was lonely, Inspector. I know that. Hayley was a 'better when' kind of person."

Kim shook her head, not understanding the term.

"Throughout her early life she convinced herself that things would be better when something or other happened. She told me she felt her life would be better when her mother came back to fetch her. When that dream died she felt her life would be better when she found a foster family that would love her. Over time that hope faded and she felt her life would be better when she could escape the care system completely and make it on her own." Louella paused. "The care system would not be categorized as a warm and nurturing environment where—"

"Is that why she had Mia?" Kim asked. She was well-versed in the care system.

"I think so. Better when she had someone of her own to love."

"Did she believe that Luke Fenton had sexually abused Mia?" Kim asked, hoping for a negative response. For some reason she really wanted to believe that Hayley would not knowingly have placed her daughter in danger.

Louella thought for a moment. "I think she did but she didn't want to."

"You think she was too vulnerable, too desperate for love to withstand Luke's persuasion."

Louella nodded. "As I'm sure you know abusers play on emotions, primarily fear. They will tell children that if they speak of abuse something terrible will happen to them or someone they love. But there are other fears. Fear of exposure, fear of physical harm, fear of being alone and I think Luke may have managed to convince Hayley that he was the only one who would love her. I think he probably played on her wish to believe that nothing had happened. He was the first man to pay any interest in her. He made her feel valued; he made her feel like somebody for what was probably the first time in her life."

Given what they'd learned about Luke Fenton Kim was surprised he possessed the charm to lure her back to his home. It wasn't a personality trait he'd displayed either at work or to his neighbors. But they didn't have a nine-year-old child, a small voice said inside her. And Mia had been the real prize. His courtship of Hayley had been a means to the end.

"We tried to give her the confidence. Her abilities were ummm...limited, so finding work was..."

"She had learning difficulties?" Kim asked, wondering if there was anything else that could have been thrown at her.

"She was barely literate but we tried to work with her. I felt we were making progress and offering her some kind of self-value and confidence."

"But despite everything she went back to him?" Kim observed.

A shadow passed over Louella's face.

"And your thoughts on that?" Kim asked.

"May I be honest?"

"It's preferable," Kim advised. This woman had an opinion and she wanted to share it.

"I'm sorry she's dead but Mia is safe now. She came here and took a valuable place from someone who might have used it more wisely. It was a waste of time. This place is a haven for abused women and children. Marianne could have done no more to give her a better chance in life. She did everything to put Hayley in a better position for both herself and Mia. As she does with all of us. I tried to counsel her; Marianne tried to counsel her."

"That was her job before she opened the shelters, wasn't it?" Kim asked, recalling Stacey's background notes.

"Yes, that's how she met many of us in the first place. She offers a helping hand to anyone who needs it. You'll find that most of us would have nothing if it wasn't for her, so for Hayley to just throw all that time and effort into the bin and go back to the man who had abused her child is, quite frankly, unforgivable."

Louella's voice had risen in volume and passion as the words had tumbled from her mouth.

"You blame her despite everything you know about her past?" Kim asked.

"Of course I do. She was a mother before anything else."

Kim couldn't argue the point even though something inside her wanted to, but she wanted to pick up on something else the woman had said.

"So, you're saying that many of the people involved here at the shelter are from Marianne's past?"

Louella nodded. "She's a very generous woman who gives everything she has to victims of abuse whether it be domestic abuse or sexual. If they need a place to go she will do her utmost to take care of them. And some people just throw that effort back in her face when all she does is think about ways to…"

Kim found herself tuning out of the tirade of hero worship coming out of the counselor's mouth.

"…and she should not be judged too harshly for what she did. If she'd had any other choice she wouldn't—"

"She had no other choice in what?" Kim asked, sitting straighter.

"Turning Hayley away," she said with a frown.

"When was this?" Kim asked. The woman had been in hiding for weeks.

"I'm sorry, I thought you already knew. Hayley was here on Tuesday night asking if she could come back."

Hayley Smart had been here the night she lost her life.

CHAPTER 83

"You didn't tell us you'd turned her away," Kim said to Marianne. They had asked Jay to call her back to the office.

Marianne's face folded into a mixture of sadness and regret.

"She was here for just a moment," she said, as her eyes filled with tears. She wiped at them before they could topple over the edge.

"That doesn't really excuse you keeping that information to yourself, Marianne. You may very well be the last person other than the killer to have seen her alive."

"Oh no, please don't say that. I can't bear the thought that I..."

"But why didn't you help her?" Kim asked.

"We're full, Inspector. I had nowhere to put her."

"There wasn't a spare sofa she could have used?" Kim asked. This response to a woman in need did not quite match the description they'd just had from Louella the counselor.

"We have regulations. I couldn't."

"I'm sorry, Marianne, but I'm not buying that. I think you turned her away because you were angry with her for going back to Luke Fenton after all the time and effort you put into her," Kim said, feeling her anger rise. "It appears to me that your help comes with conditions, that beneficiaries of your charity are held to your standards and expectations and if they fail to do so they're cut loose. That girl came to you for help and you turned her away. Surely you could have referred her somewhere else, made a few calls. She was scared and alone, beaten down and begging for help and you decided to make a point because you disapproved of her choices. You could have done more but you were punishing her."

Marianne shook her head in denial but Kim could see the truth in her eyes, and there was nothing Kim could or would say to make her feel better. Hayley Smart might still be alive if Marianne hadn't turned her away.

She tried to keep the disgust from her voice. "Did she say anything at all that you haven't told me?"

Marianne hesitated before nodding. Her voice was low and full of regret.

"She said she needed to be somewhere safe."

"And you didn't think to call the police or do anything at all to help her?"

Marianne looked away.

Hayley had been cold, frightened and alone, almost begging this woman for help. And still she had been turned away.

But that didn't make sense, Kim realized. Hayley had received the message from Luke Fenton's sister. She knew her ex-boyfriend was dead.

Unless that wasn't who she'd been hiding from at all, Kim realized, as her phone began to ring.

Her stomach turned when she saw that the caller was Keats.

CHAPTER 84

Marianne grabbed the envelope from her drawer and headed out of the office. She had no idea what had caused the detective inspector to leave in such a hurry but she was just pleased that she had.

She could not tolerate the woman's judgment of her actions. Yes, she had managed to summon the tears at Hayley's passing, but in truth she felt little for the girl who had taken her help, her resources, her time and thrown it back in her face. Whatever her reasons she had chosen to return to an active abuser with her own child. It was inexcusable and unforgivable and Hayley had learned the hard way that there were consequences to her actions.

She put Hayley out of her mind and barreled down the hallway. She had more pressing matters to attend to.

"What the . . . ?"

"Sorry, I . . ."

The envelope fell from her hand as Diana Lambert stormed out of the bathroom and they collided.

Marianne bent to pick it up.

"Sorry, I was just in a rush to get . . ."

"It's okay," Marianne said, with a smile. "And calm down. Your meeting with Child Services will be fine and you'll be reunited with your daughter in no time."

"I hope so, Marianne," she said, her brown eyes soft with fear. "But I know that bastard will lie through his teeth to stop me . . ."

"You'll be fine," Marianne reassured. "Just relax and tell the truth. You'll get her back, I know you will."

"Thank you," Diana said, before tearing off in the direction of the front door.

Marianne continued her search of the premises until she found Carl in the toolshed just outside the back door.

She held out the envelope.

Carl looked down at her hand and began to shake his head.

"Take it, Carl. It's urgent. I want this one done now."

"Marianne, it's gone too—"

"Take it," she said, thrusting the envelope toward him.

"That copper is sniffing around. She wants to see me next."

"She's gone, Carl. You can leave now. Get it done before..."

"I'm not doing it, Marianne," he said, turning away.

Marianne realized she needed to change strategy. She had felt his indecision at the last envelope she'd handed him.

She placed a hand gently on his back. "Do you remember how much help you needed when we first met, Carl?" she whispered.

His head dropped forward just an inch.

"How scared you were; how you still cried yourself to sleep when you were nineteen years old. How the fear didn't leave you even after your abuser was dead."

"I remember," he whispered.

"These women have to feel safe, Carl. They can't recover unless they feel protected. Just look at Louella and...and all the rest who have thrived and made good lives for themselves. They've overcome the pain, the fear to become successful. And that's all because of what I...we've done here. We have to keep going," she said, squeezing his arm. "They're relying on us."

He said nothing for a full minute.

Finally, he turned and held out his hand for the name.

CHAPTER 85

"Got it," Stacey said, out loud even though the room was empty.

It had taken some time to plow through all the data that had been accumulating on her desk, but she had finally pieced together that the mobile number she'd been unable to account for on the call register of Luke Fenton had also been in contact with Hayley Smart.

She had found a deleted text message on Hayley's phone from that same number as well as seventeen unanswered calls.

The text message had chillingly read

Come out, Come out, Wherever You Are

But there was one final piece of the puzzle before she could state something categorically, and she'd been thinking of the way she could get the information.

If she was as devious as Kevin Dawson, she could have probably devised a dozen different ways to be sneaky to get what she wanted. But her mind just didn't work that way.

So, what else can I do? she asked herself.

In the absence of deviousness all that was left was honesty.

Okay, here goes nothing, she thought, googling the number she required.

Within seconds she was waiting for someone at West Mercia to answer the phone.

"CID, please," she requested, once she pressed a few buttons and got through to an actual voice.

"In connection with?"

"A current murder inquiry," she answered simply.

The line went dead, causing her to think she'd been disconnected.

Suddenly a female voice answered.

Stacey was unsure why she was relieved. Maybe sisterhood and all that.

She took a quick second to introduce herself and then went straight in for the kill.

"We're working a couple of murders that we think are linked to your current investigation of Lester Jackson at Redland Hall and—"

"I'm sorry," the woman said, quickly. "But you know that I can't—"

"I completely understand," Stacey said, unwilling to lose her so soon. "And I'm not looking for any detail in your case whatsoever. But is there any way I could ask you a question and just get a yes or a no? I think it could help you in the long run too."

Silence.

Stacey didn't hear a no so she plowed on.

"I've got a telephone number here and I'd just like to know if it's come up anywhere in your investigation."

Silence again, which Stacey took as agreement.

She read off the phone number.

Silence except for the tapping of keys and then just one quiet word.

"Yes."

Stacey thanked her and put down the phone.

Now she knew for a fact that she was looking at the phone number of the killer.

CHAPTER 86

By the time Bryant pulled up at the address they'd been given by Keats, two things had happened.

The small, narrow street had been cordoned off and she was now hopping mad.

She all but rammed her ID in the face of a PC as she ducked under the cordon tape. She grabbed the protective slippers from another without speaking.

She could hear Bryant mumbling apologies behind her. He really was going to have to stop doing that. She wasn't sorry at all but getting pretty pissed off with being summoned left and right across the Black Country.

She headed into the house at speed and reached the living room area at the back.

"Keats, you are gonna have to start offering some explanation for—"

"Is this explanation enough, Inspector?" he asked, standing aside.

"Bloody hell," she said as both the sight and smell hit her immediately.

In all her years she had never come across a stench like that of a rotting corpse. Some described it as decaying meat with a hint of sickly sweetness but she had never heard a description that represented the foulness completely. And this particular corpse had released its bowels. She covered her nose with her hand and tried to take a deep breath using her fingers as a filter mask.

The sight that met her gaze was of a gray sweatshirt, bloodstained from a single stab wound to the chest. A line of blood had seeped from his upper torso to join up with the carnage that appeared to have been wrought on his genitals.

Keats obliged by lifting the lower roll of flesh so she could take a better look.

She heard Bryant's sharp intake of breath.

The penis and testicles had been stabbed multiple times. The shaft of the penis had been chopped and the testicles held on by a thread.

Her gaze returned to his face, where a tie had been doubled and used as a gag. To prevent alerting the neighbors to the noise, she suspected.

His dead gaze stared straight ahead and fleshy jowls hung limply either side of flaccid lips.

Kim tore her gaze away and looked around the room.

There were few people present but the heat was stifling.

"Fire was left on full," Keats explained. "But I'm thinking he was murdered sometime last night."

Kim was surprised by his words so soon into his examination.

"That a guess, Keats?" she asked. "Surely he wouldn't smell this bad after twelve or so hours?"

"As you well know decomposition begins the second the heart stops beating. There are some thirty trillion cells on the average human body not to mention more than double that in the intestinal tract and they all get very busy very quickly..."

"But still," she said, wrinkling her nose.

"The constant full heat of the fire added to the man's body mass added to the fact that his sphincter loosened accounts for—"

"Got it," she said, needing no further explanation of the aroma that was getting into the back of her throat.

She started looking around the sparsely furnished room for any letters or paperwork.

"I can help you with that too, if you'd like," Keats offered, as though tuned right into her brain. Not a prospect she relished.

"Go on," Kim said, testing his psychic powers.

"I'm surprised you don't recognize him," he teased.

"Why would I?" Kim asked, taking another look.

"His name is Charles Lockwood, whose life as he knew it ended around eighteen months ago."

Kim frowned, vaguely recognizing the name but still not recognizing the person.

"He didn't look like this then. He was much slimmer and while not exactly a stick he was not obese."

Kim tried to imagine him with less weight. There was something pricking at her memory.

"He had a short segment on a Friday evening magazine show, mainly reporting on entertainment around the local areas, restaurants, clubs, offering opinions and recommendations. Until it came out that he was accepting backhanders for favorable reviews."

"Aah, I think I remember. He disappeared from our screens very quickly."

Keats nodded. "And that's not all that happened. He lost everything. House, cars. His wife moved out, had no choice really. He was prosecuted and went to prison and looking around I'm guessing he's not long been out."

Kim frowned. There was nothing there that matched their victim profile.

"Again, I know what you're thinking and the answer is yes."

"Abuse scandal?"

Keats nodded. "A rumor. Hinted at in some online article and then retracted. His eldest daughter was around seven at the time."

Kim's concern about his direct line to her thoughts was pushed down by the disgust that rose within her. If he was guilty of what Keats said, she could find little sympathy inside herself for his death or the gruesome manner in which it had occurred. Her personal feelings for the murderer did not in any way diminish her need to find the killer. She believed in justice and the system.

"Postmortem will be at 9 a.m. It's already been a long day," Keats said.

She thanked him and headed for the door.

"Bryant, clearly this has to be connected to our case. The genital mutilation is the same as two of our victims, but how exactly...?"

"His wife, guv," Bryant interrupted. "She was a woman who lost everything. She had to have had somewhere to go."

Kim followed his train of thought and began to smile.

"Good work, Bryant. Bloody good work."

CHAPTER 87

"Hey, Jay, it's DI Stone. I need your help. I need to know if anyone by the name of Lockwood spent any time at any of the refuges in the last eighteen months."

"You mean Wendy?"

Kim cast a triumphant look in Bryant's direction.

"Wife of Charles Lockwood?" she asked, to confirm.

"Yeah, yeah. She stayed at this one for about four months I'd say. I can check exactly if you'd like."

"No, Jay, it's okay. I don't suppose you'd have any idea where she moved out to?" she asked, crossing her fingers.

"Sorry, Marianne's gone out and her office is locked. But if I remember rightly she was getting a place in Gornal. Her and her two kiddies."

Kim felt an excitement building in her stomach. They were getting somewhere. She could feel it.

"Okay, Jay, you're a star and I just need one more favor."

"Of course."

There was one key member of staff at the refuge she hadn't yet interviewed.

"You have control of the gates. Don't let Carl Wickes leave until I get there."

CHAPTER 88

It hadn't taken long for Stacey to search the electoral roll and find a Wendy Lockwood living in Gornal Wood.

The area of Gornal was located on the western edge of the Dudley borough and historically comprised three villages: Lower Gornal, Upper Gornal and Gornal Wood. The last being famous for the landmark the Crooked House pub and for being at the epicenter of the 2002 Dudley earthquake that measured 4.8 on the Richter scale, felt as far away as North Yorkshire.

"Ha, Pig on the Wall," Bryant said, passing a McDonald's.

"Huh?" Kim said, looking back to see what she'd missed. She'd seen no pig anywhere.

"There was a hotel there once called Pig on the Wall," he said.

"What a bloody ridiculous name for a place."

He smiled. "Local legend has it that once a military band marched through the area and caused such excitement that not only did all the locals flock to see it but one guy even put his pig on the wall to give it a better view."

She raised an eyebrow. "Bryant, please tell me we're almost there."

"Yep, this is the road and that's the one we want," he said, nodding to the other side of the street.

The house itself was a mid-terrace in a street that had cars crammed end to end along the pavement. Outside number 23 was a battered Fiat Yugo that looked older than her and Bryant put together.

The door was answered by a striking woman in her mid-thirties with straw blonde hair and a light complexion. Immediately, Kim heard children's voices in the background.

"Wendy Lockwood?" Kim asked, showing her identification.

She nodded. Alarm instantly registered on her face and then faded as she appeared to remember that her children were safely behind her.

"We're here about your husband," Kim said quietly.

She folded her arms. "I have no interest in anything you have to say about that man."

"Mrs. Lockwood, you're going to want to hear us out, but you won't want your children present."

Her irritation turned to a frown as she invited them in.

Kim followed her to a small kitchen at the rear of the house, where two girls, still in uniform, squabbled over a purple crayon.

The aroma told her the youngsters were waiting for their tea.

All activity stopped as she and Bryant stepped into the small space and, although both looked at them suspiciously, there was a touch of fear in the eyes of the eldest. Kim offered what she hoped was a reassuring smile, but the girl's expression didn't change a bit as she looked to her mother.

"Girls, go and get changed for tea," Wendy instructed.

"Don't wanna," said the older one, who had snaffled the crayon.

"Who are they?" asked the younger one, narrowing her eyes.

"I said go upstairs," Wendy repeated.

Neither moved.

"No iPad after tea unless you—"

The woman didn't need to finish the sentence as the scraping of chair legs filled the room.

"The threat of no telly used to get the same response from me," Bryant said, offering the woman a smile.

She didn't return it and only when she heard that the continued squabbling was a safe distance away did she speak.

"What about him?" she asked.

"He's dead," Kim answered, not bothering to dress it up.

Wendy's eyes widened and her hand shot to her mouth.

"Oh, my G...God...how...when...I mean..." Her words trailed away as she felt her way to the chair previously occupied by her eldest daughter. "I can't..."

Kim said nothing as she waited for the woman to wrap her head around the news.

"Please tell me what happened."

Shock, horror, but no tears, Kim noted. After what she'd learned from Keats she was not surprised. Confident that the woman could handle the truth, she continued.

"I'm sorry to say your husband was murdered, Mrs. Lockwood."

Her face creased into disbelief. "No...you're...that's not... no," she said, shaking her head.

"I'm sorry but there's no easy way to say it," Kim offered. "It was brutal and I wouldn't want you to hear that from anyone else."

"I hated the man but not enough to..."

"I understand," Kim said, meeting her gaze to indicate that they knew about the abuse. "But someone hated him enough to make him suffer; but there are other things we need to speak to you about."

"Please go ahead. Anything that will help."

"You lost everything because of your husband's actions with taking secret payments to publicize certain venues around the area?"

"His actions left me with nothing, Inspector. Because of his work we were somebodies. We had a good life, had minor celebrity status. Our girls had everything they could wish for. We were liked, we had friends and were treated well wherever we went. Little did I know that the money he was taking was going straight onto a Blackjack table along with the mortgage payments. By the time he was found out he had accrued almost seventy thousand pounds of debt and his face was splashed all over the news.

"We lost everything, me and the girls. Suddenly we were social pariahs. The girls lost their friends and so did I, to be honest. We were treated like lepers because of what he'd done."

Kim held up her hand. "We understand that you were left with nothing, Mrs. Lockwood, which as big a problem as that was must have paled against your daughter..."

"It did," she said, as every muscle in her face tensed and hardened. "I'd left him already, you see. I was maxing out our credit card at a hotel while we got ourselves sorted and I decided where to go next. The girls didn't really understand what was going on and then one night as I was putting her to bed Sasha asked me if it was all her fault. She asked if it was because she'd considered telling her schoolteacher her secret." Wendy lowered her head, and Kim didn't push.

After a moment she took a breath and continued. "Three hours later I had the whole story that her father had been abusing her for around ten months. He'd told her that if she ever spoke of it to anyone that I would die or that she would die and the child was terrified."

"Mrs. Lockwood, I can't even imagine what..."

"You're right, Inspector. You can't. Unless you've been in that position you'll never understand the guilt and self-hatred. I won't share my nightmares with you, but suffice to say I will never be able to make it up to her or forgive myself for not seeing what was right in front of me."

And so you shouldn't, Kim thought, just managing to keep the words to herself. In her opinion the little girl could not have been suffering with no visible signs; reduced appetite, unwillingness to go to bed, withdrawn into herself. Kim knew the signs well enough.

"Did you go to the police?" she asked.

Mrs. Lockwood shook her head. "Sasha begged me not to. She was terrified at the prospect of having to recount the events to a stranger. I tried to talk her into it and bought myself a whole new bag of guilt by trying to force her to do something she didn't want to. In that way I felt no better than her father and eventually I gave in." She shrugged and opened her hands. "I just pray it was the right thing to do."

"And what did you do?" Kim asked, steering her toward the subject she wanted to explore. She had no words to bring the woman comfort. That would come only with time and Sasha's continued well-being.

"Called him and made all kinds of threats. I called him every foul name I could get my mouth around and told him he would never see his daughters again. The next day he'd put a stop on the one remaining credit card with any money. I managed to pay the bill by cobbling together a few favors from people who would have anything to do with me. Few and far between after the scandal broke."

"And then you had nowhere to go?" Kim prompted.

She nodded. "I'd read about Marianne Forbes and her shelters and I turned up in Dudley with little more than three suitcases and two girls. She took me in and made room somehow, thank goodness. She pretty much saved my life."

Which was more than she'd done for Hayley Smart two days ago, Kim thought.

"Go on," she said.

"It gave us a chance to regroup as a family, the girls and I. We were taken care of while we adjusted to being a threesome instead of a foursome. Our stay there gave me time to build the strength and confidence to take care of my girls alone."

Kim heard the note of pride in her voice.

"I realized I could make it on my own and that I would do whatever I needed to do to keep my girls safe. Louella gave me that confidence and Sasha responded well to counseling there too." She smiled. "Became quite good friends, the two of them."

"And you?" Kim asked. "Did you make any friendships?"

The faint blush that colored her cheeks belied the shake of the head. Kim understood the dynamics of places like shelters. Hospitals were similar. They were unfamiliar surroundings and people bonded. Hayley had been the exception. Hayley had always fended for herself and remained closed to those around her, but Wendy Lockwood was another story. Wendy had needed to be told she could cope alone. Wendy had needed support, handholding, friends.

Kim thought about the photos she'd seen of the Lockwoods before the scandal. They had made a very attractive couple out and about being wined, dined and treated like local celebrities to garner favor and positive reviews and recommendations on the television. Advertising that could not be bought.

Alone Wendy Lockwood was no less attractive and probably stood out amongst the women at the shelter. Some of the rules set out by Marianne may have been harder to follow for some residents than others.

"There's nothing to feel guilty about, Wendy," Kim said, taking a gamble. "These things happen and especially when you're lonely and vulnerable it can…"

"Oh no, nothing happened. It wasn't even like that," she protested.

The word "it" indicated that there had been something with someone.

"Of course. It's understandable that you'd want to talk to someone, confide in and maybe just enjoy being around."

"Exactly that," Wendy said, nodding her agreement.

Kim had no idea how intimate the relationship had been and she didn't care. She had only one question left to ask.

"Which one was it, Curt or Carl?"

And she wasn't surprised at the answer.

CHAPTER 89

It was almost seven when they were allowed access through the gate back into the shelter.

They had spoken little during the journey as they had both considered the ramifications of Wendy's friendship with Carl.

The ringing of her phone appeared to startle them both.

Her stomach turned when she saw that it was Keats. Surely not another.

"Inspector Stone, I thought you might like to know something curious that happened prior to the postmortem of Charles Lockwood."

Other than the victim coming alive in the back of the pathologist's vehicle, she couldn't imagine what had happened since they'd parted.

"Not sure it means anything but as we were lifting him into the body bag a curious item fell to the floor."

Kim wondered if the man got a bonus for each time he used the word *curious*.

"Go on."

"It was a sixpence, Inspector. Bent slightly but still identifiable, and if you don't know what…"

"I know what a sixpence is, Keats," she said as her face creased into a frown.

It had been the equivalent of two and a half pence until 1980.

"Okay, Keats, thanks," she said, ending the call.

It was curious indeed. But given what Dawson had uncovered it may be not all that surprising. Perhaps she should have listened more closely to what Dawson had to say. Had she dismissed the theory so quickly because it had come from the least productive member of her team, the one who had given her the most trouble all week, or had she genuinely felt there was no substance to the idea? It was a question she would need to ask herself later and she wasn't sure she was going to like the answer.

She turned to her colleague. "Looks like Dawson might have had something with the nursery rhyme thing after all," she said, pressing the call button.

"Oh great, now the guy will be totally insuff—"

"Dawson," she said when he answered, cutting off Bryant. "I need you to stay on your nursery rhymes. We have a bent sixpence. See if there's any connection."

He answered in the affirmative as Bryant parked next to Carl Wickes's Transit van.

Oh yes, after her conversation with Wendy Lockwood she was even more eager to speak to this particular handyman.

CHAPTER 90

Dawson replaced the receiver and beamed at his colleague. "Looks like I might have been onto something after all."

"Well, I suppose it had to happen at least…"

"Ooh, not bitter eh, Stacey, cos I might have done something to impress the boss?"

She ignored him and continued working.

Yeah, maybe it was his turn to be star pupil.

He wasted no more time and entered a Google search for sixpence in nursery rhymes.

His first hit was for "Sing a Song of Sixpence."

He read through the first verse. The original was only one verse long.

Sing a song of sixpence,
A bag full of Rye,
Four and twenty naughty boys,
Baked in a pye.

The next version, dated around 1780, had two verses and the boys had been replaced by birds.

As he read on to find any darker meaning behind the rhyme, he learned there had been a version with four verses and included a magpie attacking an unfortunate maid. Other versions with happier endings began to appear from the middle of the nineteenth century.

He read through the many interpretations including the sixteenth century amusement of placing live birds in a pie.

Others had interpreted the rhyme as a tie to a variety of historical events or folklorish symbols. Or the blackbirds as an allusion to monks.

There was nothing he read that would indicate any reason for tying this victim to this particular nursery rhyme.

He returned his attention to the earliest version, looking to hang his hat on something to tell the boss to prove he'd been right.

He wondered about the four and twenty naughty boys. Could the killer be calling Lockwood a naughty boy?

His hand hovered over the phone, eager to call the boss and tell her he'd found a link that proved him right. But his hand wouldn't quite reach for the phone.

So far, their killer had been detailed on the darker meanings of the rhyme and not the actual lyrics.

His gut instinct and enthusiasm were not meeting up, but something in him so desperately wanted to make that link and prove himself right.

But this wasn't the link and he knew it.

He moved his hand away from the phone while he took another look.

CHAPTER 91

"You ever go home, Jay?" Kim asked as the security guard let them into the building.

"Hoping to soon when my relief gets here."

He nodded toward the camera room. "Everything's quiet in there and all the staff are out, except for Carl, who is on his way through to see you now."

Kim looked to Marianne's locked office.

"I can't let you into there, I'm sorry, but Jerome's here now. You can use the security office and I'll brief him outside, if you like."

Kim smiled her thanks at the man who was looking a little worn after his twelve-hour shift.

"Aah, just the man," she said as Carl entered the hallway, carrying his tool bag. Clearly, he was not going to waste time once they'd finished.

Unlike his brother he offered a smile that didn't seem to sit easy on his face.

As they all took a seat, Kim studied him briefly, looking for the slight differences between the two brothers, but other than a slightly shorter haircut she could see none.

"Thank you for hanging on to see us," she offered. "And I'm sure by now you know it's in connection with Hayley Smart?"

He nodded and drew his open legs together.

"How well did you know her?" she asked.

"Not very. We don't talk too much to the residents. Marianne don't like it."

And yet she already knew that this twin spoke more to the residents than his brother. Especially the attractive ones.

"But surely you had conversations with Hayley. She was here for six months."

He shrugged. "Now and again. I'd ask her how the little one was. The kid didn't talk too much."

Kim nodded as he again changed his seating position. It was clear she was now talking to the fidgety twin.

"Are there no residents you've struck up particular friendships with? I saw you just earlier, while you were changing a plug talking to a woman."

"Well, we can't very well ignore them," he said. "We just keep it pleasant and professional."

If she remembered correctly he'd kept it pleasant and professional for more than twenty minutes.

"Didn't you react on Hayley's behalf when Luke Fenton tracked her down and came here making a nuisance of himself?"

He shrugged. "He was gone by the time I got out there. Never saw the bloke."

There was something tapping away at her subconscious. An alarm bell that all was not as it should be.

She plowed on.

"Do you remember a woman called Wendy Lockwood?"

He looked up and to the left as his legs fell open. There was no obvious recognition of the friendship they'd built according to Wendy.

"I think so. Two little girls, married to that reporter bloke?"

Kim nodded, watching him more closely as a nagging suspicion popped into her head.

"Well, that reporter bloke was found murdered just a couple of hours ago."

Genuine surprise shaped his features. That's what she'd wanted to test. He appeared to be sincerely shocked at the news.

And if the suspicion and anger growing alongside each other in her stomach were to be believed he would be surprised by the news of his death.

"So, you didn't really talk to Wendy Lockwood much?"

He shrugged and shook his head.

"Like I said, we're not..."

"Yeah, you did say. But that girl earlier, with the fresh perm, what's her story?"

His face looked blank.

"I don't really know much..."

"What about her name. You know that at least, don't you?"

Bryant's head turned at the change in her tone. But she wasn't a fool and she didn't appreciate being treated like one.

She sat back and connected the dots, as she glanced down at his shoulders.

Tiny flecks of blonde hair. The fidgeting and body movement. The fact he didn't know who he'd been talking to earlier. But the clincher was his total detachment from the mention of Wendy Lockwood. A woman he'd been known to at least have had a friendship with.

She folded her arms.

"Nice to talk to you for the second time in one day, Curt, but I asked to speak to Carl; now where the hell is your brother?"

CHAPTER 92

I drive away from the shelter undetected with a smile on my face. There are people trying to stop me and I don't understand why. But I'm away now and they'll never find me in time.

I know they've found the body of my last offering: the obese, despicable specimen that was Charles Lockwood.

The man was bent, dishonest, crooked. He told lies to the public to line his own pockets and that wasn't even the worst of it. Wendy told me all about it. She told me how he'd been abusing poor Sasha right under her nose. Luckily I believed her or she would have been added to the list. Her voice, the slight trembling of the hand, the heavenward gaze as she'd whispered, "God forgive me." She hadn't known what the bastard was doing to his own daughter. I will leave her to live with that guilt.

Killing Lockwood revitalized me, enthused me after the disappointment of Hayley. The man showed himself to still be the vacuous, dishonest bastard I thought he was.

"Take everything I have," he offered, once he realized I was a threat. He struggled to force himself out of the armchair not knowing he would never stand again.

I told him I didn't want his possessions, pitiful as they were. There was only one thing I wanted from him, and once I explained why I was in his house the fear came. He wanted to continue his woeful existence with no friends or family. He was frightened that he was going to die. His eyes shone with it and I felt myself restored like a car spluttering into a petrol station on fumes alone.

Surely these people looking for me understand that Lockwood had to die after what he'd done?

I smile wider as I wonder if they've found my clue. Do they understand that there is no innocence in the world, that something as simple as a nursery rhyme hides evil and darkness? I learned that many years ago.

No matter, they'll never know where I'm going next. A simple conversation today and my next victim has been presented to me. A few google searches, ten minutes' research and I have a plan. I yearn for the fear and after the satisfaction of Lockwood I need to feel it again soon. I am like a vampire after it has fed for the first time.

I understand that cravings increase the more they are satisfied. The longing is a by-product of addiction, and the power of the life of abusers resting in my hands offers me a heady euphoria that hurts no one.

Another abuser will die tonight and there is only one thing left to do.

It is time to go buy an apple.

CHAPTER 93

"Anything on the phone records, Stace?" Kim asked, realizing she'd shortened the officer's name.

"Working on it and hope to have something for you soon."

"Okay, urgently I need a home address for Carl Wickes of Wickes Repairs. Maybe try Companies House to see where the business is..."

"Yeah, boss, I'll get it, and Dawson wants a quick word."

"Put him on," she instructed.

"Boss, I think I've got the rhyme."

"Go on," she said, expecting to hear about singing a song and blackbirds.

"Did you say the sixpence was damaged?" he asked.

"Keats said bent."

"Okay, it's definitely linked to 'There was a Crooked Man.'"

"Huh?"

"Listen, it goes like this: 'There was a crooked man and he walked a crooked mile. He found a crooked sixpence upon a crooked stile. He bought a crooked cat that caught a crooked mouse and they all lived together in their little crooked house.'"

"Err...I'm not sure..."

"Boss, so far our killer has linked the murders to the darker meanings behind the nursery rhymes. This one isn't about an old man with a cat and a house. It's rumored to be about General Sir Alexander Leslie and is from seventeenth-century history;

Leslie was known for his lack of loyalty and dishonesty. It's that kind of crooked."

Kim saw his point. "In reference to Lockwood's dishonesty in taking backhanders?"

"I'm thinking so, boss," he agreed.

She could hear the excitement in his voice.

"Oh, Stacey wants you back," he said, and she could hear the dip in his voice.

Too late she realized she should have forced the words out. She had allowed her feelings about his earlier performance in the week to color her view.

"Boss, I've got an address," Stacey said.

"Text, it to me," she said, thinking only of finding Carl Wickes. Dawson would just have to wait.

CHAPTER 94

There was no van parked in the street of Carl Wickes's address in Tipton.

The flat was on the ground floor of a large house converted into four separate dwellings and from what she could see the only window visible to them had the curtains drawn.

"But what the hell did he have to gain?" Bryant asked, as they approached the front door.

"We'll be sure to ask him once we find him," she said.

When asked to explain the attempt at subterfuge, Curt had explained that Carl had a hot date and needed to get away. He explained they'd done it loads of times in the past. When asked if any of those occasions had involved talking to police officers working a murder investigation he seemed to finally grasp the gravity of the situation.

Curt had tried to get his brother on the phone but it had gone straight to voicemail.

Neither she nor Bryant believed the hot date story. She believed the man was on a mission.

"I think that our killer was abused himself. Perhaps his abuser read nursery rhymes to him before inflicting the abuse. He experienced something that should have been so innocent followed by absolute horror. That's why he's acting out the darker meanings to the nursery rhymes because that's his association. The darkness."

"Makes sense," he agreed. "So, you think the twins were sexually abused as young boys?"

She nodded. "I think one of them was. Louella was clear that Marianne collects lost souls who have suffered just as she did."

"But how does that help us? Cos I don't think he's here, guv," Bryant said, as they approached the front door. He covered his mouth to stifle a yawn.

She checked her watch. So far it had been a thirteen-hour shift.

Sometimes, she had a tendency to forget the limitations and commitments of her fellow team members, especially when she felt they were onto something.

"Let's just confirm he's not here and then we'd best call it a night and start fresh in the morning."

Bryant knocked on the door and they waited.

He knocked again.

Nothing.

Kim leaned down and tried to look through the letter box. The brushes located on the other side obscured her view. But she could hear the eerie sound of empty silence beyond the door.

She suspected Bryant was right and the man was not at home.

"Just try his phone again," she said, wondering if he'd turned it back on and if it would sound beyond the door.

She couldn't rid herself of the vision of him hiding in the wardrobe.

Bryant did as she asked and shook his head. "Straight to voicemail."

She pushed at the door.

"You know, Bryant, I reckon between us we could have this down in..."

"Guv, you might not value your job but I've still got a few years left on my mortgage."

"I'd say it was an accident."

"What? We leaned against it and it fell open?" He shook his head. "We've got no grounds to enter. We don't believe anyone is in danger and..."

"Okay, teacher's pet. I get your point, but with as many murders in as many..."

She stopped speaking as a sudden thought occurred to her.

"Bryant, did Keats say he thought Lockwood had been murdered on Wednesday?"

"Yep," he said, following her back to the car.

The relief on his face that they were leaving was evident. But if she was right in what she was thinking, there was no way Carl Wickes was at home.

"Bryant, by my calculations we've had one victim every day this week. Fenton on Monday, Hayley Smart on Tuesday, Lockwood on Wednesday. We don't know exactly when Lester Jackson was murdered but it looks like our killer is on a roll."

She turned an apologetic smile on him. "Looks like the shift isn't quite over yet."

The inner groan was written all over his face.

But no one was going home yet.

If the killer remained true to form there was going to be another murder this very night.

CHAPTER 95

Stacey had no idea what had caused the sour expression on her colleague's face but it had altered when he'd got off the phone with the boss.

Had she liked him more she would have taken the time to ask.

Would he ask her? She suspected not.

She glanced again at the clock wondering when this shift was going to end. So far this week each night the boss had given them the nod to go home. There'd been no nodding yet and Stacey was beginning to have visions of the boss and Bryant having gone home without telling them.

From what she could gather her colleague didn't have a home to go to, but she did. Admittedly all that was waiting for her was a pizza and a couple of hours on *Warcraft* but it was more than he had.

In the absence of the go-home nod she returned to the phone register of the killer. She already knew it was a pay-and-go phone topped up with vouchers.

The register appeared to have days in between uses and the only numbers called belonged to Luke Fenton, Lester Jackson and Hayley Smart. There were no calls to Charles Lockwood, but he had not been lured from his home. The killer had taken the crime scene to him.

Just ten minutes ago she'd received the mobile phone tower information from the phone network. Stacey knew that whenever a mobile phone made a call it emitted electromagnetic radio waves, also known as radio frequency or RF energy. Once those radio waves were emitted, the antenna from the nearest tower received them.

She pulled up a map of the Black Country and took a screenshot of it.

Next, she plotted the locations of the phone towers in the area with a red dot.

As she began to place green dots at approximate locations a pattern began to form.

She added another overlay to the document and plotted yellow dots for the shelters owned by Marianne Forbes and realized that the killer's phone was never very far away.

CHAPTER 96

"How the hell are we going to predict who comes next?" Bryant asked.

That was exactly what Kim was trying to work out when her phone rang.

She rolled her eyes seeing her boss's name appear on the display.

"Stone, where are you? I expected an update hours ago."

"Sir, we're just following up a lead and..."

"In my office in one hour. We need to talk resources for this. We have three victims likely to have been murdered by the same killer. We need to draft in more—"

"S...rr...y...s...r...can't...hear...go...thr...tunn..." she said, waving the phone around in front of her.

She ended the call. In his opinion it was three victims and in hers it was now six. She didn't have time for a briefing right now and she certainly didn't have time to bring a whole new team up to speed. By the time she'd finished she could be heading to the crime scene of victim number seven.

Their killer was going to strike again and she had to find out who the victim was going to be.

"Wait a minute," she said, thinking back over the events of the day.

"What?" Bryant asked, rubbing at his forehead.

"Hang on," Kim said, taking out her phone. She dialed Marianne's number. The woman answered in a voice mixed with breathlessness and irritation.

"DI Stone, how may I help you?"

"There was a woman today, at the shelter; mid-thirties, cream jumper and navy slacks, looking quite smart and—"

"Diana Lambert, thirty-six years old, had a custody hearing today to retrieve her daughter from the state."

"Was the child sexually abused by her father?" Kim asked.

"How did you know…?"

"Lucky guess. What's her story?"

"Husband had been abusing their child for two years but Diana had no idea. He accused her of taking prescription drugs and endangering the child following a minor car accident when all along he'd been molesting the little girl. Diana left him and reported him to Child Services but the child refused to speak. There were accusations back and forth of neglect and abuse and drug-taking so Lily was removed from the home, and Diana sought help from us while an investigation was carried out."

"And what about the husband?" Kim asked.

"He's a doctor, a GP I think."

"And what's happening to him?" Kim asked, feeling the tension tighten in her stomach.

"It's my understanding that Child Services have still not been able to glean anything from the child, but they have deemed it safe to return her to Diana. So, in the absence of any kind of statement from the child I'm pretty sure there'll be no further action and he'll receive no punishment at all."

Kim thought back to Carl Wickes's lengthy conversation with Diana earlier that day.

She had a feeling that was about to change.

CHAPTER 97

Bryant pulled the car into the curb in front of The Full Moon pub in Dudley High Street. When asked if she could return to the shelter at almost ten to speak to Diana Lambert, Marianne had told her that Diana was celebrating at the local Wetherspoons with a few of the women from the shelter after a successful meeting with Child Services. Marianne had been invited but had been unable to attend.

Kim entered the establishment as a blur of sashes, veils and tiaras came stumbling out. The cheap beer drew in most stag and hen parties from a three-mile radius.

She spotted Diana Lambert amongst three other women on a table behind a fruit machine halfway along the space. She was immediately struck by the fact that Diana was swaying along to the background music and the other three were not. She could feel their discomfort as she approached.

"Diana Lambert?" she asked.

Diana focused on her and nodded.

Kim held up her identification. "May we have a word?" She looked around the group. "It's urgent."

The other three women grabbed at handbags and jackets hanging from the back of their chairs.

"Gotta go anyway, Di," said one.

"Yeah, time to get back," said another.

"No, girls, stay, we need to paaaaarrrrtttaaaayyyyy," she cried, punching the air. "It's my victory night."

The three women smiled tolerantly and headed for the exit.

Kim took a seat and nudged Diana's handbag and a few glasses along the table to make room for her forearms.

"Diana, I need to talk to you about Carl Wickes and your conversation earlier today."

"You like my hair?" she asked, shaking it like a shampoo advert. "New style. Carl said he liked it."

"Did he?" Kim asked, although she wasn't sure it had taken him twenty minutes to comment on her hair.

She nodded coyly.

"You talk to Carl a lot?" Kim asked.

"If I can find him," she said, with a lazy smile.

He hadn't appeared to be trying too hard to hide, she thought, remembering the camera view.

"You talk to him about your husband, your daughter, the abuse?"

Her eyes narrowed. The woman might have had a few drinks but she wasn't completely wasted.

"Everyone knows what that bastard did. There are no secrets at the shelter and I have nothing to hide."

"So what exactly did you tell him?" Kim asked.

"Told him that Steve tried to get my little girl all to himself. Tried to get me out the picture so he could do whatever he wanted without interruption."

"Sorry?"

"Bastard tried to cover himself by saying I was endangering the life of our child. But I had him good and proper."

The expression on her face Kim could only read as triumph.

A feeling started to churn her stomach. There was something not right here.

She glanced at Bryant, who also looked puzzled. She remembered what Marianne had told her.

"There was some kind of accident?" she prompted. "A car accident involving your daughter?"

Diana waved her hand in the air. "It was nothing. A scrape when I picked up Lily from school one day. She had a bang on the head and Steve said I should have taken her to hospital." She blew a raspberry and then laughed out loud. "She didn't need no doctor to put a plaster on her brow," she said, rolling her eyes.

Kim knew little of the man beside her but she was pretty sure he would have taken his daughter to hospital following any type of road accident. As would most mothers.

But hospitals ask questions, said a small voice in her head.

Kim stayed quiet for a few seconds. The woman had been drinking and her tongue was loose.

"Had a bloody massive row. Bastard accused me of being a drug addict just cos I took a few painkillers. Dickhead threatened to call the police on me but I had him."

"What did you do?" Kim asked, but she already had a suspicion.

"I left the bastard and went to the shelter."

"Oh," Kim said. That wasn't the timeline Marianne had given her. She had indicated that the drug-taking accusation had been in response to the sexual abuse allegation.

"They found you a place?" she asked. "Most shelters are for the assistance of women or children abused in some way by their husbands or a family member."

"Well...yes...I was coming to that. Lily told me about her father and then he accused me of taking tablets and..." She frowned as her words trailed away as though her muddled brain couldn't quite follow the script.

Kim took a good look into the dark brown eyes with dilated pupils. She knew there were many drugs that worked on the brain's neurotransmitters causing the iris to expand, including antidepressants, amphetamines, LSD, ecstasy and cocaine.

Kim's left arm twitched violently and Diana's handbag fell to the floor. Before Diana had even realized what had happened Kim was bending to pick up the bag and the contents that had spilled out.

As she raised herself back to a seated position her right hand held the bag and her left hand held pills. Three bottles of pills.

"A couple of painkillers?" she asked, waving the bottles in the woman's face.

Diana grabbed for them, finally understanding what had happened, but Kim kept them out of her clumsy grasp.

"Mrs. Lambert, did you lie about your daughter being sexually abused by your husband to deflect from your addiction?"

Despite the shake of the head the truth was in the color that filled her cheeks.

Kim jumped up from the table and rushed toward the exit.

"Slow down, guv," Bryant said, reaching her outside.

"We don't have a minute to lose right now, Bryant. Our murderer is about to kill an innocent man."

CHAPTER 98

"Okay, pass me to Dawson," Kim said, once she'd finished speaking to Stacey, who had informed her of the killer's proximity to the various shelters whenever the phone was switched on.

That was no surprise to her now. Both Carl and Curt carried out the maintenance tasks for all of the sites.

"Right, Dawson, I need you to get digging on nursery rhymes. We need to try and think ahead of the killer. I have to know where this murder is going to take place. I don't care how outlandish your theories might be. We have to do something. And pretty much all I can say is our guy is a doctor."

"Okay, boss. I'll get right on it."

She could hear the fatigue in his voice but no one else was going to lose their life if she could help it.

"Thanks, Dawson," she managed to say.

"No probs, boss, and Stacey wants you back."

Kim had to hand it to the detective constable, who already had an address.

CHAPTER 99

"Not bad," Bryant said, as they pulled up outside 27 Redlake Lane.

Located on a new estate in Hagley, the house was detached with faux stone pillars either side of a racing-green front door.

A BMW 5 Series car sat in the drive.

She knocked on the door, hard.

She waited a few seconds before looking through the darkened windows.

She could make out only vague shapes of furniture and yet one of those shapes could be a dead body.

"Guv, I think…"

"Forget it, Bryant. This time I'm going in because I really do think someone is in danger."

"I was actually going to suggest it."

She smiled in his direction.

"Okay, you get the top and I'll get the bottom."

In the absence of officers with the big key, their combined strength would have to do.

"Okay, on the count of three."

"One."

"Two."

"Thr…Jesus…" she cried as they both fell into the hallway.

An attractive woman wearing satin pajamas, an eye mask on her forehead, had opened the door a split second before they made contact with it.

"What on earth do you think you're doing?" she asked, looking from her to Bryant and back again.

"Police," Kim explained.

The expression didn't change.

"And?"

Kim frowned at her. "Who are you?"

The woman folded her arms.

"I'm pretty sure you should be introducing yourself seeing as you were just about to break into my home."

"Your home?" Kim asked, showing her ID.

She was going to be seriously pissed off if Stacey had given them the wrong address.

It wasn't that she minded complaints landing on her boss's desk, but she could do without needless ones on top of the genuine ones where she'd seriously pissed people off for a reason.

"Well, that I share with my partner."

"Who is?"

The woman's head went back and the frown deepened.

"I'm sorry but..."

"Can you just tell us his name, please?" Bryant offered with as much patience as he could muster after a fourteen-hour shift.

"Steven Lambert. That's Doctor Lambert."

Kim breathed a sigh of relief. Good job, Stacey. At least this complaint would be excused. They were trying to save the man's life.

"May we speak to Doctor Lambert?"

"I have no idea what this is all about but you'll have to come back tomorrow, at a more reasonable hour if you want to talk—"

"Miss...it doesn't matter. We really need to speak to him now."

"Well, you can't. He's not here."

The exact words she did not want to hear.

"Where is he?"

She shook her head in exasperation as Kim pictured this particular complaint making it onto two pages.

"He's a doctor, a GP, he gets called out. He left about half an hour ago."

CHAPTER 100

"Please tell me you've got something, Kev; we are seriously running out of time."

Kim could not rid herself of the feeling that someone was going to die tonight. And that it was going to be her fault.

"I'm trying, boss. I'm looking at the 'Doctor Foster' nursery rhyme."

"Put me on hands-free and read it out."

She heard Stacey's fingers tapping furiously as Dawson read out loud.

" 'Doctor Foster went to Gloucester, in a shower of rain; He stepped in a puddle, right up to his middle and never went there again.' "

"Okay, Stace, you listening?" she called out.

"Yeah, boss."

"Search for places in the local area with Gloucester in them. I want roads, avenues, anything and then look for ones that are close to a body of water."

"Thing is, boss..."

"Dawson, get onto the doctor's call-out service to see if there were any emergencies funneled through them."

There was hesitation behind his silence until he eventually gave her the answer she wanted.

"Okay, boss."

Good. She would have hated giving him a dressing-down on loudspeaker in front of the whole team.

"Got something," Stacey called in the background. "Just outside Romsley there's a Gloucester Street with a fishing pond that backs onto some of the houses."

"Give me the post code," Kim said, feeling like they were finally getting somewhere.

She just hoped they weren't already too late.

CHAPTER 101

Dawson could feel the excitement for the lead from the boss through the phone line.

When the call ended he saw his colleague's eyes alight with achievement and pride that she was potentially sending the boss to a murder scene.

Except he wasn't so sure they were following the right clues.

He had been in the process of researching the possible meanings behind the "Doctor Foster" nursery rhyme when the boss had called in.

So far, he'd read that it was based on a story of Edward I of England traveling to Gloucester, falling off his horse into a puddle and refusing to return to the city again.

There were two other interpretations of the rhyme and neither of them were dark in origin, unlike the others the killer had used.

His gut was saying that the murderer was unlikely to change his MO now for convenience. The darkness behind the rhymes had been consistent throughout: the killer wasn't making the murder fit the wording of the nursery thyme. Though he'd looked into what possible darker meaning could lie behind the rhyme and behind Doctor Foster, he simply hadn't been able to find anything sinister.

"Cheer up, Dawson," Stacey said, still breathless with excitement and anticipation.

"You wanna check the doctor's call-out for me?" he asked.

"Still trying to get folks to do your work for you?" she said, raising one eyebrow.

He considered every possible response, in every possible tone, and then settled on the truth.

"Stacey, I could do with your help."

She hesitated and he wasn't sure he blamed her.

"Okey dokey," she said, simply.

He returned to the internet and carried on looking for nursery rhymes containing the word "Doctor."

The next listing in his search came from "An Apple a Day."

He read through the rhyme.

> *An apple a day keeps the doctor away.*
> *Apple in the morning, Doctor's warning.*
> *Roast apple at night, Starves the Doctor outright.*
> *Eat an apple at bed, knock the Doctor on the head.*
> *Three each day, seven days a week, ruddy apple, ruddy cheek.*

He read it again and then learned that it was suspected of being parental propaganda to get children to eat their greens.

But it really hailed from the sixteenth century and a deep distrust of doctors.

Something stirred inside his stomach. A memory. A snippet he'd heard just recently on the news or in a newspaper.

He ran a search on doctors and trust and got nothing.

He ran a second search on doctors and malpractice suits and found what he was looking for.

He read the half-page article twice and then without hesitation he reached for the phone.

CHAPTER 102

"Dawson, what the hell are you talking about?" Kim asked, putting her mobile on loudspeaker so Bryant could hear. They were approximately two miles from the target area in Romsley.

"I think you're going to the wrong place," he urged.

"The two words that start that sentence do not convince me to change my mind," she snapped. Her adrenaline was running high as they got closer to Gloucester Street.

"Please, just hear me out. So far our killer has left clues that allude to nursery rhymes that have a darker meaning behind them. There's no darker meaning I can find anywhere behind the 'Doctor Foster' rhyme. It's about some guy falling off a horse into some water and never going back there again. It doesn't make sense for him to change his pattern now."

A mile and a half.

"Dawson, I think we're going to stick—"

"One more minute, boss. There's a different rhyme about an apple a day. It's all about the mistrust of doctors, of them not being the pillars of society they're supposed to be. It was a warning not to put too much trust in them, to try and resolve health issues without—"

"Dawson, how the hell does this help me right now?"

"There was a private clinic, boss, The Willows, just outside Quinton. Three doctors, all cosmetic surgeons…"

"I'm hanging up now, Dawson," she said. She couldn't listen to this any longer. She had to start forming a strategy for when they reached Gloucester Street and they had one mile left.

"Boss, the place went out of business eleven months ago. Doctors were sued for all kinds of things both medical and admin based but especially of sharing personal details of their clients."

Half a mile.

"Boss, at the final court case just two months ago the judge said it was the worst case of trust abuse he'd ever seen by any doctor. The newspaper headlines screamed that line."

A quarter mile and they were going to be at the point where Gloucester Street met the reservoir.

"Dawson..."

"The whole clinic is abandoned now, boss. It's a totally empty site, derelict and perfect if you don't want anyone to hear the screams."

Kim thought about the details on the wipe boards back at the squad room and everything Dawson had said. She considered how long he'd spent working this lead and what they had learned because of it.

They were one street away from the location they'd been speeding toward and she had to make a decision. Now.

She held the phone away for a second as she made up her mind.

"Bryant," she said, "we need to turn the car around."

CHAPTER 103

"Can you just put me onto someone who can give me the information?" Stacey shouted down the phone.

She'd been passed from one unhelpful voice to another at the out-of-hours call service that she'd been forwarded to when she'd called the emergency number for Doctor Lambert's surgery.

Each time she had tried to explain that she had no medical emergency she'd been put on hold and shunted to another operator. She understood that the operators were probably prioritizing her against people who were calling with serious ailments, but she wasn't going to keep anyone talking for long.

Call center healthcare was something she couldn't quite fathom. She imagined the operators sitting at tiny cubicle desks with headsets staring up at target-oriented wipe boards of how many people they could convince that they would be fine until the surgery re-opened in the morning.

"I don't want to hear the data protection laws again," she said to the next voice that answered. "I'm a police officer and I know them pretty well, but if someone doesn't tell me soon where Doctor Lambert has been sent on a call-out I'm pretty sure he's gonna die."

Silence.

Finally. Maybe some assistance.

"Excuse me, madam, but did you just threaten me? These calls are recorded and..."

"I said the doctor is going to die. He's in danger so will you...?"

The line went dead again. Stacey recognized the sound that came out of her mouth as a growl.

She was about to throw the phone down into the cradle when another voice came on the line.

"May I help?" asked the female voice cautiously.

Stacey threw back her head in frustration as she began to tell the story again.

"My name is Detective Constable Stacey Wood and we have reason to believe that Doctor Lambert may be in danger and that the call received by yourselves was a bogus…"

"One second, officer," she said.

Stacey expected the line to die again in her hand, but instead she heard the dialing of another phone. She also heard a generic voicemail kick in.

A pause before the woman did it again and got the same result.

"Strange," she admitted. "We're getting no response from the patient's phone either."

"Because they're not a patient," Stacey explained. "The call was made by someone with a grudge against Doctor Lambert, who has lured him out to a—"

"Number 24 Cedar Close, in Belle Vale. That's where he was called to."

Stacey thanked her and ended the call.

"So you got an address?" Dawson asked, with a glint in his eye.

She reached for the phone. "Yeah, I'm just gonna call…"

"Right, the boss is on her way to a potential crime scene in action and right now we don't know for sure if Doc Lambert is even involved. You have the address that the call-out service sent him to, and if you want to speak to them again and ask them to make contact, be my guest but I don't think the boss will welcome a progress report right this minute. You want to rethink?"

Stacey's patience was wearing thin after the phone conversations and she was in no mood for long speeches or cryptic questions.

"What the hell do you suggest I do, Einstein?" she snapped.

For the first time all week she saw a genuine smile.

"You wanna come with me for a ride?"

CHAPTER 104

Kim was counting down both the miles and minutes as Bryant drove. The satnav on her phone had told her they'd been eleven minutes and 4.6 miles away from Quinton, and each passing minute was torture.

For just one second she'd considered telling Dawson and Stacey to head toward the site in Quinton. They were one mile closer, but her dynamic risk assessment of the situation had persuaded her otherwise. She didn't know either of them well enough to be sure of how they'd react to a potentially dangerous situation, but what she did know was that Dawson was unruly and impetuous and Stacey was inexperienced and at her most comfortable behind a desk.

Neither of those things were deal breakers for her as team members, but for first response to a serious crime in action those qualities could get either or both of them killed. Not something that would go down well on her first-week assessment.

She had briefly considered calling Woody and asking for backup. She played the request in her head:

Sir, I think I need assistance at a site where I think torture and murder might be about to take place to a doctor I've never met by a handyman of whom I have not one shred of physical evidence but the nursery rhymes say so.

He would politely refuse the reallocation of resources and issue her with a direct instruction to return. Which she couldn't do if she was hoping to save a life and catch the person responsible for six other deaths. No, any further assistance at this point was not an option.

If Carl Wickes had persuaded his brother to impersonate him during questioning then this murder was going to happen tonight. It had to happen tonight, but she didn't have the time to try and explain her certainty of this to anyone. She only knew that he had guessed they were onto him and he was still desperate to add another victim to his tally.

It was just her and a man she had known for four days against a killer whose thirst for blood was increasing by the hour.

She glanced sideways at her colleague as she took out her phone and typed in a search of The Willows. She couldn't read his expression in the darkness of the car. She realized that she barely knew the man beside her any better than she knew the other two.

But right now, he was all she had.

CHAPTER 105

"Jeez, slow down, Dawson," Stacey said, hanging on to both the door handle and the underside of the passenger seat. As someone who had been terrified her whole life of taking driving lessons this experience was not instilling her with confidence.

"Come on, you can't tell me you're not getting a buzz out of what's going on right now. And if you're not then you're in the wrong job," he said, taking a bend at what felt like sixty miles per hour.

"Have you forgotten that there's a man's life in danger here?" she asked.

"And we're involved in trying to save it," he said, taking another corner at speed.

Why the hell had she agreed to come with him in the first place when she could be watching or coordinating events from the safety of the office? It was almost 11 p.m. and she could no longer remember what had happened today and what had happened yesterday. In fact, the whole week was rolling into one long shift.

If she gave him her honest answer she'd say she was having the time of her life, but she was keeping that fact to herself. There was something obscene about them both rejoicing in current events. People had died.

He turned another corner and slowed into Cedar Close.

"You wanna bet that's his car?" Dawson asked, pulling in behind a gray Range Rover a few spaces away from the address to which the doctor had been called.

"What do we do now?" she asked.

Dawson turned off the engine and thought for a second. "We knock the door."

"Dawson, do you know what time it is?"

"Lights are still on."

Stacey had already seen the outline of ice-blue flashing Christmas lights behind thin curtains. That didn't make it any more acceptable to frighten the life out of people. Late-night door knocks never brought good news. "You could still cause someone a heart attack knocking their door at this time of night."

"You don't think the boss would want to know if Doctor Lambert is in there tending sick folks right now?"

She opened her mouth but it was not a point she could argue with.

"I'm just not comfortable..."

"Bloody hell, Stacey, man up or woman up, whatever. You go check around the car, see if the doors are open while I go and ask."

Stacey got out of the car and approached the vehicle. Her heart hammered in her chest with the unnerving feeling that she was doing something wrong and the police were going to arrive any minute. Her actions would look suspicious to anyone taking a glance out of the bedroom window before closing the curtains.

She watched as Dawson knocked quietly on the door. It was answered within seconds by a bearded man who towered over Dawson. The facial hair did nothing to hide the look of annoyance on his face.

"Sorry to disturb you at this—"

"There'd best be a fucking good reason for—"

"Sir, have you called a doctor to this address this evening?" she heard Dawson ask with more politeness than she'd heard from him all week.

She shrank back against the side of the car and then jumped away in case she set off the alarm.

"What the fuck are you talking about?"

"Thank you. That's all we needed to know. Is that your car?" he asked, nodding her way.

The man looked beyond him. "I bloody wish. Now fuck off."

"Thanks again," Dawson said, moving away from the door which was already closing in his face.

"Anything, Stacey?" he asked.

She moved toward the driver's door and reached for it. Her palm instantly recoiled from the metal as she felt a cool stickiness on her hand.

"Dawson," she said, holding her palm upward.

He took out his phone and shone it toward her.

There was no mistake.

Her hand was covered in blood.

CHAPTER 106

Kim's trepidation was tempered with relief as they pulled up outside the clinic building. A car was already parked. A Mondeo Estate that had been at the shelter both times they'd visited. And both times Curtis and Carl Wickes had been present.

Dawson had called it right.

Now she had proof. Now she could request backup without losing her job or being called back to the station.

She got out of the car. Her colleague followed.

"Bryant, call it in," she said, stepping toward the car.

She quickly surveyed the area. The last house they'd passed was half a mile back down the road and the abandoned facility lay on the outskirts of Woodgate Valley Country Park: a 450-acre site previously made up of rural land and smallholdings.

From the aerial view she'd seen on Google Maps and the now defunct website, the facility was split into two distinct sections. To the east lay the administration, maintenance and welfare functions and to the west were the treatment rooms and a surgical theater. A reception suite linked the two sides.

As she heard Bryant giving their location she stepped toward the car. She touched the bonnet. It was still warm. Thank God, they might have a chance.

She tried the door handle but it was locked. What kind of murderer had the bloody foresight to actually lock their car while escorting someone to their death?

She peered into the darkness of the car but could see nothing.

She beckoned Bryant over and motioned a clicking action while he continued speaking.

He took his torch from his pocket and handed it to her. She shone it through the front windows and saw nothing but bits of rubbish. She shone it on the rear seats and two things caught her attention.

In the foot well of the rear passenger seat was a medical bag and the seat was stained with blood.

Damn it, the doctor was already injured and she was willing to bet it was some kind of bang to the back of the head.

She looked longingly toward the glass door to the reception area that had clearly been breached.

She knew full well it would be foolhardy to enter the premises. There were two of them and support was being requested. Training and experience told her they should hold tight and ensure that the killer could not get away. Wait for more officers, form a plan to cover the area while keeping it secure. Flush him out. Safely.

"Okay, guv, backup is on the way. ETA is eight to ten min—"

"Ugh, what the hell?" she said, lifting up her shoe.

A squashed apple lay beneath her foot.

An apple a day.

Suddenly the image of an innocent man being tortured and made to suffer flashed through her mind. Backup would not arrive in time. If she waited patiently for the agonizingly slow eight to ten minutes to pass Doctor Lambert was going to die. They might get their man but another life would be lost. And this one had done nothing wrong.

She turned to her colleague. "Okay, Bryant, I'm going in."

CHAPTER 107

Despite her best efforts Bryant had insisted on entering the building with her. She had tried to dissuade him but the time she was wasting arguing with him could be better spent trying to save the life of their potential victim.

"Okay," Kim said, once they were inside. "We need to divide this up. You head around the admin block and I'll head to surgical."

"Okay," he said, thrusting his hand forward. "But you take the torch."

She considered arguing some more but took the torch.

"You got phone signal?" she asked.

He took out his phone and nodded.

"Me too. You find anything at all, just ring. No need to speak but just call my phone."

"Will do, guv," he said, using his mobile as a torch and heading off toward the double doors leading to the facilities block.

She shone the torch around the space. Behind the reception desk sat a couple of chairs and a small filing cabinet with the drawers pulled out.

She gasped out loud as something scurried past her right foot and past a metal cupboard marked "Incident Post." It hadn't taken the local vermin long to move in. A building infested with rats didn't thrill her, but she wouldn't let it stop her either.

She turned the torch to the floor onto mauve carpet with random spots. She looked closer and cast the torch in a wider arc. The pattern was too random to make sense.

She leaned down and touched one of the larger droplets and brought her finger to the torch. Damn, the doctor was still bleeding.

Kim found herself hoping the blow had been to the head. She knew the head could bleed profusely from even a minor cut. Many tiny arteries and veins serve the individual muscles and skin on the head and some wounds aren't life threatening.

She stepped through the double doors, shining the torch down on the ground, hoping to follow a blood trail right to the crime scene.

"Damn it," she said, out loud. There was no trail. If the killer had brought the doctor this way he'd realized that the wound was leading anyone straight to them.

She shone the torch around the corridor, which appeared to be more like a tunnel curving out of sight. She remembered that the shape and layout of the medical wing had reminded her of a donut. Plastic chairs still lined the walls waiting for customers to attend consultation appointments. Medical warning posters still hung from noticeboards that dotted the wall between doorways.

She shone the light on the direction board to her left.

Arrows pointed to consultation rooms for nonsurgical procedures including Botox, fillers, permanent makeup, chemical peels and microdermabrasion, which sounded far too painful not to require a general anesthetic.

Another arrow pointed to surgical procedures, which seemed to include every part of the body with a name.

Where the hell would he have taken his victim? she wondered, looking over the rooms and procedures again, and how could she move silently along this corridor with enough speed to save the doctor's life?

She had the sudden feeling she was running out of time. She was moving stealthily to avoid being detected but by her reckoning there were more than thirty rooms to be checked.

She paused before moving too much farther along the corridor. Her current and pressing objective was to save the life of Doctor Lambert. Catching the killer came in a close second.

She looked back toward the double doors and realized that she was doing this all wrong.

CHAPTER 108

Kim threw open the double doors to the reception with a different plan in her mind.

If her prime objective was to save the doctor's life, then what she needed was a distraction. She needed to make her presence known and hope that the killer thought the preservation of his own life was more important to him than killing this one man.

It was a gamble she had to take. Running in and out of rooms until she found them would most likely sign Doctor Lambert's death warrant.

She smashed the end of Bryant's torch against the lock holding the metal doors of the incident cupboard together.

It took two more attempts for the flimsy lock to break open.

She shone the torch into the space and smiled. Amongst the safety chair, fold-up stretchers, emergency kit and first aid box she found exactly what she was looking for.

Perfect.

Before she reached into the cupboard she took out her phone and called her colleague.

"Bryant, they're over here somewhere," she called out.

"Shhh..." he replied, whispering on her behalf. "He'll hear you."

"Yeah, there's been a change of plan. Just get back over here as quick as you can," she said, ending the call.

She stepped back through the double doors into the curving tunnel corridor. She listened keenly first but heard no sound.

She lifted the loudhailer to her mouth and switched it on.

"This is DI Stone and the place is now surrounded. Come out with your arms in the air."

No sound and she hadn't expected any. This man was not going to give himself up easily.

She raised the loudhailer again.

"Okay, fella, get running cos I'm coming to get you."

CHAPTER 109

Kim began moving along the corridor opening doors and shining the torch inside. Contained within each space were the remnants of the business it had been. A desk here, a chair there, boxes of gloves, syringes.

Even if her plan had worked this was taking too long. If the killer had left the area, Doctor Lambert could still be bleeding to death.

Think, think, she told herself. Where would the killer want to make his point? Where was the most important area of the building?

The operating theater.

She recalled the information board and remembered it was halfway around the other side.

She dropped the loudhailer as something scurried up ahead. She put it out of her mind and began to sprint, shining the light at the ground and then up toward the signage.

She was only twenty feet away from the theater when she heard a sound. She slowed and tried to drown out the sound of her own breathing. She took a second outside the door. Took a deep breath and threw the doors open.

There was a small anteroom that led into the operating theater. Two steps in she could see a writhing form on the ground.

She rushed forward and shone the torch down. Doctor Lambert's eyes were wide with fear and pain. The groans of agony were being held back by a gag that indented the flesh of his cheeks. A trail of blood was seeping from beneath his head but that wasn't the reason for his pain.

His trousers and underwear had been pulled down to his ankles and blood from his genitals oozed over his thighs.

She reached down and eased the gag from his mouth. A loud groan escaped.

"Police," she said. "You're safe now. Did you see which way he went?"

Doctor Lambert shook his head and groaned again as his head rolled from side to side.

Kim reached underneath him and untied his hands. They immediately came around to his genitals.

He cried out. "What the...?"

"Try not to move too much; help is on the way."

She heard a sound in the corridor as the man's eyes rolled back in his head. She shone the torch and her colleague walked into its beam.

"Bryant, stay with the doctor," she said, glancing down at his central region. "And help him to apply pressure."

Bryant didn't flinch as he knelt beside the man.

"What are you going to do, guv?" Bryant asked, using his palms to bear down on the doctor's genitals.

"I'm going to find our killer."

CHAPTER 110

Kim stepped outside of the operating theater and wedged the door open. Once emergency services arrived they'd be able to hear the doctor's cries and be guided quicker to offer assistance.

She turned right and headed around the corridor in a clockwise direction. It made sense to her that if she'd scared him off he would have headed away from where she was making the noise with the loudhailer.

She threw open every door as she went, shining in the torch and listening for just a second before moving on. She found herself back at the double doors leading to the reception. Would he have made a dash for his car, not believing her bluff of them being surrounded? And if she went out to check would he somehow give her the slip?

She sprinted outside but the car was exactly where he'd left it.

She took a second to look around. Nothing had been disturbed. If he had disbelieved her he would have been out and gone by now. He had only needed to be ten feet ahead of her in the winding corridor and she'd been slowed tending to Doctor Lambert.

She was now sure he had not ventured outside, which meant he was still in the building somewhere.

She reentered the clinic with no choice but to retrace her steps. She headed back through the double doors for the third time and instantly felt a frisson of fear. There was something not right here. She should have found him hiding in one of the rooms.

And she couldn't hear the doctor groaning.

Why the hell hadn't Carl Wickes gone back to his car and left while he had the chance? He could have...

Her thoughts slowed down as she pondered another question that came to mind after seeing the car out front again.

Yes, she'd seen the car parked at the shelter the times she'd been there. But she'd seen it at the same time as the two vans. It would have been physically impossible for the handyman to drive two bloody vehicles to work.

But if it wasn't Carl Wickes carrying out the murders, who the hell was it?

All the events of the week began tumbling around in her head and some were bouncing around louder than others. She had fixed her attention on one man because of his behavior toward the women at the shelter. Her suspicion had increased when he had used his brother to avoid answering her questions. But what questions had he been afraid to answer?

Another common denominator at the shelter and beyond suddenly came into her mind.

Damn it, how the hell could she have been so stupid? she asked herself as she reached the doors of the operating theater.

They were closed.

She had left them open.

As she stormed back into the theater her torchlight illuminated the figure of the man she was now expecting to see.

And he was holding a knife to her colleague's throat.

CHAPTER 111

"Move the knife away from his throat, Nigel," she said to the shelter's hairstylist.

He didn't move a muscle as he stared back into the torchlight. Bryant was on his knees with a blade poised at the left-hand side of his neck. Doctor Lambert groaned behind them, much quieter than when she'd left the room a few minutes earlier. Without Bryant applying pressure to the wound the man was losing too much blood. He was dying right before her eyes.

She guessed that Nigel had remained ahead of her during the chase with the sole intention of coming back to finish the job. Killing the doctor was more important than trying to get away while he had the chance. That single fact made him dangerous and capable of anything to achieve his goal.

How the hell had she not seen sooner that Nigel was behind the murders?

Because of his charity work he visited other shelters and cut hair for free, especially around the festive period. The season of goodwill, of giving back.

Her brain quickly worked through the murders on the board. All of them.

He knew of Marianne's story, as did everyone at the shelter. He'd witnessed Hayley's story for himself. He knew that Luke Fenton had sexually abused little Mia and that Hayley had gone back to him and viewed her equally guilty as the man himself. He'd spent time at the shelter with Wendy Lockwood and he'd styled Diana Lambert's hair earlier that day for her meeting with Child Services. Right before the woman had been seen chatting to Carl Wickes.

She remembered his reaction to the children in the pop-up salon. She recalled now they'd been singing "Ring a Ring of Roses." He'd turned up the radio to drown out the nursery rhyme.

She tried not to let the fear show in her expression as she faced him, but she had to get that blade away from her colleague's throat. Less than a second and he would be dead. She had no weapon. She was twelve feet away from them both. This was a man who wanted to kill and didn't care much for the consequences.

She briefly considered throwing the torch at him as a distraction so that Bryant could scramble away, but just the raising of her arm could prompt him to do something drastic in response. It would take less than a second.

Think, think, think, she told herself. By her reckoning help was just a minute or two away but any sudden activity could cause him to pull that blade across Bryant's neck. Whatever she did she had to remain perfectly still.

She had an idea and just prayed that Bryant would understand.

"People talk, don't they, Nigel, while they're having their hair done? Did Butcher Bill tell you all about Tommy Deeley's past?" she asked, quietly.

Hell, the homeless guy who had confessed had pretty much told her who the murderer was on the interview tape.

Snip. Snip.

No response from Nigel as he continued to stare right at her.

"You were leaving the refuge when Hayley turned up seeking help from Marianne, weren't you? Hayley liked you, trusted you. You bought her food while you made your plan because you were surprised by her presence at the shelter. She was a gift to you. Just placed right there when you weren't expecting it. And then you took her and murdered her."

No response.

"John Doe, six years ago. That was your abuser, wasn't it?"

A slight tremble to the hand. Bryant's eyes widened but he kept perfectly still.

"Who was it, Nigel?" she asked.

"My father," he said, quietly. The voice was gentle, pained and not what she'd expected.

His suffering found a spot inside her but she pushed it aside. Six people were dead because of this man and two more could be added to that list if she didn't tread carefully.

"He would read nursery rhymes to you, before—"

"Every night," he said.

"The words were innocent little rhymes but you knew what was coming after…"

"There is nothing innocent about nursery rhymes. They are dark and evil like sexual abusers. Everyone I've killed deserved to die. They all inflicted pain and fear on victims who couldn't fight back because they were too little, but the little people grow up, you see, and turn into people like me."

"Not all abused children go on to commit murder," she said, trying to plant the word in his mind.

"You think that's what I did?" he asked, genuinely surprised. "You think I murdered people?"

"Didn't you?" she asked.

"I provided a service. I didn't go looking for these people. They were presented to me. Everywhere I went. What choice did I have? I couldn't ignore the obvious signs. None of them are innocent, you see. Many of them pretended to be good fathers and—"

"You see that guy kneeling in front of you," she said, to bring his attention back to the people in the room. The details they could discuss further in the police station interview room. "He's a father, but he's a good father. He has a teenage daughter who is loved and protected. He's a hard-working man with integrity and passion for his family. He's innocent, Nigel. He has hurt no one."

He considered her words and then nodded slowly. "But while I have this knife to his throat you won't come near me and the man behind me will die. That's all I want. It's not murder. I've committed no crime. I've helped people to heal, knowing that these monsters are gone. That little girl will sleep easier knowing he's never going to get the chance to hurt anyone again."

She paused before speaking. "The problem is, Nigel, that the man behind you is innocent. You only have to look at him to know I'm telling the truth. He didn't abuse his daughter. Diana Lambert made it up. It was a vindictive lie to cover his accusations of her own drug addiction. His daughter has not been harmed."

For the first time he appeared unsure of himself.

"It's true, and if you look at him I think you'll see that the man is innocent," she said, offering Bryant his second cue.

"No, he can't be. She said that's why she was at the shelter. You're lying."

"It's the truth, Nigel. You've looked into the eyes of the guilty. You know the fear that lives there. You've seen the evil in their eyes but killing this man is murder; even in your own eyes it's a crime."

"No, I don't believe—"

"Nigel, you know these people. You've seen it up close. Now take a look and..."

"You're wrong. You're—"

"Take a look, Nigel," she repeated.

He began to turn his head and that was all Bryant needed.

With Nigel's focus on something other than the blade, Bryant reared his head backward away from the knife.

Nigel stumbled.

Bryant didn't take the time to get off his knees. He turned, grabbed Nigel's legs and pulled him to the ground.

Kim closed the space between them in a second and took the knife from Nigel's hand at the exact second she heard footsteps in the corridor.

"In here," she called out as she rolled the man onto his front and sat astride the small of his back.

Bryant moved around Nigel to get back to Doctor Lambert.

"Is he okay?" she asked, tightening her thighs around the man beneath her to keep him in place.

"Still breathing," he said, placing his hands back at the man's crotch.

Suddenly the room burst into light as uniformed officers stormed into the space.

Confusion reigned on all the faces at the sight that met them.

"Get the paramedics to the doctor over there and then I need you guys to do me one more favor."

"Yes, Marm," said the one at the front.

"Give Wolverhampton station a call and tell them we got their man."

CHAPTER 112

Stacey stepped into her flat at 1:30 a.m. after an eighteen-hour shift.

After finding the blood smeared over Doctor Lambert's car she and Dawson had headed straight to the medical center, arriving just as Bryant was insisting he needed no help from a concerned paramedic. The boss had told them both to go home, but neither Stacey nor Dawson had wanted to leave until they'd been debriefed.

The meeting had been short, just long enough for the boss to neck a strong coffee, but it had been intense, as they'd recounted the events of the night. Her mouth had opened, closed and opened again as though she was watching some kind of action film. She'd started the week attending a crime scene that had almost made her throw up and had finished it by learning that one of her new colleagues had been held at knifepoint. Oh yeah, her first week had sure been a baptism of fire.

She threw down her satchel and fell back into the sofa, unsure if she would even make it as far as the bedroom tonight, but they'd been told to take tomorrow off, today now, and she wanted a moment to reflect.

She found it hard to believe that they had been working this case for only four days. Not four shifts as she knew them. They'd exceeded that by a long shot. But only four days in real hours and in that time she had learned a lot.

She'd learned that she had an aptitude for digging for information. When given a task, a path to that information lit up in her mind like a route planner. She enjoyed the analysis of a problem and could just as easily work alone as with company.

She'd learned that the boss was passionate, intuitive, driven and maybe a little bit rebellious. Stacey had felt a seedling of respect for the woman when she'd been sent away from the gruesome sight of Luke Fenton. She had wanted to repay that gesture by returning and showing the boss that she wasn't a quitter. She had seen the brief smile of acknowledgment upon her return to the crime scene and her regard for the woman had begun right then.

The events of the week had done nothing to detract from that and what Dawson had told her in the car about his night at the Travelodge at the boss's expense had simply blown her away. Somehow, she knew that information would never have come from her.

Additionally, she had learned that Kevin Dawson wasn't the arsehole she had thought he was. If she was talking scoring systems she'd thought ten on the dickheadometer and he was most likely a nine. But still it was a tiny improvement.

Once the boss and Bryant had headed off to prepare for the interview of the hairdresser, Dawson had offered to drive her home. She'd refused but he'd insisted.

And finally she'd learned that she would give her left arm for the opportunity to remain with this team. It wasn't a perfect group of people. She knew that. The boss wasn't exactly warm and nurturing. She lacked social skills and had to be reminded that folks needed to go home. Bryant was steady and reliable but not what she'd call dynamic. Although a knife to the throat hadn't sent him scarpering for home at the earliest opportunity. He had continued to do his job and for that she admired him. Dawson was an arrogant and cocky so and so, but despite his personal problems had managed to get into work every day and stay until he was told to go. He had shown commitment and he didn't even know it himself.

Yes, it had been one hell of a week. The job, like the people, had been a challenge but she knew so much more than she did four days ago.

She wanted more weeks like this. She wanted to continue to learn from these people and only hoped she would be given the chance.

CHAPTER 113

Dawson eased the car onto the drive of the house he shared with Ally. He turned off the engine and sat for a moment. Although he'd never really believed in God he did believe in fate when it suited him and he had decided to trust in it tonight.

Whatever the time of day or night, Ally always seemed to know when he parked on the drive. He had no idea how because the bedroom they shared was at the back of the house. They had forsaken the additional space in the master bedroom for the privacy of the back, which looked out onto an empty field. Both of them liked to sleep naked and both of them liked the curtains left open.

He had once lain on the bed when she'd been due home and he hadn't heard a thing from the front of the house, yet somehow she always knew when he had arrived home.

It had been two weeks since he'd walked out of this house in a fit of rage and there had been some surprises for him in that time.

Little had he known how his old team felt about him. He had thought they were a close-knit, bonded group yet not one of them had called him since Gary's outburst to declare their disagreement with his opinion. Which told him one thing. They all felt the same way.

Initially he had put it down to jealousy and there was still a part of him that thought they were envious of his skills, but despite his best efforts some of the things Gary had said had stayed with him. Maybe he did try and pass along jobs he found less interesting and perhaps he didn't make as many coffees as the next guy, but he was a damn good detective and he knew it.

Other surprises had come from his new boss who shouted him a night at the Travelodge. He understood that she didn't want the embarrassment of one of her team members spending another night on the car park but in truth it was the best night of sleep he'd had in weeks. No lumpy sofas, no musty, dubious-smelling pillows pulled from the back of airing cupboards, no angry partners giving him shit in the morning. Just a hot shower and a decent breakfast that had set him up for the day.

Unlike the night he'd spent at Lou's. As he remembered it the color flooded into his cheeks and he wished he could take that back. The sour feeling returned to his stomach every time he thought about what he'd done. As Gary had pointed out, he wasn't averse to using people but he had treated Lou in the worst possible way. He had danced all over her emotions to get a bed for the night. It wasn't the proudest moment of his week. Neither was his attempt to belittle DS Bryant at the beginning of the case.

In truth, he still thought the bloke was a bit of a plodder but the man had been on his knees with a knife at his throat earlier that evening and still come back to work to interview the culprit. Fair play to him. Dawson had changed his opinion of the man just a little bit.

Even the young, green detective constable wasn't as bad as he'd originally thought. A couple of times during the week she'd shown a bit more spirit than her continually beaming face reflected and he liked it. He had no time for pushovers or doormats.

But his most drastic change in opinion was for the boss. Initially, he'd thought he could play her, outwit her, find her weaknesses to exploit and aggravate like scratching an angry boil. He now knew that there wasn't a morning he could get up early enough to pull that one off. She had surprised him at every turn. She'd remained silent when he'd expected rage. She'd blown up at him when he'd expected silence and she had paid for a bed for the night when he'd expected to be thrown off the team.

But right before she'd headed off to prepare for interview, she'd hesitated beside his desk.

"Good work on the nursery rhymes, Dawson."

He was glad she'd gone by the time the smile had formed on his face.

It was then that he'd realized this wouldn't be a bad place to settle for a while. Not that he'd get a chance to try it, he reasoned. The boss would be summoned to meet DCI Woodward on Monday morning for an evaluation of the team. He knew full well that he would be transferred to another squad. She wouldn't keep him and he couldn't blame her. The work on the nursery rhymes was too little too late. He felt genuinely sorry. It could have been a good team to be a part of but he'd shot himself in both feet.

And was he about to do that again? Was he really going to base his future on whether the downstairs light came on? Was he truly going to wait for fate to decide if he and Ally had a chance?

No, he wasn't.

He got out of the car and let himself into the house.

As he entered the lounge he knew she was already sitting there. In the dark. Waiting to see what he would do. Come in or run away. Again.

"You're up?" he said, switching on the light.

She sat at one end of the sofa, dressed only in an ivory dressing gown, her legs curled to the side. Her blonde hair was ruffled from the pillow, her face clear of makeup. His heart missed a beat. It was how he loved her the most.

She said nothing. She wasn't going to make this easy for him.

"Ally, I—"

"What are you doing here, Kev?" she asked, her eyes full of emotion. He tried to read them all, anger, disappointment, regret and something else he couldn't read. "You run out of places to crash for the night?"

Any honesty there would not help the cause.

"I wanted to see you," he offered, sounding lame to his own ears.

"Why? Do you want to carry on the argument we were having? You remember accusing me of trying to trap you into marriage right after you asked me if I'd deliberately forgotten to take my pill?"

Ah, that's the emotion he was missing; hurt.

Regardless, he felt his own jaw tightening at her tone. This wasn't how he'd imagined his homecoming.

"Give me some latitude here, Ally. I was in shock at the—"

"I'd known myself for twenty minutes. I hadn't even had a chance to work out how I felt about it myself before you launched into attack mode. We were supposed to talk about it, share how we felt, discuss all the options, but instead you blamed me and then walked out."

"I'm here now," he said, trying to keep his temper. Did she not see what he was trying to do?

"Don't do me any favors, Kev," she snapped. "We don't need you in our lives if this is how you're going to react."

When had she become a we? he wondered, as though battle lines had been drawn.

"I'm the child's father," he said.

She nodded. "There's no doubt about that and I'm keeping your child regardless of any decision you have to make or process you have to work through. I've done that already, alone."

Dawson began to realize that his return was not the slam dunk he had thought it would be. He had thought a smile and a hug and a few sorrys would make things right. He had fucked up big.

And right there in that second he knew that he did not want to lose this woman or their unborn child. He had been a fool of the biggest kind in not even realizing how much he valued what was right in front of him.

"I'm sorry," he said, and meant it. He was sorrier for more than she knew but that could come later. "I shouldn't have run away. It was the shock," he said, glancing down to her stomach.

"You think I wasn't surprised?" she asked, quietly.

He had said some terrible things because secretly he had blamed her, wondered if she'd done something to trap him into fatherhood.

"I know and I'm sorry for all the things I said," he offered, stepping toward the sofa. He sat down. She didn't move away. "I panicked because despite all the bravado I know what kind of man I am. I know I'm arrogant and selfish, self-centered. I didn't know if I was ready for the responsibility of another life, to have that life reliant on me. All I saw ahead was failure on my part. Failure for you and for our child."

"You do know that's a perfectly normal reaction, don't you?" she asked, inspecting her hands.

He could hear the emotion in her voice and was desperately sorry for the hurt he'd caused. He'd left her to deal with everything alone.

He took her hand and she let him.

"I love you, Ally, and I know I'll love our child. I can't promise I'll be perfect but I want to be a part of this small family if you'll let me."

All week he'd been faced with child abuse, suffering, fear and he now knew that these were not feelings he ever wanted a child of his to experience. And he could only protect the child if he was around.

But that was it. He'd said his piece. He'd told her the truth. Most of it. Would she forgive him and allow him to be a part of her and their child's life?

The tentative smile that began in her eyes told him that maybe he had a chance.

CHAPTER 114

Bryant hesitated before knocking on the door. He wasn't sure if this was appropriate or not but he felt it was a conversation he needed to have.

He was glad of the day off today. He hadn't slept much. Every time he'd closed his eyes he'd felt the sensation of the cool metal at his neck. Once he opened his eyes the panic went away.

Jenny had woken and asked him if everything was okay when he'd climbed into bed at 4 a.m. but he hadn't had the heart to keep her awake to recount the events of the evening. He would talk to her about it later, but that wasn't why he was here. There was something else that needed to be cleared up.

The door opened and two things hit him at once. The look of surprise on her face and the smell of burning behind her.

"Sorry to come to your home, guv, but..."

"Everything okay?" she asked, stepping aside for him to enter.

"Yeah, I just need a word, privately."

"And you couldn't have managed that during the lifetime we've spent together in your car this week?"

Maybe he'd called this wrong and he shouldn't have come here, but a quick glance at her face told him she wasn't angry. He'd seen that look enough times to know.

"I won't keep you long but what the hell is that smell?" he asked, following her through a sparsely decorated lounge to the kitchen. A small round dining table was covered in newspaper and parts of an exhaust.

She lifted the lid on the bin at the side of the breakfast bar. "Scones."

He glanced inside and saw a pile of black, flat, disk-shaped objects that would have looked more at home on a hockey pitch.

"You sure?"

She shrugged. "They wanted to be."

"Not a natural cook, eh, guv?"

"Hate cooking," she said, holding up the coffee pot. "And I'm shit at it."

He nodded as he glanced back at the bin. "Err...so why do it?" he asked. He hated mowing the lawn so avoided it at every opportunity. And scones were not a difficult thing to get hold of.

"Because I'm shit at it. I'll master it someday."

Somehow he was not surprised by the response.

She reached into the top cupboard. "Mugs only, I'm afraid."

"Mug is fine," he said, wondering how to start the conversation. He took a breath. "Look, guv, I need..."

"Kim," she said.

"Yeah, guv, it's just..."

"Kim," she repeated.

He frowned and she met his gaze as she pushed a mug of coffee toward him. "I'm not at work. I'm in my home. It's Kim, not guv."

He wasn't sure he would ever be comfortable calling her by her first name.

"But call me Kim at work and I'll have you transferred."

He hesitated.

"Jeez, that was a joke."

He knew her angry face very well. He clearly needed more practice on judging her jokey face.

She picked up her own drink. "This about what happened last night?"

He shook his head. "It's about the promotion thing. Me going for DI."

"It's never too late," she said, standing back and folding her arms. He appreciated the gesture but the doubt in her voice was obvious. He had tried twice and failed both times.

"But that's the thing, guv... sorry, Kim. I don't bloody want it." She frowned. "Go on."

"The last two DIs I've worked with have kind of pushed me into going for it and I'm ashamed to say I've let them. But the thing is I like the work I do. I like being part of a team but I don't want to run a team. I love my job and I like to think I do it well. I'm not cut out to be a DI and I'm getting a bit sick of trying to explain that."

He knew that everyone in the force who had responsibility for other team members was required to encourage them up the ladder, to fulfill their potential, but he had come to realize that he was perfectly happy where he was. He was sick of being pushed into applying for a role to satisfy someone else's team management objectives. And he wanted to make sure she understood.

"It's just..."

"Consider it explained," she said, holding up her hand. "But quite honestly, Bryant, I have no clue what's happening with this team. I have a 7 a.m. meeting with Woody on Monday to discuss it."

He felt a sinking feeling in his stomach. Despite the fact that the week had ended with him on his knees with a knife to his throat, he thought it had been a reasonable week. He wouldn't mind another few just like it, but right now he'd just relax and enjoy the weight that had lifted from his mind.

He glanced around the kitchen and back into the lounge. Not one Christmas decoration or fairy light in sight and the main event was only six days away.

"You going away for the...?"

"I don't do Christmas. Hate it. I'm on call. I take it every year."

He wasn't sure what to say. He'd never met anyone who didn't do Christmas in one form or another. He thought back to the little he'd learned of her past and wondered just how much more there was to know. He knew one thing. If she didn't tell him he'd remain in the dark, and somehow he didn't think she was the confiding type.

"Ha, missus would kill me if I volunteered. Plans it by the hour from present opening at eight in the morning to cold meat buffet at eight on Christmas night. There's a program of events on the kitchen…"

"You're kidding?"

He smiled. "Yeah, I'm probably worse than she is, truth be known. But I don't drink, so although it's more than my life is worth to volunteer myself, if I happened to get called out in an emergency, you know, it'd be fine."

She met his gaze and understood. If she was called out and needed a second, he'd be there.

She took a sip of her coffee. "So, your wife know you're visiting the homes of other women during the day?"

He rolled his eyes. "Yeah, she told me to come and as I want to stay happily married there are few things she suggests that I don't do."

She laughed out loud. It was the first time he'd heard the sound. He liked it.

"It's not gonna become a habit though, is it, Bryant?"

He shook his head. "I shouldn't think so, Kim."

CHAPTER 115

DCI Woodward read through his page-a-day diary as he waited for his first meeting of the day.

List-making was a habit he'd formed early in his career. He liked to see things on paper, written down. Any task, however small, got noted and transferred to the master list in his diary. As he completed the tasks a satisfying line was drawn through the item and no shift was deemed complete until he had carried over the items not accomplished to the following day. It served many purposes, not least of which it showed him any tasks he was either consciously or subconsciously avoiding by the number of times it had been transferred to the following day.

The meeting at 7 a.m. with DI Stone he was expecting but the impromptu request for a chat by one of her officers had taken him by surprise. Did this team member want out already?

A double knock sounded on the door.

"Come in, DS Bryant," he called out.

Although he'd never worked with this officer before, he'd heard nothing but praise for his work ethic, his reliability and his impeccable judgment. A good pairing with Stone, he thought.

The man entered looking smart, alert and ready to start another week. All good except for the pensive expression on his face.

"Please take a seat, Bryant."

"I'm fine standing, sir. I won't take up much of your time. I just need to ask you about something that's been bothering me."

Woody sat back in his chair. "Please, ask away."

Was the man wondering how he had ended up on this team? Did he want to know if he had been requested? Was he wondering how quickly a transfer request would take?

"I saw a photo, sir, earlier in the week. It was an old photo of a six-year-old girl being carried from Chaucer House on Hollytree, right behind the body bag of her dead brother. There were police officers all around and one in particular that looked just like you."

Surprised by the question, he stood and moved to the window, considering his answer carefully.

Yes, he had been there when the door had been broken down into the flat on the seventh floor. The stench of the dead body had hit him immediately but little had he known that there was a little girl attached to the decaying body of her brother.

At first he had thought she was dead too but her eyes had opened, stark with fear, and then closed again. He had immediately known that she was close to death herself and he had not been prepared for the fight that had come from her thin, emaciated body when they had first tried to remove her dead twin from her side. No amount of soothing would comfort her until she passed out from exhaustion. When she came to her brother was gone. And he would never forget the look on her face as she turned to the empty space beside her.

Both the incident and the name of the girl had remained at the back of his mind and had been brought to the fore almost fourteen years ago when he had read about the bravery of a young female officer who had risked her own life by entering a service station to assist the owner, who had been injured during a robbery. She hadn't known if the assailant was still present but she had entered anyway. The sixty-two-year-old man had lived to tell the tale and she had received a commendation.

He had attended the award ceremony to see her. She had not turned up.

Since then he had followed her career with interest. He had raised a glass when she joined CID and another two following her promotions. What he hadn't celebrated was her inability to gel with any kind of team for longer than a case or two. Something in him had wanted to see that level of stability in her life, but she had bounced into almost every station in the borough and bounced right back out again. Except for Halesowen. When he'd heard about her most recent run-in he'd requested her presence on his team. He hadn't had to shout loudly or more than once to get his wish.

He took a breath, turned to the sergeant and opened his mouth. "Bryant, I—"

"Because, you see, sir," Bryant said, meeting his gaze, "if I think it's you in that photo, I'll always know that I'm keeping something from her, and if I am to remain a member of this team I want to give the DI my full support and not be privy to something about her past that she doesn't already know. It wouldn't be fair to her and it wouldn't be fair to me."

Woody nodded his understanding and took another breath. "It isn't me in that photo."

"Thank you."

"Is there anything more you need from me, DS Bryant?"

"No, sir. Thank you for your time."

DCI Woodward watched as the door closed behind the sergeant and realized that from this point forward he had to forget what he knew of her past. He had to erase the picture of the frightened, vulnerable, six-year-old girl and replace it with the independent grown woman she had become.

He was not her father, he was not her uncle and he was not her friend.

From this point forward he would be only one thing to her. He would be her boss.

CHAPTER 116

Kim headed up the stairs to the executive suite, still surprised by the fact that Bryant had made it in before she had. He'd mumbled something about needing to dot an I and cross a T and that he was ready and raring to go. She'd left him filling the coffee machine in preparation for the day ahead.

She knew what this meeting was about and after much thought over the weekend she was pretty sure about her answers. Almost.

The case was complete as far as they were concerned. The interview had elicited a confession which included dates, names and methods. There was no question Nigel Hawkins was responsible for them all.

There was a part of Kim that wondered if Nigel had wanted to be caught. His determination to leave clues to the dark meanings of nursery rhymes had formed his signature. Some killers insisted on leaving a personal stamp based on a need or compulsion. Some offenders posed corpses or carved something into the flesh, inserted items or took souvenirs away with them to relive the crime. All actions to do with the personality factors rather than the tools needed to commit the murder. Nigel hadn't needed to leave the clues to get the job done. It was something he had chosen to do to send a message.

Butcher Bill had been released over the weekend to return to his favorite shop doorway. From what she'd heard he hadn't been all that keen to leave. She was guessing he'd be back confessing to another crime for the benefit of a bed and a meal, especially over the Christmas period.

She had eventually caught up with Carl Wickes, who had sat in the interview room trembling with fear before she'd even begun to take his statement. When she'd raised the subject of Wendy Lockwood he had almost collapsed with relief and admitted that he'd had sex with more than one of the women at the shelter.

His initial reaction had set off alarm bells in her mind, as though he was more than happy to admit to a lesser charge. She'd wondered if he'd been involved in the murders somehow alongside Nigel or had at least known about them. Further probing had revealed that he and Marianne had been engaging in another illegal activity for more than two years. Blackmail.

A seventeen-page statement that she had been unprepared for had followed as the young man had unburdened himself. She had watched the real fear behind his eyes diminish as he'd listed names, dates and methods. Only this last week he had been sent to a man named Derek Hodge armed with photographs of his naked body in a hotel room after sex with Marianne, to extort funds for the shelters. He confirmed that Marianne had issued him with a second envelope that he hadn't even opened. Because of the police presence at the shelter he'd ripped the thing up and headed into town to get pissed before explaining to Marianne that he wasn't going to do it anymore.

Marianne had been questioned on the strength of Carl's statement and predictably was admitting to nothing while hiding behind an expensive lawyer.

Kim couldn't help her feeling of disappointment in the woman's methods. There was no doubt that the shelters had helped hundreds if not thousands of women recover from physical and psychological abuse over the years and Marianne's passion for their welfare was commendable. But not when it included breaking the law, Kim reminded herself.

The case had already been handed over to another team who would investigate Carl's claims individually and charges would be brought, a process in which Kim believed wholeheartedly. Yet she couldn't help but wonder what would happen to the shelters in Marianne's absence. There was no team of directors or managers waiting in the wings to install another force of nature, no deputy manager to step up and keep things ticking over. Marianne Forbes had been a one-woman army and Kim feared for the vulnerable women in her absence.

Doctor Lambert was still in hospital and had endured two surgeries to try and put him back together. The long-term effects were not yet known, but the man was alive and for that she was grateful.

She had placed a courtesy call to Mrs. Roberts to update her even though she'd never met either Nigel or Hayley but she was relieved for Mia that it was over. Kim was pleased to hear that the family were taking steps to bring Mia into their family more permanently. Kim hoped that worked out for Mia's sake. Her foster mother loved the child very much.

Lisa Bywater had accepted the news with little emotion and a response Kim could have anticipated. She couldn't talk for long as she was heading off to work. Kim hoped there was some part of the woman that might begin to heal now that it was over, or at the very least she received an employee of the month award for her efforts.

"So, shall we talk about the case first?" he asked.

"We caught the bad man who killed six people," she said.

"Is that it?"

"We caught the bad guy even though no one believed he killed six people."

Woody peered at her over his glasses. "I watched the interview. Good work getting the confession."

She shrugged. "Not really. He wanted to talk. Somehow, he thinks that the more he tells people the more they'll understand and that he'll be back to his old life in no time. He honestly does not see himself being sent to prison." She paused. "Did you watch it all?"

He shook his head. "Just the confession. First twenty minutes, I think."

"Bryant and I were in there for an hour. Once he started talking he couldn't stop. Pretty horrific, sir. His mum died when he was five and a half and the abuse started about six months later."

Kim couldn't help but feel for the six-year-old boy grieving for his mum and then being subjected to such horrific acts by the one person left in the world to protect him.

"His father would read him the same book of nursery rhymes every night before abusing him. Nigel came to hate those rhymes as he knew what came next. There was no innocence in the little ditties, just darkness and fear."

"And the grown man held a knife to your colleague's throat," Woody said, bringing her back to reality.

To her the boy and the man were two separate people. Nigel the man had coldheartedly murdered six people while convincing himself he was providing a service. Nigel the boy was still terrified and trying to make himself invisible beneath the bedcovers.

Woody's reminder of what he'd done was unnecessary. The picture had been in her mind ever since. Bryant had been put in that position because of her. She had decided to enter the building and he had followed her.

"He's a grown man," Woody said, as though reading her thoughts. "And you're a grown woman and although I don't blame you for what happened to Bryant I do think your decision to enter the building was foolhardy at best, for your own safety."

"The man was dying, sir," she said, simply.

He accepted her point.

"So, you know what comes next. I assume you've heard about the CID team at Wolverhampton?"

She nodded. Following the failure of the team to identify that Butcher Bill was not the murderer and their willingness to accept such a flimsy confession, the team of six had been disbanded. And they all needed to go somewhere.

"There are some good people going spare," he added, unnecessarily.

She knew and had worked with at least three of them.

"It's time to pick and choose."

She considered the bright lights who were being reassigned.

Spencer Adkins was a DS in his early forties and had one of the highest arrest rates in the borough. He was unmarried, diligent and needed little to no supervision. He was first at his desk and last to leave and always had a kind word for everyone.

Rory Mason was a DS in his mid-twenties whose ambition and drive did not distract him from the job at hand. He responded well to supervision, was respectful and worked hard.

Lisette Wilson was an Oxford University graduate in her early thirties with a brain that could analyze and separate data like a piece of software. She was married with one child and although mainly office bound had contributed to more successful prosecutions than anyone Kim had ever worked with.

She considered the team she'd been given at the beginning of the week.

DC Stacey Wood, inexperienced, nervous, squeamish at a crime scene, lacking in confidence. And yet she had suffered her colleague's inertia without a word of complaint. She had stayed at her desk until told otherwise and had contributed wholeheartedly and consistently throughout the week. What she had lacked in experience she had made up for with enthusiasm and integrity.

DS Kevin Dawson, arrogant to the point of cocky, sarcastic, insubordinate and at times insufferable. He had challenged her at every turn throughout the week. Clearly the man had been experiencing some kind of personal crisis at home, but still he'd had moments of brilliance. His determination to find the link between the anomalies at the crime scenes had led to the nursery rhyme theory. Kim had berated herself for not listening sooner because the theory had come from him. That was a reflection on her own quick judgment of his character and she would not let it happen again with any team member. She knew they would have never found Doctor Lambert in time without Dawson.

And finally, DS Bryant. The man had been at her side the whole week. He lacked ambition and was not the most dynamic officer she'd worked with. His demeanor, while not forceful, was steadying, fair and sensible. He was not easily offended, which could only go in his favor. The man had ended his first week with a knife to his throat and hadn't moaned about it once.

The team as a whole was inexperienced, unpolished and statistically way behind the three officers who needed a home.

She met Woody's gaze, signaling she was ready with her response.

"So, tell me, Stone. Who do you want to lose and who do you want to keep?"

She took a breath before she answered. "Sir, I want to keep them all."

A LETTER FROM ANGELA

First of all, I want to say a huge thank-you for choosing to read *First Blood*. If you'd like to keep up-to-date with all my latest releases, just sign up at the website link below.

angelamarsons-books.com

The idea of writing a prequel to the Kim Stone series has been playing around in my mind for some time. The more I reveal of Kim's journey the more I want to understand how things began in the early days when the team first formed.

Over the course of the books I've watched as Kim has come to regard her team as a surrogate family, the one she never had, even if she doesn't realize it herself. She is fiercely loyal and protective of them all despite her limited social skills and inability to form emotional connections, and would give her life for any one of them.

Additionally, as I've grown to know the team better with each book I find that questions are constantly buzzing around my head.

Where had Kim been before heading this team? Why was she transferred to Halesowen police station? How did she gain the respect of her superior officer, Woody?

What type of police officer was Bryant before joining the team? How did he grow enough patience to work with and support Kim with the loyalty he does? How did she learn to trust him so that he becomes her only true friend?

How did DS Dawson become so cocky and how did he adapt his working practices to fit into the team? How was the relationship between him and Kim on the first case they worked together?

How did Stacey cope with being a newly promoted detective and being thrust into a major investigation?

The more I've thought about these questions the more I wanted to explore the forces that brought them all together and to see how the team began.

Since releasing the *Silent Scream* I have been overwhelmed by the public reaction to Kim Stone and how readers have taken her to their hearts despite her faults. Many want to mother her, others want to protect her but the majority of readers tell me they simply want to be her friend.

If you did enjoy it, I would be forever grateful if you'd write a review. I'd love to hear what you think, and it can also help other readers discover one of my books for the first time. Or maybe you can recommend it to your friends and family…

I'd love to hear from you—so please get in touch on my Facebook or Goodreads page, Twitter or through my website.

If you haven't read any of the previous books in the DI Kim Stone series, you can find them here:

Silent Scream
Evil Games
Lost Girls
Play Dead
Blood Lines
Dead Souls
Broken Bones
Dying Truth

Fatal Promise
Dead Memories
Child's Play

Thank you so much for your support; it is hugely appreciated.

Angela Marsons

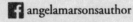 www.angelamarsons-books.com

 angelamarsonsauthor

@WriteAngie

ACKNOWLEDGMENTS

Never have I needed more to acknowledge the role my partner, Julie, plays in every part of the process of writing the Kim Stone books. Not once has she ever sighed heavily, spoken harshly or shrugged off my need for meetings, confidence boosts and pep talks. She is honest and open in her opinions and will never allow the words "I can't" to come out of my mouth. She is involved in the process from the moment an idea is born to the moment the book is finally complete. She is my absolute partner in crime.

Thank you to my Mum and Dad, who continue to spread the word proudly to anyone who will listen. And to my sister, Lyn, her husband, Clive, and my nephews, Matthew and Christopher, for their support too.

Thank you to Amanda and Steve Nicol, who support us in so many ways, and to Kyle Nicol for book spotting my books everywhere he goes.

I would like to thank the team at Bookouture for their continued enthusiasm for Kim Stone and her stories and especially to Oliver Rhodes, who gave Kim Stone an opportunity to exist.

Special thanks to my editor, Claire Bord, whose patience and understanding are truly appreciated and who has never been more important to me on both a professional and personal level than in recent months.

To Kim Nash (Mama Bear), who works tirelessly to promote our books and protect us from the world. To Noelle Holten, who has limitless enthusiasm and passion for our work.

Many thanks to Alex Crow and Jules Macadam for their genius in marketing the books. I still need a translator for Alex's explanatory emails as there are many words I don't understand. Also to Natalie Butlin, who works hard to secure promotions for the books. To Leodora Darlington, who works hard on the books behind the scenes, and to Alexandra Holmes, who looks after the audio production of the stories. Huge thanks also to Peta Nightingale, who sends me the most fantastic emails.

A special thanks must go to Janette Currie, who has copyedited the Kim Stone books from the very beginning. Her knowledge of the stories has ensured a continuity for which I'm extremely grateful.

Thank you to the fantastic Kim Slater, who has been an incredible support and friend to me for many years now. Despite writing outstanding novels herself, she always finds time for a chat. Massive thanks to Emma Tallon, who has no idea just how much I value her friendship and support. Also to the fabulous Renita D'Silva and Caroline Mitchell, without whom this journey would be impossible. Huge thanks to the growing family of Bookouture authors, who continue to amuse, encourage and inspire me on a daily basis.

My eternal gratitude goes to all the wonderful bloggers and reviewers who have taken the time to get to know Kim Stone and follow her story. These wonderful people shout loudly and share generously not because it is their job but because it is their passion. I will never tire of thanking this community for their support of both myself and my books. Thank you all so much.

Massive thanks to all my fabulous readers, especially the ones that have taken time out of their busy day to visit me on my website, Facebook page, Goodreads or Twitter.